LARK & KASIM

START A REVOLUTION

For everyone who is learning to love themselves

Cataloging-in-Publication Data has been applied for and may be obtained from the Library of Congress.

ISBN 978-1-4197-5687-0

Text © 2022 Kacen Callender
Illustrations by Sabrena Khadija
Book design by Jade Rector

Published in 2022 by Amulet Books, an imprint of ABRAMS. All rights reserved. No portion of this book may be reproduced, stored in a retrieval system, or transmitted in any form or by any means, mechanical, electronic, photocopying, recording, or otherwise, without written permission from the publisher.

Printed and bound in U.S.A.
10 9 8 7 6 5 4 3 2 1

Amulet Books are available at special discounts when purchased in quantity for premiums and promotions as well as fundraising or educational use. Special editions can also be created to specification. For details, contact specialsales@abramsbooks.com or the address below.

Amulet Books® is a registered trademark of Harry N. Abrams, Inc.

ABRAMS The Art of Books
195 Broadway, New York, NY 10007
abramsbooks.com

LARK & KASIM

START A REVOLUTION

BY KACEN CALLENDER

AMULET BOOKS
NEW YORK

Chapter One

MY PHONE BUZZES. I SPIN AROUND IN MY CHAIR SO FAST I almost fall. Birdie laughs. Frank Ocean plays. I chew on some strawberry Pocky. Another notification, phone vibrating against my desk. *hey are you ok??* I pull at my hair in frustration. A ton of my followers are tagging me, mutuals DMing me, asking if something's wrong, where've I been, am I all right? I usually post every night, but it's been over a week now. I type and delete and retype drafts, the cursor blinking at me on my laptop's screen, but my brain is blank, empty, nada, nothing is going on up there and, oh no, I'm also pretty cute, please, God, I don't want to be a thembo—

I groan and toss my phone, my poor phone whose only crime was that it was in my hand—shit, a little too hard, it bounces off my desk and somersaults through the air and I scramble to catch it and this time I really *do* fall, crashing onto the hardwood, shaking my whole room with an echoing *thud.*

My mom calls from downstairs. "Lark? You all right?"

"Yeah!" I hiss and cringe and check my elbow. God, that really hurt. "Yeah, I'm fine!"

Wait, isn't exercise supposed to stimulate the brain? I jump to my feet and run in place for ten, nine, eight—

Yeah, no. Never mind. I flop onto my back on my bed and stare at my ceiling. And I sigh.

It's not the end of the world if I can't figure out a post, but that's kind of how it feels. Like all of my dreams are crashing down around me with every second that ticks by.

My mom says I'm just addicted to the likes. I don't know. Maybe she's right.

Music starts playing downstairs, the kind of R&B song that my mom swears was "the shit" about twenty years ago. She calls my name. "Lark? Lark! Come down!"

Gladly. I push myself up and thump down the wooden stairs. The windows are wide open, begging for any sort of breeze since PECO is practically snatching arms, legs, torsos, everything in exchange for electricity. I sneeze, sneeze, sneeze so hard I slip down a few stairs. Survived a pandemic, just to be taken out by pollen. I leap over the last two steps onto the landing and turn into the kitchen—and stop short.

Kas sits up on a counter, looking way too relaxed for a house he doesn't live in. "Bless you," he says with a grin.

I rub my nose and look at my mom, the traitor. Why does she always let Kasim inside? Just pretend you don't see him or hear him knocking on the door. She sits at the white table pushed up against the wall. Her open laptop is streaming music. *My whole life has changed . . .*

She gives me a look.

Right. My face.

I wipe away the *what're you doing here?* stare and force on a creaking smile. "Oh. Hey."

2

CHARACTER PROFILE!

NAME: Kasim Youngblood

PRONOUNS: He/him

AGE: 17

BIRTHDATE: November 19

ZODIAC: Scorpio

HOMETOWN: West Philly

OCCUPATION: Student

Kas hops down from the counter, leaning against it with his arms crossed. He has beautiful dark brown skin, the kind of shade that reminds you of night. The top of his hair is loc'd and usually tied up, the sides shaved and ends bleached. He's in a black crop top, black cutoffs, worn black boots, a spiral gauge in one ear. He always has this vibe that he thinks everyone should feel honored to be in his presence. Like he was a pharaoh or a king in a past life and I should be on my knees. To be real, I'm jealous of that energy. I mean, that's the kind of attitude that doesn't question, not even for one second, if he deserves to be here. If he, too, gets to take up space in the room. *This crown is already bought and paid for, and I'm wearing the fuck out of it.*

It could just be my imagination, but I'm pretty sure his smirk grows by a couple of centimeters when he sees me. That smirk. *That smirk.* Kasim should trademark that freaking smirk, I swear to God. "Hey, Lark."

We watch each other. Kind of like we're in a nature documentary, two natural enemies staring each other down before the attack. If this was an anime, lightning would spark between our eyes. Neither of us says a word. My mom's gaze flits between the two of us like she's worried we're going to fight for no reason other than the fact that we're breathing the same air. I'd like to think I'm pretty loving. I believe in world peace. I hate getting into fights and arguments with anybody. But Kasim, somehow, is the only exception, and not in that romantic Paramore kind of way. There's got to be some sort of chemical explanation for why Kas and I can't be in the same space without shit blowing up. I don't know. Science isn't exactly my strong suit.

My mom attempts to break the awkward silence. "Still up there staring at Twitter?"

Kasim's gaze slides to me and judgment radiates from his pores. My defensive walls were already up, but they climb a few miles higher.

"I wasn't *staring* at Twitter."

"Uh-huh." She recognizes my tight, clipped tone and raises an eyebrow. I can practically read her mind. *One day you're going to figure out that you need your friend more than you need the fight.* I still don't know if she meant *the fight* as in *the struggle* or *the fight* as in *the literal fight me and Kas have been in for the past year.*

"Kasim, honey, are you staying for dinner?" she asks.

"No, thanks, I don't want to bother—"

"You know you're not bothering anyone."

Kas meets my eye, glinting with an *Oh, really? Lark, what do you think about the fact that I'm not bothering anyone?* smile.

My mom notices. "Right?"

My voice is monotone. "Yeah. Stay for dinner."

Kasim barely holds in a laugh. "I'd love to. Thanks, Ms. Winters."

I'm *really* not in the mood for Kasim tonight, but my mom never turns anyone away. Even in the height of the pandemic, she would help anyone who needed it, especially Kasim and his big brother Taye. And I love that. Yes, community is important. But it's also okay to have boundaries sometimes, right? Especially boundaries from ex-best friends who love to purposefully piss me off.

"Eggplant's almost done," my mom says, groaning as she pushes herself to her feet. "Set the table, okay, my love?" She puts a warm hand on my shoulder and kisses my cheek before she walks past me, leaving me and Kas alone. Seriously? She knows she's wrong for that one. She knows this isn't going to end well.

There's a beat of silence.

I ask, "So what're you doing here?"

My mom calls from the other room. "Don't be rude."

Kasim answers my question with a shrug and a grin, white teeth shining. Why is it that the most chaotic of queers have the sharpest canines? "I was just saying hi to your mom. I didn't think I'd see you."

Why wouldn't you? I *live* here. "Yeah. Okay."

We repainted all the cabinets white a few months ago, but some of the old brown wood still streaks through. Kas opens one of the cabinet doors to pull out three glasses with different patterns of fruit on them—strawberries, oranges, grapes. "Why do I get the feeling you're not happy to see me, Lark?"

"You came over last week, too," I tell him, scraping open some drawers and pulling out utensils. "Plates, please."

"Are you that mad at me for coming over?" Kasim opens the cabinets above the sink.

"I'm not mad."

"Are you sure about that?"

"You know you're only here for the free food."

He puts a hand over his chest like he's wounded. "Come on. I'd never take advantage of your mom like that."

I have to admit he's being sincere for once. Kasim's mom died when he was four, and about three years ago his dad was charged for a few ounces, so now it's just Kas and Taye, who's been fighting to keep Kasim with him. When Kasim's dad got arrested, my mom started offering to let Kas stay over whenever his brother had to do a night shift for one of his jobs. Kasim would stay here for weeks without leaving.

And the thing is, I actually *liked* it when Kas lived with us. We were best friends. We spent every second together. Skateboarding around the basketball courts. Going to the records store on Baltimore Avenue. Making TikToks with us dancing, falling, dying laughing, the sort of laugh where you can't even make a sound and you're just wheezing and gasping and crying and smacking each other and then falling over again, just to laugh even harder. He's straight-up got the personality of Bakugou when he's mad, so I'd call him Kacchan, and he'd call me Deku, and we'd watch bootleg anime on my laptop all night beneath the covers when we were supposed to be asleep, and any time we heard my mom walking by outside we'd drop and play dead, snorting and shoving each other whenever we made a sound. I could tell him anything. Anything. And he never judged me. "I'm afraid I'll end up alone someday." He shook his head. "Why? You've got me, right?"

But when high school started . . . I don't know. I don't hate him. I don't hate anyone. Honest, I don't. And I don't think he hates me, either. (Most of the time.) But things definitely aren't the way they were before.

Kasim's smile grows as he watches me, like he knows how annoyed I am. "Something's got you pissy."

"I'm not pissy."

"Really?"

"Yes, *really.*"

"You seem pissy to me."

Birdie inspects one of their wings. "You're being kinda pissy, Lark."

I grind my teeth. "I'm fine."

Kasim snorts. "Yeah. Okay. You're so calm. So peaceful."

I take a tight breath. Maybe he's right. I'm on edge. It's always stressful, writing something for 20.1K people (and more) to see, to read, to give their opinion on, to like or not like, to agree with or to quote-tweet with a *look at how fucking stupid this kid is* comment. The fact that I'm stressed isn't Kasim's fault.

Besides, there isn't any point in being annoyed. I learned from an early age that I don't get to be angry or frustrated. Some people are allowed to take up space in this world, while other people are expected to disappear. When we don't disappear, we're hated and then blamed for that hatred. *If only you'd been nicer. If only you'd smiled. If only you'd just sit down and shut up, maybe people wouldn't hate you so much.* It isn't fair, but there's a lot about this world that isn't fair, right? I sigh, shake my hands back and forth to get some of the tension out, hum a Solange song. *Well, it's like . . .*

Kasim puts the last plate down. "What's your post about?"

He knows that if I'm staring at social media, it's probably because I'm planning out a new thread. I wouldn't say I'm *famous*, but my posts can get around 50K likes sometimes.

"Um." I can't meet his eye. "Not sure yet."

He gives a half-smile. "Maybe it can be *how to kiss white people's asses to make them feel more comfortable with your existence*."

Jesus Christ on cheese. See what I mean? Kas likes to piss me off. It's a game to him. Poke at me until I snap. He knows that I'm not radical, like him and his new group of friends. He knows that I'm all about peace. "Fuck peace," Kasim told me once. "They don't give us peace. Why should we give them ours?" He wants to rile me up. To make me angry so that he can smirk and say that I'm a hypocrite, and I'm not as peaceful as I pretend to be.

I pull out my phone. I've got more than twenty new notifications. More tags and comments and DM's. *lark are you alive?!!* I scroll. "Maybe I could write about how anarchy hurts community." Another argument we've had a million and one times. We always fall into the same patterns, the same cycles, the same fights whenever we come near each other. It's like an addiction. We can't stop.

Kasim cuts his eyes at me, fire shining in them. He's like a volcano, tectonic plates shifting and pressure building. I can always tell when he's about to erupt. "Tearing down a hierarchal society that's built from racism is a *good thing*, Lark."

"But what about community in the meantime?" I ask.

"We take care of each other."

"Can't take care of each other when resources are being destroyed."

"We take that shit and redistribute it to the people."

"Take it from people *in the community*, you mean?"

"No, from corporations—"

"People's businesses in the same community get fucked up, too—"

"They aren't the target."

"But that's what happens, right?" I say. "While you're busy burning down the system, people are gonna struggle in the process."

"People *been* struggling, Lark," Kas says, his voice getting louder. "Damn, your head's so far up liberal white people's asses that you can't see shit except theirs."

"Christ, Kas, that's disgusting."

He ignores me. His smirk is gone. "Open your fucking eyes. Seriously."

The argument's really heated now. It usually is with us. I know my mom can hear, but she doesn't step in. Kas stares at me for one long second, not saying a word. He can get pretty intense like that. Like an explosion contained in a human body, and even if you can't see the blast and the fire and the debris, you can feel it coming at you.

"What?" I say. My voice cracks.

He only shrugs, looking away again. "You could write about dogs. For your post, I mean. Can't go wrong with that. Might even get more followers."

I roll my eyes. "You're an asshole," I say, and immediately regret it, because, yeah, that's not very nice or peaceful of me at all.

He has the perfect opening, the perfect opportunity, to point out that I called him an asshole and take me down with a FINISH THEM! blow, but he only lets out a laugh. A real one, too—not hollow or forced at all. Kas can be in a fight one second, laughing lightly like it was no big deal the next. Even when being insulted. Like he really and truly couldn't care less. Yeah. I'm definitely jealous of that energy.

"I guess I'm an asshole sometimes," he says. "But isn't everyone? Even if no one wants to admit it, we've all hurt someone else in our lives. You have, too."

I feel a spark of shame. Of defensiveness. I want to argue with him. But I force myself to stop. He's right. It's true, isn't it? I've probably hurt someone also. We're all human. We all make mistakes, and we all hurt each other, even when we want to think that we haven't, or think that the other person shouldn't feel hurt, because we don't want to be the kind of person we point fingers at and say are bad people. We don't want to be the bad person. Ever since I was a kid, I wondered about that—why we humans always like to point at someone else and say they're the enemy while they point at us and say we're the enemy. Maybe no one is actually good or bad, but a mix in between. Maybe the same is true with me and Kasim.

"Just as long as we learn and grow," he says.

Dinner's so freaking good, and as we're clearing the table, my mom leans back in her chair, satisfied. *I remember that night, I just might remember that night for the rest of my days.* My mom has brown skin and dark freckles that grow around her eyes. Her curly hair is already turning silver, which kind of scares me, because—and, yeah, this is kind of dark and depressing since even I can't force myself to be glass-half-full-optimistic every second of every day—but I don't want my mom to die and leave me alone. I was freaking out that she would get sick when the pandemic first started, and I'm still nervous about it. She had me when she was in her early forties, so she's older than most moms of people who are seventeen, and I just think about that a lot, I guess, her dying before I'm ready and me needing to figure out how to exist in this world by myself.

My mom was alone, too—never married. My other parent is an unknown person who donated their sperm. Sometimes I wonder if I've got a huge biological family with a group chat, siblings and cousins that call just to hear your voice. I'm scared that I'll end up like my mom, too: someone who deserves to be loved, just like everyone else who wants to be, but will always be alone for whatever reason, just can't figure out why, and maybe that's the scariest thing of all—never really knowing what I'm doing wrong, why everyone else in the world has love and a ton of family and friends and just knows, inherently, without a doubt that they *belong*. But maybe that's too whiny. I'm being really self-conscious, right? I think that's what most people would say.

Birdie shrugs. "Whatever another person thinks of you is just a reflection of themselves."

My mom asks, "Kasim, baby, are you staying over tonight?"

Even Kas knows that's a terrible idea. "Oh, no thanks, I should—"

"Didn't you say Taye had to leave for the week? You've been in the house all by yourself for four days."

"Yeah, but he's coming back tomorrow."

"Classes start at the Commons tomorrow." The Commons, aka the Common Ground Community Center. My heart leaps at the thought of going back to class again—and of a certain person who posted on their Insta that they'll be there. "You should have someone to see you off," my mom says.

"It's not a big deal. I'm seventeen. I stay home alone all the time."

"Isn't that lonely?" she asks. I try not to laugh. I can see Kas internally starting to regret that he even came over. "The center is closer to us. You two can leave together."

Kasim pauses as he struggles to find another reason why he can't, then almost desperately bursts out with, "But I don't have a change of clothes."

Kas is playing checkers while my mom is playing chess. She replies smoothly, "You still fit into Lark's, right?" We always used to wear each other's clothing. My mom gets up from the table. "It's getting late and the sun's already down. I'd feel better if you stayed over instead of walking home, okay?"

He closes his eyes for a second, maybe biting back a sigh. Kasim can never say no to my mom. He really does love the hell out of her, as he and everyone in the world should. "Yeah, okay. Thanks, Ms. Winters."

I grin smugly at Kasim when my mom turns her back to leave the kitchen.

"Lark, help Kas settle in," she says.

Grin wiped clean. Crap. I forgot this means I'll have to share my bedroom with Kasim. The last time he stayed over was about six months ago, and that was only because he got sick and Taye wasn't around to take care of him. We were scared it was the virus, but it turned out to be a bad mix of allergies and the cold, and the doctor just ordered lots of fluids and Benadryl. It was actually kind of nice. Not the Kasim-getting-sick part, but us talking into the night and watching anime again like when we were kids. We laughed so much that night. But then Kas got better, and we got into another argument about something I can't even remember now, and when he left the next day, everything went back to business as usual.

Kasim won't meet my eye, and I wonder if he ever thinks about the way things used to be between us—if he ever regrets the way our friendship ended, too.

Maybe not. Maybe he doesn't give a shit.

Hmmm.

Chapter Two

MY MOM'S BEEN RENOVATING THE HOUSE EVER SINCE WE MOVED here a few years ago, but it's been a slow process, with most rooms half-finished, some walls with different patches of paint and others with carpet ripped from the floors. Kasim follows me as we clomp up the steps. Is it just me, or does it feel like we're being led to our executions?

"Sorry that I'm all up in your space," he says.

Are you, though? Are you really?

My room has pale blue walls and scuffed and worn-down wood paneled floors. My shoes are in a pile in my half-open closet. I painted my dresser green, and there are plants everywhere, so it feels like I'm in a tree. There is lemongrass incense and half-melted rosemary candles on my nightstand and piles of books and journals and clothes scattered across the floor. To the outside eye, it might look like *a tornado flew around my room before you came, excuse the mess it made*, but it's my organized chaos, and I like it exactly the way it is.

My laptop's still on my desk, which is covered with textbooks from school. I sit on my chair and spin around slowly, looking anywhere but at Kasim. God, this is going to be an awkward night.

There's a beanbag chair at the foot of my bed. Kas immediately drops into it. "Wanna watch something?" he asks. He's decided to go the *pretend this isn't weird* route, I see.

"Can't. I still have to figure out what to post." I stop spinning and fold over with a groan, hitting my head on the desk with a *thud*. "Ow."

He gives a low laugh. "You're acting like it's homework."

I rub my forehead. "No, I'm not." I sound defensive, so I pause. Take a breath. "I didn't know you were doing classes at the Commons again." He's probably doing the writing class, like me. Kasim considers himself to be a *serious writer*, and, well, I kind of hate that he's actually really good. He writes super autobiographical stuff, fiction based on his life, and sometimes essays, too. Honestly, he's probably going to grow up to win the Pulitzer or the Man Booker Prize or something.

"Yep." He scrolls on his phone. Different voices, music. *The giant horse conch weighs over eleven pounds.* "Why do you even need to post something?"

"Because that's what people expect."

He squints at me. "Why?"

"I don't know. People follow me because of the kind of stuff I say, and they've been messaging me to see why I'm not posting anything when I usually do every day. So now I have to post something."

Twitter's a millennial breeding ground, but I get nervous when I have to speak, so TikTok—on my own, not dancing and falling and laughing with Kasim—is a no-go for me, and I've never liked Insta much. The other teens on Twitter are usually my kind of people anyway. Queer, nerdy, neurodivergent writers and readers who talk about books and anime and social justice. I've gotten a bunch of likes and followers for the most random posts—

Lark Winters (they/them) @winterslark
i thought it was fruit loops not froot loops

💬 1K   🔁 3K   ❤️ 11.1K

—and millennials are obsessed with anyone from Gen Z—I think they wish they could be us or something, I don't know—so that's boosted my account, too.

Kasim stretches out. "Okay," he says. He looks like he's seconds from laughing at me. Not like that's new. "I don't get it. Why're you letting a bunch of strangers control you?"

"They're not *controlling* me."

"It's not like you're getting paid for it."

"I'm doing this for fun."

"*This* is what you do for fun?" he asks, and the judgment actually stabs me through the heart. Yeah, sorry, Kas—since you dumped me as your best friend, I haven't been left with a ton of options.

Besides, it's not *only* for fun. My dream is to be a published author. I have so many ideas—like, a single document with literally over one hundred ideas—that feature dozens of characters who look like me and speak like me, appearing center stage in my daydreams. They talk to me, sometimes, like they're real—and sometimes, I answer back. (Not a good thing to do when other people are around, let me tell you.) Contemporaries with teens who fall in love with each other and fantasies where genderless heroes save their kingdom and sci-fis, too, where multi-gender human beings have to contain an exploding star—

I want to write books where Black is the default. Where it's understood that we are beautiful. I want to write books where readers wouldn't have to see a single blond-haired, blue-eyed character with *eyes like the ocean/sky*, where my curls aren't described as unkempt and wild, where the character's eyes are so dark you can't even see the iris and I understand the power and beauty in that, instead of writing *but at least they had a nice smile.* I want to see *me* for once, not just fragments of me, like books are puzzle pieces and to see myself, I have to read them all. *I wanna be the very best—like no one ever was.*

"Why're you humming the Pokémon theme song?" Kasim asks.

"I'm not humming."

God. I want to be published so freaking bad. Maybe then, I'll be seen. My writing will be vulnerable in the way I'm afraid to be vulnerable in real life, because the last time I was—well, it didn't exactly work out for me, did it? Kasim glances up at me just as I look over at him. People will know me. The real me. People will love me. They'll want to be my friends. My queer found family. I won't be so freaking lonely.

"You're still humming, Lark."

"I don't know what you're talking about."

I started querying my first novel about a teen named Birdie who starts to grow wings—well, okay, so I did the one thing everyone says not to do and started querying the book before I'd finished writing it, but what's the point in writing an entire novel without knowing if an agent will even want to see the full manuscript? I wanted to test the waters, so I started querying my top wishlist agents a few months ago, but so far, Birdie has only gotten rejection after rejection. *Best wishes to you on your path to publication.*

"Their loss," Birdie says, legs crossed as they sit on my desk.

To be real, finding fame on Twitter is pretty much the only path I see opening up to this dream of mine. Agents and publishing houses pay attention to how many followers a writer has, so if I gain over 50K, the chances of getting my book represented by an agent and finally published will skyrocket.

And that's exactly why I've started to stress out about my posts so much. Twitter used to be fun, but now, one bad decision could make me lose a shit ton of followers. All of my plans could go up in flames.

Kasim waves around a hand with chipped black nail polish. "Why don't you just take a break for the night? You look like you need a vacation from your—uh—*fun.*"

"I've got to keep my followers by posting regularly."

"I don't get the point of Twitter."

"And I don't know what to say to that."

Kasim pulls out some weed and a lighter, edges of his paper already burnt. Click, sizzle. "I can help you brainstorm if you want."

"You already helped enough, but thanks."

"Come on. I've got some good ideas."

"Sure. Fine. Let's hear them."

"Hot white boys."

"Fuck off."

He laughs and blows out a haze. "Okay, okay. Seriously. One topic I haven't seen you cover yet is mental health in the Black community."

I spin in my chair to face him. "You read my posts?"

Trademarked smirk tugs at his lips. "Unfortunately."

"I thought you hated Twitter." I assumed that Kasim wasn't on there. He talks enough shit about it.

He ignores me. "You could write about—you know—how depression and anxiety and shit affects Black people."

I watch him for a second, then spin back around. "That's actually a good topic. Thanks."

"No problem."

I begin typing, and we fall into a silence that's more comfortable than I've experienced between us in a while. But with just the sound of my clacking keyboard, a question thickens the air. This topic about mental health was really specific. I want to ask if something's wrong—if Kasim is struggling. Is he depressed? His mom died when he was four, so he says he doesn't miss her. More like he misses the idea of her, the relationship they might've had together. His dad hasn't been around much since he was released, and they haven't been in touch for about a little over a year. I don't know much about the situation, but I heard he had a breakdown and disappeared, leaving Kasim and Taye behind. Kasim told me once that his dad was so traumatized that when he got out of prison, he'd been a shell, his life and hopes taken from him, and all because he was a Black man with some weed. Prisons shouldn't exist. People who can't imagine a world without prisons probably couldn't have imagined a world without slavery, either.

I want to ask Kas how he's feeling, but we're not as close as we used to be. Maybe this is something I could've asked him, once, when we were still friends—but now . . .

Kas smokes while he scrolls on his phone. I know my mom wouldn't be happy if she saw Kasim carrying weed. Not when there're too many white people who'd be happy to lock him up, too. But my mom doesn't care if we smoke. She likes the health benefits. Emotional, physical. It helps my anxiety, helps her back pain. Weed's only illegal because of racism, since Black people profited from it—

Birdie snorts. "Meanwhile, prescription opioids are more addicting and fatal and yet are still legal. Hmmm, I wonder why?"

—and now, after generations of people of color and especially Black men have lost their freedom and lives for a few ounces, white people are starting cannabis businesses and making money while continuing to villainize *us* for smoking a few puffs.

I can't begin to imagine how Kasim must feel, knowing his dad had been arrested and imprisoned for having weed and then seeing smiling pictures of Karens and Marthas as they give the grand tour of their cute Colorado cannabis shop. The thought alone makes me want to cry and scream and curl into a ball, lying inside of a soft pink shell, where I know I'll be safe. Sometimes I think I might see flashes of that same pain in Kasim's eyes before he blinks, walls back up again.

He glances at me now, and I realize I've been staring, but he doesn't seem to care. "Is it all right if I play some music?" he asks.

"Yeah, sure." I reach for the weed and smoke a little, calmness tingling over my skin. He presses the screen on his phone. Teyana Taylor. *And are you gonna love me?* The song hits the mood, and I lean back and forth in my chair as it squeaks beneath me.

I type the last word. I read and re-read the thread, making edits until it's perfect. I hold my breath as I hit *tweet all*.

"You finished?" Kasim says.

"Yep."

"Can I read?"

"Just look at it on your phone."

"I don't have the app."

"What? Why not?"

"Because I'm not a weeb."

I roll my eyes, grab the laptop, and hand it over to him before I get up from my desk and flop onto my bed, scrolling through my notifications on my cell. I see 20, 23, 26 likes and counting.

Lark Winters (they/them) @winterslark
why don't we talk more about mental health for black people?? tbh i have been struggling so much with anxiety lately & i don't even feel like i can talk about it openly
💬 0   🔁 7   ♥ 31

it's like we as black people don't get to have mental health breaks. so many of us are brought up to just smile through it and keep pushing and keep working and be grateful and pray the anxiety and depression away
💬 2   🔁 15   ♥ 45

and so many of us are brought up to believe that therapy and mental health isn't for us. just ignore the pain so that we can keep working hard
💬 5   🔁 21   ♥ 63

but thats so capitalistic right?? we aren't only as valuable as the work we do. i'm not worth more than another person if i grow up to get a job that makes me a millionaire.
💬 7   🔁 29   ♥ 70

the idea that we're only as valuable as our work and money is literally created by slavery!! we shouldn't have to work so hard. we deserve breaks too.
💬 10   🔁 33   ♥ 81

Looks like it'll be another popular thread—but inevitably a troll finds it and quote retweets: *jesus christ this kid is so annoying*

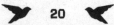

Birdie hugs me from behind. "You aren't annoying, Lark."

If only everyone else agreed. White people, straight people, cis people, neurotypical people, adults—practically everyone is always quicker to consider someone like me annoying: unlikeable, unempathetic, unrelatable.

I went to a charter school in Brooklyn when I was a kid. I was one of the only Black people in my grade and the only person that used my pronouns. Teachers said I was a "disruption" in class for always raising my hand, too eager to answer questions, while white students who did the same were called *hard workers*. I was the only person in my class to get in trouble almost every single day. I would talk and laugh, just like everyone else, but I was the only one to be sent to the office. I was given detention because I didn't smile at a teacher, once. She said I was trying to intimidate her. I had no friends. Whenever I spoke, my classmates would scream at me to shut the fuck up, no one likes me, go away, Lark. The school bullies made a game of following me, spitting at me, shoving me around, and then there was that day when I fell asleep at the back of the bus and had my legs stretched out and everyone got mad and yelled at me for taking up too much space because I am not supposed to take up space in this world and it wouldn't stop escalating and then finally one girl who had never spoken to me before made fun of me for buying sneakers from Payless and then punched me in the eye—

"Breathe," Birdie reminds me.

Teyana's song ends. Arlo begins. *Just know it won't hurt so much— won't hurt so much forever.*

Birdie is from the future. They say it's different there. We've evolved so much that we realize we're all one and can't even tell the difference between each other, from one human to the next.

"Maybe I'm from the future, too."

Kasim looks up at me. "What?"

I duck my head. "Nothing."

Kasim gestures at the laptop. "We deserve breaks, too? Really?"

"Yeah. What's wrong with that?"

"Lark—you're literally not taking a break by posting this."

I throw a pillow at him. "Shut up."

He catches the pillow and laughs, then goes back to reading in silence for a minute. "You've always been good at getting your point across."

My neck gets hot. "Thanks, I guess." I sit up, more than ready to change the subject. Compliments always embarrass me, but there's something about a compliment from Kasim especially that *really* makes me feel awkward. Like it forces me to remember the days when we were so close and leaves me wondering why things changed.

"Does it ever feel like a waste of time?" he asks.

"What?"

"Social media. The talking, without any action. I'm not sure it actually does anything."

"And you just want to burn down the world, right?"

"Not the entire world. Just the systems that're killing us."

"Even if the fire spreads and burns us, too?"

"Well, it's the best option we've got."

"According to who?"

He squints at me, small smile growing. "People who don't agree with you aren't automatically wrong. Still waiting for you to figure that one out."

It's like he always knows which nerve to slam. "I never said you're wrong just because you don't agree with me."

"No. You just imply it."

"Forget it. I'm not in the mood for another argument right now."

"I wasn't trying to fight with you."

I don't know how to answer that. When is Kasim ever *not* trying to fight with me?

"I'm just saying, there's nothing wrong with going against the status quo to try something new for a change."

"Right—because you want the world to know you don't give a shit about what anyone thinks." Okay, maybe I didn't need to say that so meanly. My shame builds in the silence. "Sorry."

Kasim shrugs. God. How did shit get so unbearably awkward between us?

"I'm going to sleep, okay?" I tell him. "Don't shut my laptop down when you're done with it."

He nods, already focused on whatever he's doing, typing away. "Got it."

Chapter Three

Lark Winters <winterslark@gmail.com>

Dear Ms. Jenkins,

I am seeking literary representation and hope that you will consider my speculative contemporary YA novel, BIRDIE TAKES FLIGHT.

Sixteen-year-old Birdie is from a future where humans grow wings. When they accidentally slip through a crack in time and end up in our current world, they are mistaken as an angel and are treated like they are the second coming, toured around the world and praised by millions, while others treat them like they're a monster.

When they meet eighteen-year-old Alexandra, Alex vows to help Birdie get back to the future—but then Alex vanishes without a trace, leaving Birdie to follow clues and solve the mystery of her disappearance, which might just give Birdie the answers they need to go home, too.

Not everything is as it seems, however, and not every lost person wants to be found.

BIRDIE TAKES FLIGHT is complete at approximately 50,000 words. The first fifty pages are attached per your website's instructions. I am a high school student with a passion for writing, with the goal of creating more visibility and representation for people like me. I currently have over 20K followers on Twitter. Thank you for your time and consideration.

Sincerely,

Lark

—

Jenkins, Susan <sjenkins@ytliterary.com>

Hi Lark,

Thank you for your query. The concept is intriguing, but I didn't connect with the voice. Though this is a YA, the voice was just too *teen*, and I struggled with the rambling, repetitive, incohesive, and, frankly, exhausting monologues throughout.

I wish you every success in your writing journey.

Best wishes,

Susan

Birdie makes a face. "Well, damn."

I sigh and rub my eyes, dropping my phone onto the floor. Kasim groans and rolls over beside me. I shouldn't be surprised, right? This is my thirteenth rejection. The rambling, repetitive, incohesive, exhausting monologues—I mean, ouch, that hurts, especially since it's because I think and write differently than neurotypical people, and that just means not only is my writing being rejected, but *I* am being rejected, too, with just a small undercurrent of ableism. But there's a bubbling of anger inside the hurt. *Though this is a YA, the voice was just too teen.* What does that even *mean*?

"What time is it?" Kas asks, voice hoarse.

"I don't know."

"Check."

"My phone is on the floor."

He sighs.

Too teen. As if it's a bad thing to be a teenager. Why do adults always act like we're the worst? They think they're smarter and more mature than us. From what I can see, adults do the same exact things as teenagers. They bully each other. They're self-conscious. They have lessons they need to learn to grow as people. They get all up in their feelings about one another, and they have the same emotions, too. They get afraid and they laugh and they cry.

Birdie sits cross-legged on my floor. "Just another way for one group of humans to think that they're better than another group of humans. That's what your civilization tended to do a lot, at this point in the timeline."

"Ageism is weird," I say.

Kasim sits up, hand shaking out his locs so that they fall into his face. "What?"

"Think about it. It's one of the few ways you can go from a person with less privilege and power and become a person with more privilege and power. Adults take advantage of that and treat us like crap." When I'm an adult, I'm going to remember how shitty

26

this feels, and I'm going to treat teenagers like what we are: human beings.

Kasim squints down at me, still half-asleep. "You're so random, Lark."

I shrug, then throw my sheets back and bend down to pick up my phone, checking the screen. "It's ten."

"We should get ready to go, then."

It's funny that we're going back to the place our friendship started. We're in the same school up by Chestnut, but we'd never really talked at all until our classes at the Commons. School is over for the year. Our classes were on Zoom, but it was kind of impossible to pay attention on my laptop, especially since I'm neurodivergent and all. I mean, I'm assuming I'm neurodivergent, anyway. I don't want to be officially diagnosed, which my mom says is fine, as long as I keep a handle on managing everything that's always spiraling around me, but I might have autism, or I might have ADHD, or I might have both. It'd explain why I was bullied. It was almost a relief, to find out that a lot of people who have autism are severely bullied. Like—ah, finally, somewhere I really *do* belong.

Getting ready in my house is always a mess, since I can be in the middle of brushing my teeth before I think about the outfit I want to wear and then I go to see if I can find my favorite tee but then I can't find where I put my freaking toothbrush and I think about fluoride that's in toothpaste so then I sit down at my laptop to look up fluoride and then my mom yells that I'm going to be late and especially when there's another person, it feels like we're in a dance, tripping over each other every three seconds. Kas barges into the bathroom while I'm in the shower.

"Jesus, Kas, get out!"

"Fuck, sorry, I didn't know you were in there—"

"The water is literally *on!*"

He doesn't look at me when I storm into my bedroom, towel tightly wrapped around me. I rummage through my dresser, piles of folded clothes tangling up with each other. I don't even know if I'm actually that mad. It's not like Kas saw anything. I was behind the shower curtain. Maybe I'm just *acting* like I'm mad, because I think that's what I'm supposed to do when it comes to Kasim. His mouth is in a tight line as he brushes past me to walk out into the hall, slamming the bathroom door shut behind him.

Birdie rolls their eyes. "You two fight about the stupidest shit."

My mom's in the kitchen when I go downstairs, hair still damp, drops of water on my neckline. "Good morning, love," she says, looking up at me from the table.

"Morning."

I'm wearing a yellow collared shirt, floral-patterned scarf that doubles as a mask, wide-legged jeans, and white platform sandals. I basically look like Jaden and Willow Smith combined with an Afro that's like a halo or a cloud, ends faded pink. My style is like a hippie from the seventies. Flare jeans and tucked-in bright graphic tees. I couldn't have the name *Lark* and not turn out to be a sunbeam flower child, right?

"Do you want breakfast?"

"No, thanks." I have my phone in my hand, trying to get to my Twitter notifications. They've blown up more than I was expecting. That thread must've gone viral last night after I went to sleep. But my mom grabs my attention.

"You two are going to be late if you don't hurry."

"It's just the Commons, Mom."

"So, it's okay to walk into the center's classes whenever you want to?"

"No, but—"

"Good morning," she says when Kasim walks into the kitchen, a backpack he borrowed from me slung over his shoulder. My gray tee and black sweatpants are usually clothes I sleep in, and it's probably too warm for my beanie, but it all looks extra cozy on him now. A mask is down around his neck. He isn't binding today. He told me once he doesn't always mind his chest. He yanks on one of my beanies, locs down around his face. My mom gives him a huge hug.

"Wait, why didn't I get a hug?" I ask her, but she ignores me.

"Are you hungry, Kasim?"

"Not really."

"You two should probably get going," she says.

"Time's just a construct," I tell her as she smiles at me knowingly, gesturing at us to hurry. "Seriously, it isn't even real. Have you ever noticed that one month can feel like a whole year, and then a year can feel like it just flashed by in the blink of an eye? According to Einstein's theory of relativity—"

But she isn't listening. She practically pushes us outside with a "have fun" before she shuts the door.

I shake my head at Kas. "She does the most."

"You're really lucky to have her."

True. No point in trying to argue with that.

I clutch my hand around my phone in my pocket, but I can't scroll through Twitter and walk at the same time. I usually end up tripping over my own feet, and the sidewalks are cracked, tree roots pushing up the concrete. I'll have to check out the notifications later.

We walk across the porch, down the steps, and into the sunlight. Another day in West Philly, aka Best Philly. My mom and I moved here from Brooklyn about four years ago for multiple reasons, the first being that we couldn't afford to live there anymore, and the second being that the city was really loud and always moving and it turned out that the noise and lights and millions of people weren't helping my anxiety, go figure, and the third being that the bullying had gotten so bad, to the point where the teasing and social ostracization had escalated to me being pushed around and spat on and punched in the face, and, yeah, those are all memories I don't like to think about too much, but, anyway, the point that I'm trying to make is that we left New York and ended up here.

I like West. My neighborhood is a tree-lined street with townhouses that have beautiful porches with potted plants and chairs where our neighbors sit outside and drink tea and watch their kids run around. It's quieter and slower and the people here smile. I haven't had a ton of problems at school. Most of my classmates think I'm weird, and no one really talks to me, but that hasn't mattered much since school basically became little boxes on a screen. Plus there's space for gardens. Only rich people could afford gardens in New York.

But, well—I'm also super self-conscious of the fact that I'm not actually from here, but I'm living comfortably in a house while people who're from this neighborhood are houseless and hungry. A guy riding a bike pulled up to me while I was walking home from school one day and asked for some change and I felt bad that I didn't have any and he told me about how his family had lived in this neighborhood for like fifty years but then they lost the house and they're living on the streets now and I said I was sorry, which felt so meaningless, and I didn't know what else to say, and then he rode away. It's fucked. I hate that I'm a part of the same system that hurts so many people.

Kasim and I walk in an awkward silence, because that's the only way we know how to live our life. The sky is a beautiful blue with fluffy white clouds. Gardens explode around us, huge flowers with bees and butterflies floating by, and pollen dances through the air. Did you know that city planners planted a shit ton of sperm trees but not enough egg trees to take in the pollen and now people living in cities don't have access to free fruit and are forced to buy food and that's why allergy season is the fucking worst? Colorful townhouses compete to have the brightest trims and someone walking their dog calls out to another person across the street, "Hey! How're you doing? Haven't seen you in a while!" It's the perfect spring weather, you know? That cool breeze with that hot sun, and everything buzzing with life. Spring is my favorite season by far.

"Kas," I say, "what's your favorite season?"

"Winter."

The season where everything is cold and dead. Of course it is.

A couple of kids on the corner shout, "Water! Gatorade!" as they sell bottles from a cooler. Signs in windows read BLACK LIVES MATTER and FUCK THE POLICE and ABOLISH ICE and JAWN CROSSING. A mural on the side of an abandoned warehouse shows a child cupping a handful of dirt, a green sprout growing from it, and I think of the poem by Ross Gay, "A Small Needful Fact," which makes me tear up. Kas notices but doesn't say anything. He knows I'm always crying.

My mind wanders, and I think about everything this country's been through these past couple of years. The police brutality, Black people murdered by cops, and there's an epidemic of violence against Black trans women and feminine people, too, and no one can even be sure that the numbers are accurate for nonbinary and gender non-conforming and transmasculine people, when so much visibility is erased. I get scared thinking about that. Worry that I might not even make it to my twentieth birthday. As much as this world feels like everything is falling apart, I love life. I want to live. When the pandemic hit and the world screeched to a stop and people were forced to look and there were protests everywhere, I started to feel more optimistic. Hopeful, that things would really start to change. I remember telling Kasim this, about a year ago now—things had already gotten weird between us, but this was one of the last real conversations we had before we stopped talking altogether—and he'd shaken his head, like he was disappointed in me. "Jack shit's going to change," he said. "There's still prison. There're still cops. They refuse to give us reparations. They talk a good talk, because they don't want to be seen as racist, but they still support the same racist system. Nothing is going to fucking change."

My house is just a five-minute walk away from the Commons. The sidewalk slopes down until we reach the trash bridge, the underpass for a train that rumbles past every night and where all the trash of the neighborhood rolls down the hill and collects in piles and where people dump off garbage, too. There's a muddy pool of water at the bottom. We pause.

Kas gestures. "You first."

"Nuh-uh. You go."

"Same time?"

I pretend to take a step just as he does also, and then we grab arms and elbows, trying to push each other to go first. We end up almost falling into the water, laughing so hard I feel tears prick the corners of my eyes and he gasps, "Wait, wait," until we both manage to leap across. I slip and he catches my arm and holds me up, laughing even harder now.

"Holy shit, you saved my life."

"I'm a hero, right?"

"You're my hero, Kas."

He grins at me, and I grin at him. This feels good. I can't remember the last time we laughed like this. With Kasim, everything used to be so easy. We could look at each other and burst out laughing for absolutely no reason. Maybe our relationship doesn't have to be so weird. We care about each other, right? Isn't that all that matters?

And then we get to the Commons, and the laughter dies. Smiles gone, frowns back on, awkward silence like the entire scene under the trash bridge had only been in my head.

"It wasn't, right?" I whisper.

Birdie pops up in between us. "Nope."

Kasim glances at me. "Huh?"

Before the arguments, we'd spend every minute together—but now, whenever we go to school or to the Commons or basically anywhere in public, we cross into our separate lives again with a brief nod and silent understanding. Kasim has his new friends, after all.

The Common Ground Community Center building used to be an old warehouse. The center kept the industrial feel, and the walls are brick, the floor concrete. It looks more like the inside of a college

lounge or maybe the lobby of a startup tech company with sofas and benches. Almost everyone who's here for the summer classes are people I go to school with. Summer classes were canceled last year, but this year we're back, as long as everyone's gotten their vaccination and wears a mask when they're not in class, since the classes are basically small enough to be their own pods. My mom was still nervous about me coming, and, I mean, with good reason—but I felt like I was crawling out of my skin at home, and besides, I've really missed the Commons' writing class. It might be a good chance to have Birdie's story critiqued. Figure out why I've only been getting rejections from agents.

Kasim pushes open the heavy glass doors.

We step inside, and everything stops.

Heads turn. Chatter and laughter quiets.

There's one long, collective, silent pause.

. . .

Whispers start up, people craning their necks to get a look at us—no, not at us, but at *me*. I know adults say that teens are only imagining it when it feels like everyone's whispering, but right now I am, without a doubt, one hundred percent sure that it's true. You know that feeling of being chased in a nightmare? I feel like I'm running in slo-mo, the monster just a few feet behind. Something must've happened on Twitter—I fucked up on my thread last night, said something I shouldn't have, made a mistake for everyone to see, and now . . .

I look at Kasim for confirmation. "Um. Is everyone staring at me?" I mutter beneath my breath.

"Yep."

And how many fucks does he give?

Zero.

He's already seen his friends Sable, Micah, and Patch sitting together on the staircase, so he walks off without another word. They all look like they belong in an alt fashion show: black shirts and baggy black pants, dyed hair and piercings and tats. A TikTok they made blew up a few months ago, one of those clips where they're walking in and out of the screen and flipping off the camera and sticking out their pierced tongues, song shouting *I don't need your opinion, I'll do what I fucking want*, and all the comments are like *omg I want to be in your friend group so bad!!!!!*

Kasim walks up to Sable and kisses the corner of her mouth, and she interlocks her fingers with his. Sable's a few inches taller than Kas and wears a deep purple lipstick that matches the color she dyed her hair. She catches me staring (*can the girl with the combat boots pls step on me*) and raises a single eyebrow. I can't raise one eyebrow. I've tried. I've practiced in the mirror for hours. How the hell does she do that?

I have a familiar thought: Maybe if I'm nice enough, smile enough, Sable will realize I'm not so bad. She might even want to be my friend, and then Kasim will realize he misses me, and then things can go back to the way they used to be. My mom's told me that I can't make everyone love me. "Not everyone is going to like you," she said. "You'll spend your entire life trying to mold yourself into someone else, but then you'll realize you wasted all that time getting others to like someone who isn't even you."

But if I can mold myself into someone else and change the parts of me that people don't like, then why shouldn't I? This world already has enough excuses to hate someone like me. There's been a bunch of info on social media recently about trauma and how that shapes who we are, but sometimes I look at Black people and queer people and trans people and neurodivergent people and any person this society was built against, and I wonder if we all experience a trauma from the moment we're born into a world that automatically hates us, instantly wants to kill us, already has a system in place to destroy us. Maybe this world itself is a trauma, and in that case, if I have to mold myself into someone who can be accepted by as many people as possible so that I can survive, then I don't think anyone can blame me for doing that, right? I'm already hated by so many. It's okay to want to be liked, too.

Birdie hugs me and rests their head on my shoulder. "I like you, Lark."

"Thank you, Birdie. But you're not real."

There are people I talk to, people I hang out with, people who *are* real, but I don't have a best friend the way Kasim was for me, and yeah, that can be depressing, to see everyone paired up with their ride-or-dies who look like they trust each other with their lives, tell each other their deepest secrets, make you feel like everything will be all right. God. I hate that I miss Kasim.

"Hello? Lark?"

A hand waves in front of my face.

"Huh? What?"

Asha is standing beside me, eyebrows raised and a smile growing on her face, like she thinks I'm weird for standing by the doors, totally zoned out, and, well—she might have a point. Her hair is wrapped behind her pink scarf and she has glittery makeup that shimmers, a pink floral dress and polka dot stockings. Asha can't stand Kasim, but I know she and Sable are best friends—I think they grew up next door to each other—and I'm pretty sure they're in a coven for femmes together. "You okay?" she asks.

"I don't know," I tell her. "I walked in and everyone started staring at me, and that gave me major anxiety, so I kind of froze, and then I started to think about shit, and then I guess I forgot I was standing here."

She eyes me. "You really don't know why everyone's staring at you?"

I twist to her so fast my neck hurts. She knows? "What happened?"

She looks around, adjusting the bag strap on her shoulder. "There's Jamal. Come on, let's go sit down."

Okay, I said earlier that I don't have any friends, but maybe that was an exaggeration. Or maybe not. There's like that gray area, you know? The hard-to-define friends. The friends you hang out with, but only when they're bored and their other friends are busy. The friends who text, but only because they need to know the answer to number fourteen on the history homework. The friends who stop and say hello when they see you staring off into space and will sit with you in class and eat with you at lunch but you kind of get the feeling that it's mostly because you're acquaintances at school and here at the Commons you're one of the few people they know and their best friend is always with her annoying boyfriend, and the second summer is over and we're back in school again, you'll go back to being the sort of friends that only wave and smile at each other in the hallways, until even that dies down into awkwardly pretending you don't see each other by the lockers. But, well, I'm not complaining. Asha's cool peoples. And it's nice to have someone to hang out with, too, so that I'm not completely alone.

We walk across the lobby. Jamal's hanging out on the sofas, reading, like usual. They glance up when we flop onto the couch beside them.

CHARACTER PROFILES!

NAME: Asha Williams

PRONOUNS: She/her

AGE: 16

BIRTHDATE: June 14

ZODIAC: Gemini

HOMETOWN: Orange, New Jersey

OCCUPATION: Student

NAME: Jamal Moore

PRONOUNS: They/them

AGE: 17

BIRTHDATE: September 3

ZODIAC: Virgo

HOMETOWN: North Philly

OCCUPATION: Student

The three of us are a weird group that hibernates during the school year and materializes just for the Commons. Asha has a shit ton of friends—like, seriously, she's probably got fifty friends—while I'm pretty sure Asha and I are Jamal's only friends, since they're home-schooled, which honestly makes me feel special, like we're the chosen ones. They're not shy, not really—but they're a major introvert, and they just don't have a whole lot of patience for other human beings. They stare straight at anyone who ever tries to talk shit about another person, and if anyone tries to complain to them about something that isn't fair, Jamal will reply with a stone-cold face, "Is there something you plan on doing about it, or are you only interested in wasting your energy and mine?" They're really freaking intimidating, and some people think they're just mean, but I can see how kind they are, how thoughtful. "I have a limited amount of time on Earth," Jamal told me once, "and I put a lot of thought into how I intend to spend that time, and who I spend that time with."

You'd think that they wouldn't be able to stand someone like me, but we balance each other out perfectly. They help me calm down and I help them laugh, and we talk a lot about shit that's important to us, like being nonbinary, and books, and we exchange writing with each other outside of class at the Commons. They've even given me feedback on Birdie's story, telling me that it's beautiful, it really is, and they could absolutely see it getting published as a real book one day.

"Okay," I say, lowering my voice, "what the hell is going on? Why is everyone acting so weird?"

Jamal looks up at me like *I'm* the one who's being weird. They've got beautiful dark brown skin and hair they cut short. They're starting to grow wisps of a beard. Most people look at Jamal and assume that they're a guy because they look the way society taught us men are supposed to look, but, welp, society is wrong.

"Don't worry," Birdie whispers. "More people will eventually figure out that gender is infinite."

"What the hell is going on?" Asha repeats. "I was going to ask you the same thing."

I give both of them a blank look, waiting.

Jamal finally puts me out of my misery. "Your Twitter thread."

My throat goes dry. I must've fucked up after all. I'm probably getting torn apart in my notifications. I search my pockets for my phone.

"I don't get why I'd be in trouble, though. Black people do need to think about mental health more, right?"

Asha squints at me in confusion. "What're you talking about?"

"What're *you* talking about?"

"Your post. It definitely wasn't about mental health."

"Yes, it was. I just wrote it last night."

Jamal pulls out their phone and scrolls through their Twitter app. I see my thread about mental health pop up on their feed, which has gotten a good amount of attention. First post has 1.5K likes, almost 500 retweets. But they're right . . . When they click on my profile, I see that it isn't my newest tweet.

My mouth falls open and I grab the phone.

Lark Winters (they/them) @winterslark

How do I tell them that I love them?

💬 3K   🔁 12K   💜 46.1K

Chapter Four

I

Lark Winters (they/them) @winterslark

How do I tell them that I love them?

💬 3K   🔁 12K   ♥ 46.1K

Maybe it's too late to tell them how I really feel. That I've had these feelings for months, for years, as long as I've known them.

💬 3K   🔁 1K   ♥ 10.3K

It'd kill me if they pushed me away. If they told me that they don't feel the same. Maybe it's better, then, to just keep loving them silently.

💬 688   🔁 557   ♥ 6.2K

Just be grateful for the relationship we have now, even when I'm afraid that they might hate me.

💬 96   🔁 238   ♥ 3.3K

How do I tell them that I love them? That's the question I asked, but I already figured the answer out, all on my own: I don't.

💬 973   🔁 803   ♥ 8.5K

I don't tell them that I love them. No matter how much it hurts.

💬 1K   🔁 6K   ♥ 12.2K

All right—so I'm a crier. I cry at everything: kittens curling up when they're asleep and cute romances on TV and when I read the last line of a book that I really loved and never wanted to end. So it's no surprise that this thread makes me feel like I'm going to melt into a sobbing puddle of a mess.

"That's so tragically beautiful," I say, hand covering my mouth, my eyes welling up. "Oh, my God. I feel so sorry for whoever wrote this. I kind of think they *should* tell the person they're in love with, right?"

Asha snaps her fingers. "Lark. Focus."

Jamal squints at me. "You really didn't write that thread?"

I mean, it's not like I *forgot* that this thread was written on my account, but I guess I did confuse my priorities a little. "No," I say. "I really, really did not."

They both stare at me.

"I swear, I didn't write this!"

I read and re-read the thread, look at the huge number of likes and retweets. Did I get hacked? Who would hack me?

Jamal glances back at the book they were reading, *Heavy* by Kiese Laymon. Asha crosses her arms and legs, frowning. "Well, whoever posted it must've gotten into your account somehow. Maybe it's a prank. Have you shared your password with anyone?"

I open my mouth to tell her that I haven't, but the words freeze on my tongue. I haven't shared my account's password, but I *did* share my laptop last night. I look up across the hall just when Kasim glances over at me.

Asha notices. Even though she can't stand Kasim, for some reason she's always joking around and pretending that we're secretly in love with each other, like she has a theory that we're in some

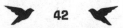

forbidden romantic affair. "You two need to get those smoldering, longing stares under control."

I resist the urge to roll my eyes. "I'll be right back."

"Mm-hmm."

I get up from the sofa and cross the suddenly way-too-big room, my platforms squeaking against the concrete floor, eyes still trailing after me. Maybe everyone's staring because it's only the first day of the center's classes, and we haven't had enough time for anything interesting to happen yet, so everyone's thirsty for drama and gossip—and since most people at the Commons go to my school, everyone's probably assuming I wrote this thread about someone we all know. I'm not Mx. Popular like Asha, but I'm still kind of weirdly well-known, I guess, for having a ton of followers on Twitter and just for standing out with my fashion and just for being—well—me. The fact that the thread is going semi-viral hasn't helped, and to suddenly talk about something as personal as my love life is bound to get views and shares. I can already see the millennials commenting about how *adorable* this is, wanting to hype up *young love*. God. This isn't going to end well.

I approach Kas and his group, hanging on the staircase. I feel like I'm a lowly peon who has just dared to approach the king's throne, Kasim standing higher than everyone else, his courtiers between me and him like bodyguards. Sable notices me first and stares at me blankly. Sable's the sort of person who doesn't feel the need to follow . . . *social norms*. She never smiles, and I've rarely heard her speak. Some people might think she's straight-up weird, but I can feel the power in her. The same sort of *don't give a fuck* power that probably attracted Kas to her in the first place.

The truly judgmental stares come from Micah, whose glare screams *what the fuck do you want?* and Patch, who eyes me and my extremely non-alt outfit. Kasim pretends he doesn't see me as he whips out his phone and starts scrolling. I stand on the second step for a heartbeat, waiting.

"Um. Kasim, can I talk to you?"

He barely glances up.

"It's kind of important."

He sighs and pushes off from the railing. "Fine."

He follows me up the stairs to the second level. I open a door. The room's walls are a burnt orange, and there are two park benches painted a light blue, a longer table against the far corner, and a sofa sectional in the center of the room.

Kasim strolls inside, taking the hat off and tossing it up and down as he sits on the edge of one of the bench tops.

"What's up?" he says, still not looking at me.

I stare at him for a second, unsure of how to begin. "Last night. On my laptop," I tell him. "Did you mess with my Twitter account?"

He raises a brow. "How so?"

"Well, I posted that thread about—you know, mental health."

"Yeah, I know. I was there. My idea, remember?"

I go to my app, then hand him the phone. Kas has always been good at hiding his feelings when he wants to. He eyes the screen, not speaking.

"Was it you?" I ask him. "Did you write this?"

He glances up at me, and I can see the truth in his flinch of shame. I grab the phone back. "What the hell, Kas? Are you trolling me or something?"

He closes his eyes for a second. "It was a mistake, all right?"

Actual confirmation! I don't even know what to feel. There's anger that he'd mess with my account, yes—but there's curiosity, too. This was some seriously heartfelt shit that he wrote. We're not close friends anymore, but I never would've thought he was secretly in love. Pining after someone like this? I feel bad for him, I really do. "How—what—why?"

"I thought I logged you out. I meant to post it on my account. I don't know. I must've been too high to notice."

"Wait, so you *do* have a Twitter account?"

"It's private, anonymous. Not a big deal," he says. "It's like a journal. It's just where I get my feelings out."

"Why don't you—I don't know—keep an actual journal?"

"I like the idea of sending my thoughts and feelings out into the universe. I didn't think so many people would actually see this."

"Well, practically everyone has, and now they think *I* wrote it."

"Yeah. I got that part."

"I have to say that it was you."

This grabs his attention. "What? Why?"

"What am I supposed to do? Everyone will think I'm in love with someone when I'm not. It's going viral. I need to post an explanation." I can already see the backlash. Trolls will just say that I'm lying, that I posted the thread for attention and I planned to say it was an accident from the beginning. I might even lose followers for this. Shit.

"Just say it was some rando."

"Some rando hacked into my account to pretend to be me and say I'm in love?"

Kas rolls his eyes, but from the clench in his jaw I can tell the idea of me sharing his secret makes him upset. "Look, I can't have everyone knowing that I wrote this."

"Why not?"

"I'm . . . you know . . ."

I raise my brows, waiting.

"I've got an image. People see me as . . . kind of hardcore."

I was watching the older version of *The Powerpuff Girls*—it was my go-to background show for a while, I always had it on while I was doing homework or writing—and there's an episode where Bubbles says, "I'll show them. I'll prove that I can be *hardcore*." That's all I can think of as I stare at Kas, who stares back at me, one hundred percent serious. I want to laugh, but I swallow it down. "So you're not allowed to feel love because you're *hardcore*? You've got a girlfriend. Aren't you in love with her?"

The bell rings. The doors are going to open any second, students filing inside.

Kas scratches his cheek. "I have a different way that I survive this world, all right? If everyone finds out that I'm in love with someone who doesn't love me back, they could use that to hurt me."

"No one would—"

"You don't know that. We have different experiences. You've got privileges I don't have."

I bite my lip. He's right. For every difficulty I've ever experienced, Kasim's darker skin means he's dealt with the same bullshit one hundred times over.

"I can already hear the crap people will say. *There's a reason they don't love you back.* I have to protect myself."

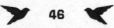

I rub the side of my head. "People are never going to believe it was just some hacker."

Quiet passes. I can already hear voices outside, laughter and the squeak of shoes.

"So?" he says. "Aren't you going to ask me who the thread was about?"

I shrug. I mean, hell yeah, I'm freaking curious, but it's also not my place to ask, right? "Well, I guess you'd tell me if you wanted me to know." He squints at me. "But there're about ten other people besides me who use they-them pronouns at school, though I guess it doesn't necessarily have to be anyone I know, and maybe . . . What?"

He's staring at me, an *are you fucking kidding me?* look on his face before he lets out a laugh of disbelief, shaking his head. "Okay, Lark."

I frown in confusion. "Okay, what?" There's an awkward beat, and he stares at me with that quiet intensity I'm so used to seeing from him. "I mean. It's not like it's me, right?" My laugh is too sudden, too loud.

Kas doesn't look away. The doors open, and a few people from our writing class start to file inside. He pushes off from the bench. "Right. It's definitely not you."

He joins his friends on the sofa. Before I even have a chance to catch myself, to think about how weird that moment was, a guy named Francis comes bounding inside and slings an arm around my shoulder. "Lark," he says. "Spill. Who were you talking about in that Twitter thread?"

This grabs *everyone's* attention, Kasim's included. I shouldn't judge his need to protect himself. I hear my mom's voice all over again, telling me that I can't keep molding myself into someone different, just to please other people. But I'm not just trying to make

everyone happy this time. I'm trying to help Kas. That has to count for something, right?

Birdie whistles. "Sure. If that's what you want to tell yourself."

I swallow, then put on a grin. "Well . . ." I say, then look away from Kasim, at Fran and around the room. "If I said who I was talking about, then it wouldn't be a secret."

Chapter Five

THE COMMONS IS OPEN ALL YEAR, WITH FREE AFTER SCHOOL programs and summer courses any teen can take. There're a ton of classes to choose from, but I only ever do the writing class, where about ten of us sit around the picnic tables and sofa and share our writing and critique each other and talk about books and usually end up having philosophical debates about the meaning of life. It's technically a creative writing course for novels, but Mr. S doesn't care and lets us write whatever we want. I always look forward to class at the Commons, because I love writing, and, well, because of other reasons, too.

CHARACTER PROFILE!

NAME: Eli Miller

PRONOUNS: They/them (and sometimes he/him according to their Insta profile)

AGE: 18 (they're a senior)

BIRTHDATE: ???

ZODIAC: I heard Asha say they're an Aquarius once

HOMETOWN: I *think* West Philly??

OCCUPATION: Student

eli miller instagram

Eli rummages in their backpack, then pulls out a notebook and pencil. They've got golden brown skin and dark brown eyes with long lashes and short hair, almost shaved, that's dyed a bright green. Their septum piercing is intricate and shiny. Their smile is like—how should I put this? If I were writing a story, I would say it's like a warm blanket, hot cocoa, like the sun shining through rain, a sunflower growing, petals blooming—

Birdie shakes their head. "Please. Please, stop."

I'm pretty sure Eli and I are soulmates. Not in the old-school way where there's only one soul out there waiting for us, but in the sense that there are multiple souls that we've all known and loved before in past lives, over and over and over again. From the first moment our eyes met, I felt like I've known Eli a thousand years, and I'm pretty sure from that slowly growing smile they always give me, hooded eyes and tilt of the head, they're also thinking, "Don't I know you from somewhere? I think I do . . ." Maybe we were nonbinary warriors who fought battles side by side until the day we ran away to escape the war, hiding together and loving each other for the rest of our lives.

Birdie sighs. "You're such a hopeless romantic."

Eli notices me, glancing up through their lashes. Crap, I didn't mean to stare. I snap my gaze away so fast it's a miracle my eyeballs don't go flying out my head.

"Hey, Lark." Their voice is so gentle, so soft, and *they're* soft, and I've loved them ever since my writing was critiqued in class a couple of summers ago, and Micah said that my characters were boring, and Eli said that they didn't think my characters were boring, just that they were kind, and kindness is underrated because we're all used to drama and snarky comments and meanness, so anyone who is kind isn't seen as entertaining enough. I think that's the thing I love about them the most: their voice. Every time they speak, it sounds like the beginning of a song. I love to sing, too. Maybe we were two world-famous bards who sang about our love for each other until we were pulled apart and spent the rest of our lives trying to find each other through the songs we sang.

"Hey, Eli." I don't know what else to say, so random words spill out of my mouth before I can make myself stop. "I didn't see you there."

How could I *not* see them? They're literally sitting right in front of me. Asha winces beside me on the bench, feeling the secondhand embarrassment, and pulls out her phone to excuse herself from the awkwardness. But Eli just gives an easy laugh. Maybe that's one reason I've always liked them. I can be weird as fuck, and they only ever laugh like they think my weirdness is cute or funny and not something that makes me a freak. As if maybe—just maybe—they could possibly like me, too. In reality, I mean, and not just in my wildest dreams.

"I saw your thread on Twitter last night," they say.

God? If you're there, if you're listening, show me mercy and smite me out of existence right here and now, please. I would've already been super self-conscious if I'd actually written the thread—to have all my vulnerabilities exposed to the entire world, my crush included—but it's made about a hundred times worst needing to pretend that I've bared my entire soul to the world, and keeping the secret that it wasn't actually me. Isn't that plagiarism? That's technically plagiarism, right? Kasim looks up from the sofa where he's still sitting with Sable and watches, eyes gazing across his royal court.

"It was really beautiful," Eli says. "It made me cry."

"Really?"

"Yeah."

Kasim blinks and looks away. How does he feel, knowing his thread made Eli cry?

"It was brave of you to post."

"Thank you."

Maybe we were two nonbinary pirates who sailed across the world together, looking for lost treasure, only to discover that the treasure we've needed was—wait for it—each other.

Birdie gags.

Eli lowers their gaze. Are they blushing? "I related to it," they say. "A lot."

Wait, hold on—they're in the unrequited love department, too? Seems impossible, since anyone would be over-the-moon happy to date them, clearly. Who the heck doesn't love them back? Who? I just want to have a talk, I swear.

"So—I don't know. Thanks, I guess," they say. "For being so vulnerable and posting it."

I don't know what to say to that. I wish I was witty and charismatic enough to have the perfect response right here and now instead of in two hours, when I'll be torturing myself over this incredibly painful conversation. I force a laugh to cover up the internal panic, and it's a second of silence before I realize what I've done, and now I look like an asshole for laughing at Eli. "I'm sorry," I say. "I don't know why I did that."

They shrug like it's not a big deal, but the damage is done. There's a flinch of hurt in their eyes, and they don't look at me as they flip through their notebook, conversation over. I'd like to shrivel up into nothingness right about now. Why? Jesus Christ, why do I have to be the most awkward being alive?

Maybe that's why Kas decided he couldn't be friends with me. Kasim scrolls on his phone with one hand, other hand playing with Sable's fingers in between them. My chest aches at the tenderness. What is it like, to be touched like that? I wonder if Sable knows who Kasim is in love with. I'm embarrassed. I actually asked Kas if he was talking about me. It wouldn't make any sense. I mean, why would he love me?

Mr. Samuels saves me from this awkward hell and strolls inside. He's probably somewhere in his fifties, his short Afro and beard sprinkled with gray, wearing a tucked-in collared shirt and faded beige slacks that're a couple of inches too long. I like Mr. S. He doesn't act like he's supposed to know everything just because he's an adult.

"All right, all right," he says, clapping his hands together as he walks to the front of the room. "Welcome back to the Commons. None of you are new, right?" He peers around, just to make sure, and when he's satisfied that we're his regulars, he does that teacher one-leg sit/lean thing on the edge of the table that's in front of the room.

"Let's start out class with the usual question," he says. "Hopefully it'll get your juices going, get the creativity flowing, get you burning with excitement and anticipation for what might just be the best writing class of your lives."

"Sounds like we'll need a cream for that," Kas mutters.

Micah snorts.

Fran raises his hand.

Mr. S points at him. "Yes, Fran."

"I have to pee."

Mr. S sighs. "You know this isn't school, right? You don't need permission—"

Before Mr. S is even finished speaking, Fran pushes off the bench, jumps to his feet, and runs out the door.

Mr. Samuels takes a breath. "As I was saying—"

I raise my hand.

"Jesus. Yes, Lark?"

"I want to answer the question."

Patch gives me a look. I know they think I'm annoying, because they've said it before—both behind my back and to my face. "He hasn't even asked it yet."

"But I remember what the question is," I say. "It's always the same question, every semester and summer."

From the way Micah and Patch smirk at each other, I can tell I've fucked up, even if I don't know how, which is honestly confusing to me, because what's so wrong with wanting to answer a question? Asha and Jamal won't meet my eye, and I'm afraid to look at Eli, too.

Mr. S takes a breath for patience. "Go ahead."

My voice is quieter now, throat closing up from the embarrassment. "Well, I've been writing a novel, and I was thinking about this recently, and I realized—what makes a story good—I think it's a trick question, because every single reader will always want something different, right? So to one reader, a book is good, and to another reader, the same book is bad, and in a way, that means every single book in the world is both good and bad, and that cancels each other out, so the answer is nothing makes a story good, in the end. They're just . . . stories. Kind of like people. There are no good people or bad people, and stories are just an extension of people, so . . . Yeah."

Mr. Samuels squints at me, and I'm not too sure I'm making any sense. "Okay. All right. That's certainly one way to look at it. Anyone else want to add? Yes—Kasim."

Kas stares at his phone, not looking up at me or smirking at me, maybe because of the way this morning has gone so far, and he knows I have the power to ruin his life if I wanted to. Not that I want to. "That's bullshit. There're good people and bad people. There're good stories and bad stories." He says it with a finality, like the king has spoken, and anyone who goes against what he's said will be dragged out to the guillotine.

I frown. "No, I disagree. There're just people."

"There are harmful people," Kasim says.

"But we all make mistakes, right? It's just easier to say that we are the good people and other people are the bad people, when in reality, we've all done something harmful, and other people are saying *they're* the good people, and *we're* the bad people, and the cycle just goes on like that forever and ever."

Patch sneers at me. "So you're saying that racists are good people?"

"No—well, I'm not saying it's good that they're racist, but—"

"And transphobes? Misogynists? They're all good people, too, according to you."

"That's not what I'm saying at all."

"Sounds like that's what you're saying."

Mr. S holds up his hands. "I think we've gotten off track."

Patch shakes their head at Micah and mutters, "Lark's so fucking stupid."

My feelings get hurt a lot. I found out that was another thing about maybe possibly having ADHD or autism or both: hypersensitivity to rejection. It's like I can feel everyone's hatred bubbling up around me, and something goes off in my brain from the caveman days when we would literally die if we weren't accepted by other people. That's what it feels like. It feels like I'm dying. Old thoughts start to find me again, thoughts that I've been pretty good at avoiding because I know they'll suck me in like a black hole. I'm not really sure, I guess, what the point to being alive is when I'm not accepted anywhere I go. If I'm just going to be hated by everyone for the rest of my life, what's the point?

Birdie sits on top of the table beside me. "There are people who already love you and don't even know you yet."

Fran waltzes in through the door and jumps into his seat on the bench. "What'd I miss?"

Eli raises their hand. "I kind of get what Lark is saying," they say. "One person's favorite book in the entire world might be a book that another person hates. It's kind of impossible to say what makes a good story, when everyone's definitions are different. Maybe it's not that a book is good or bad, but that we like and don't like certain books because of who we are, personally, and that's okay, too. We could say that a book doesn't work for who we are as a person instead of just saying that it's bad."

Mr. S nods. "That's really thoughtful, Eli."

I'm not super proud of it, because I try to be as happy and peaceful as possible, but I feel a glimmer of annoyance. I don't get why Mr. S says that Eli is thoughtful, when I just said pretty much the same thing. Why does it feel like people just don't understand me whenever I open my mouth, like I'm speaking a different language?

Mr. Samuels continues. "I always ask that question on the first day of class because I like watching how the answers change. Sometimes, you all decide a good book is based on character—sometimes, you say it's whether the plot has enough action or not. You're right that the definition of good changes from person to person. But, now, maybe the next question is whether you as writers should be trying to please as many people as possible, make the story work for as many people as possible, regardless of the question of whether a story can be defined as good or not."

"Well, yeah," I say, forgetting to raise my hand. "I mean—isn't that the point of writing?"

Mr. Samuels considers. "Some of the greatest creatives were hated in their time. It was only until after their deaths, in many cases, that their work changed the world. What if people just aren't ready for your story? Should you bend yourself to write what they want, what they expect? Should you write what is different, and what is true to you, even if your work will be rejected by others?"

If I even want to get an agent and get a book sold, I have no choice but to bend myself to what other people want, right? But I'm not going to say that, because Asha has nudged me with her knee under the bench to let me know that I'm talking a lot, which I don't always realize I'm doing until an hour has gone by and it's too late and everyone is already pissed at me for taking up too much space.

"Well," Mr. S says when no one answers him, "I'll leave you all with that as something to chew on."

For the rest of the hour, I write and write and write, and even after class is technically over and everyone else has gotten up, talking and laughing as they walk out the door, I stay glued to the same spot

and keep writing some more. I haven't finished Birdie's story yet—the plot is a mess, I can't figure out how to make things actually *happen*, and I end up writing like twenty pages and then dumping it all because it's trash. I want to have a full manuscript ready to go in case an agent requests it, even though the possibility feels more and more impossible with every rejection I get. But I'm still holding out hope. My number-one wishlist agent, Janet Fields, still hasn't responded. All it takes is one *yes* for everything to change, right? That's what all of the published authors on Twitter say. You could get a zillion rejections, and it just takes one yes for all of your dreams to come true.

Asha texts me and Jamal, asking us to hang out with her at the Dog Bowl, an hour after class ends and everyone else has already left. I don't know, maybe her plans with her other friends fell through and she's bored. I take the scenic route, heading up to Baltimore Avenue and pass by the twinkling lights strung in trees, the record store with the white cat that always sits in the window blinking sleepily, the diner where I used to eat with my mom on Saturday mornings before the pandemic, the tattoo shop where I know Kas and all his friends go to get their work done, something I wish I was brave enough to do, but, well, I don't like the idea of pain, and also, my mom would kill me. The closer I get to the intersections that'd take me up to UPenn, the more white people there are, holding hands on the sidewalk or sipping coffee at the café on the corner, some not socially distancing like they probably should. The townhouses up here are like miniature mansions that're probably worth a million dollars. Things have always been tense around this area, with UPenn gentrifying the neighborhood.

I cross the street into the park and head over to the Dog Bowl, a small valley that slopes down in the middle of the park, where people like to unleash their dogs and let them run free. The park's busier than I'd expected it to be for a Monday afternoon, with couples booed up and snuggling together on blankets. I'm about to walk around the rim when I hear a whisper.

"Hey."

I turn around, but I don't see anything.

"Hey, kid."

I see someone half hiding behind a tree. They wave me over. They're older than me, maybe in college, and they have a shaved head and they're wearing a graphic tee. Something tells me I shouldn't go over, but I do anyway, stopping a few feet away, pulling my scarf up over my nose and mouth. "Yeah?"

They look around, over their shoulder. "Wanna try some drugs?"

Seriously? "You're really going to be *that* person offering drugs at the park?"

They shrug. "You look like the type."

"I only do weed. I don't want to overdose and die."

"No, no," they say, waving a hand around. "I'm not offering crack or meth or any shit like that. That stuff'll kill you. I'm talking shrooms. The ancients, I'm telling you—they used this as medicine. If you take it with intention, to help heal your wounds, not just for fun or any shit like that, it'll break open your brain. Gives you a mind-bending, alternating reality kind of experience that the government doesn't want you to know about, because then we'd all be free of this system we're trapped in, and we'd have the power to save the fucking world."

I hesitate, but only for a second. "Still no."

They nod. "Yeah, maybe you shouldn't. You're probably not in the right place in your life to try it. Besides, people reading this book wouldn't like it if you did."

"*What?*"

Before I can say anything else, they've already vanished behind the tree again. I hear someone calling my name, and I turn around to see Asha hurrying over. She grabs my arm and starts to pull me away. "What did I tell you about talking to weirdos at the park?" she mutters under her breath.

"I can't help it. There's something about me that attracts them." Maybe it's because I'm a weirdo, too. Maybe we're all weirdos, but we want to be liked, so we try not to be weird, which is kind of sad, when you think about it, the fact that we're all wonderfully weird and trying to hide it.

Asha takes me over to a giant tree that has its roots dancing in and out of the ground. Jamal is sitting there, looking like they're already regretting coming out at all, book open in their lap. Asha plops onto the ground beside them, rummaging into her backpack for something, and I see the real reason she invited us out: there's a shiny, glittering deck of cards in her hands.

She grins apologetically. "I have to practice using my oracle cards on somebody."

I sit down opposite. "Maybe you can ask the universe how I should get out of this mess with my *how do I tell them that I love them* thread."

"Oh, yeah, it's getting reposted everywhere," Asha says, picking up the cards and starting to shuffle them. "I can't believe how much it's blown up. Isn't it almost at one hundred thousand likes now?"

It'll probably be my most viral tweet, and I didn't even write it.

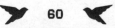

"Reminds me of those Reddit posts," she says. "Remember, the ones where people say they're secretly in love with their best friend, and—?"

Jamal raises an eyebrow at me. "But this morning, you said that it wasn't you."

I hesitate. If I tell them the truth that it was Kasim, then there would've been no point in lying to the entire class—no point in trying to protect him. I love Asha, but she's the biggest gossip in the world, and if she finds out that I lied to protect *Kasim* of all people, especially when she doesn't even like him to begin with, well . . . Chances are, the entire center would find out by the end of tomorrow that the thread was really by Kas.

"I was just playing around," I say.

Asha stops shuffling and tilts her head to the side. "Huh?"

"Earlier," I say, nodding, and trying not to feel bad about the fact that I'm lying yet again. "I lied. It was me."

Asha and Jamal exchange glances, and I can tell neither of them are buying it.

"I didn't want to admit that it was me," I say, releasing a breath. An Oscar-worthy performance, if I do say so myself. "I really did accidentally post it to my main account. I meant to post it to my side one, and it was super embarrassing, so I pretended that I didn't write it and then rushed off so I wouldn't have to deal with any questions, and . . . yeah. It was me."

Asha's nodding slowly. She seems to believe me more now. But Jamal only frowns. Not sure what their expression means.

"There's nothing to be embarrassed about, Lark," Asha says as she goes back to shuffling. "You didn't have to lie about it. What's so embarrassing about being in love? Ask a question. Any question."

I shrug, unable to meet her eye. "It's more about how vulnerable I was, I guess." I go for the obvious. "Will the person I love start to love me back?"

Jamal snaps their book shut. "I have to go," they say.

We both look up at them, startled. "Oh. Okay," Asha says. I try to wave bye, but they're already on their feet, back turned, before I can even raise my hand. Asha snorts and shakes her head. "You two are so weird."

Right. It's because Jamal is weird that they suddenly left, and not because they can probably see right through my lie and have decided they can't even stand to breathe the same air as me, the liar. Lark the Liar. Maybe that's what everyone should start to call me. I try to remind myself that I'm doing this for a good reason. I'm just trying to help out Kas.

I pull out my phone and text Jamal, even as I can see them far off in the distance, crossing the street. **everything ok?**

Asha scrunches up her face in concentration as she shuffles. One card flies out, and then another. She places them in front of me. "According to these cards, you are a starseed, and your purpose in life is to raise the vibration of the earth."

"That's cool," I say, nodding excitedly. "It doesn't really answer my question, though."

She sighs and begins to shuffle again.

My phone buzzes in my hand. **why are you telling everyone that you wrote the thread? you're obviously lying**

Shit. I hadn't planned on Jamal being a human lie detector, but that definitely fits them, now that I think about it. They've always had a zero-tolerance policy for bullshit. But Jamal will understand if I explain it to them.

"It's kind of cool, when you think about it," Asha says. "I mean, I know you were sort of famous before, but you're legit famous now."

I bite my lip. "I didn't really expect the post to get so much attention."

ok ok, its just a misunderstanding, I text Jamal back.

pretty big misunderstanding.

yeah. itd take forever to clear up, so thats why im just saying it was me

why would it take forever? you literally just have to say that it wasn't you

I still can't reveal that it was all for Kas. And then there's the other reason, too. The other reason that's probably even bigger than Kasim, if I'm going to be honest with myself. **um kinda? i have to figure out a way to do it with more *finesse* or i'll get a lot of backlash**

"So, who *were* you talking about, anyway?" Asha asks casually, as if she doesn't really care if I tell her.

"I'm going to keep that a secret," I say, forcing a laugh that I hope looks embarrassed and self-conscious. "I'm pretty sure they don't feel the same way."

I check my phone, but Jamal hasn't texted back. Why do I have the feeling that I've royally fucked up this time?

Birdie stage whispers. "Because you have."

Three cards fly out of Asha's deck. "Okay, so, you're surrounded by your soul family, and you need to remember that you are loved, but

also that you need to love yourself and not be dependent on the love of others to realize you're worthy of love." She grins at me. "I think I'm getting better at this."

Love myself. Easier said than done. But it's something I would like to figure out how to do one day. I want to learn how to love myself. Really, seriously, truly—energetically, down to my bones, love myself in the same way that I love other people around me. *I love myself.* How do you really begin to believe that, feel that? That's what I would like to know.

I nod at her with a small smile. "Sounds like a message from the universe to me."

Chapter Six

I

I'VE BEEN DREADING LOOKING AT MY NOTIFICATIONS, BUT ON THE walk home I manage to open my Twitter app to look at my (*Kas's) thread without tripping over my own feet.

> **Lark Winters (they/them)** @winterslark
> How do I tell them that I love them?
> 💬 11K   🔁 39K   ❤️ 97.1K

Oh, my God. At this point, it's hit the level of viral that a shit ton of bots are probably liking and retweeting, which will just make this go into an uncontrollable spiral on overdrive. I know I have to seriously sit down and deal with the comments, and I have to post something new, too. It's been almost a full day of silence. I can't just ignore that this is blowing up, and it could also be a huge opportunity to promote myself and Birdie. But honestly? I *wish* I could just drop into bed and read and do nothing else.

It's only when I unlock the front door that I hear voices in the kitchen. Taye's voice. I slow down, then close the front door super softly so that I can sneak up to my bedroom. Taye's an amazing person—he's got the vibe of someone who has lived a million lives and has one of the oldest souls of anyone on Earth and is really patient and kind and compassionate and will do anything for Kasim, absolutely anything—but I always feel bad whenever I see him. Like when Taye looks at me, I can feel him silently wondering why I'm not friends with his little brother anymore, and I don't really have an answer, so it's just easier to avoid him.

I make it halfway up the staircase before I hear Kas's name.

"I'm worried about Kasim," Taye says. "He's not talking to me about it. Not anymore. Trying to pretend he's better now. I've dealt with that shit too, you know?"

My mom's voice is soft, warm. "He might need space. Maybe he needs to feel like he can come to you when he's ready."

"This shit's scary," Taye says. He sounds so tired. He's twenty-eight, but he sounds like a sixty-year-old man with the world on his shoulders. Why is life so much harder for some people than it is for others? "I can't sleep worrying about Kasim. Not knowing if he's going to be all right. Not knowing what I can do to help him."

His voice breaks a little, and hearing that—God, it breaks my heart, it really does. I start to cry right there on the stairs, just listening to Taye. I'm intruding. I shouldn't even be here, eavesdropping on them, but it's hard to get my feet to move.

"You're doing everything you can for him," my mom says. "Everything and more."

There's a pause, and I hear Taye taking a few deep, long breaths.

"Listen," he says, "I really don't know how to say thank you for all that you do. Letting him stay over . . . I feel guilty leaving him home alone."

"It's not a problem."

"The new manager—shit, he said he'll fire me if I don't go. I tried explaining I need to be able to stay here in Philly, that I've got a kid brother."

"You know I love having Kasim around. And even if they're in a rocky place, I know Lark's happy to have him around, too."

Aaaaand that's my cue. My feet—wow, suddenly they can move. I make it up about three more steps before the wood squeaks beneath my shoe. I wince.

"Lark?" my mom calls. "That you?"

I close my eyes and take a deep breath before I turn around, thump down the stairs and into the kitchen. Taye's hunched forward in his chair, hands clasped together like he's in prayer, beer bottle sweaty with condensation on the table. Taye's really handsome: dark brown skin and dark brown eyes, so dark you can't see the irises, and hell yeah, I see the power and beauty in that, a wide nose and lips. Kas looks a lot like him, I guess. Which means, I guess, that Kasim is also pretty handsome. I guess.

"Why're you trying to sneak by without saying anything?" my mom asks.

"Hey, Taye."

Taye gives a small smile and nods. His eyes are red, maybe from crying or from being so exhausted or both. "Good seeing you, Lark." He finishes off his beer and stands up. "Should get going. Security shift starts in a few."

Taye claps my shoulder as he passes. He leaves with a wave, closing the door behind him. I try to back out of the kitchen, hands behind my back.

"And where're you going?" my mom asks, leaning back in her seat, arms wide for a hug.

I hold in a groan and drag my feet over to her. "I need to work on my Twitter account. My notifications are crazy."

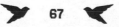

My mom gets up and holds me close, smoothing down my hair. "*Notifications.* I thought you said you were going to cut down on social media."

"I have!" I haven't been posting every single day like I normally would, but this doesn't mean I want to stop completely.

My mom frowns. "The amount of time you spend on Twitter can't be healthy."

"You're always on Facebook."

"Because I like looking at photos of coworkers from the library. I'm not on there getting into fights with white supremacists."

"I'm not fighting with white supremacists! Besides, social media isn't all bad. It spreads education and helps us connect." That may or may not be a line I've practiced in my head.

"True," she acknowledges, "but I don't like that you think you've got so much responsibility. You're still only seventeen, Lark. You don't need to dedicate your entire life to saving the world just yet."

I know that she says this with love, but hearing those words from adults always annoys me. Yeah, I *know* that I shouldn't need to dedicate my life to trying to save the world, but our generation doesn't really have a choice. We have to fight for gun control so that we don't get shot at school. We have to fight for the environment so that we'll actually live on a breathable planet that isn't half-flooded, half on fire. Mari Copeny has *been* fighting for people to have the right to drink *clean water*, something that every human on this planet should have access to, and corporations have been finding ways to bottle and market it as if it's something only people with money should be able to drink.

Birdie stretches their wings. "Fear."

The earth creates food, water, and shelter naturally, right? So how—seriously, how is it possible that we've decided so many people don't deserve something that has been created by this planet we all live on? That some people don't deserve a house, or clothes, or food, because we're so brainwashed to think it's a crime to not have money, when it's really because of the same system of money, which is fake, it's not even real, and then takes that fake resource of money away so that people will suffer while Jeff Bezos goes into space. *A rat done bit my sister Nell with whitey on the moon.* Why are there people who actually *want* others to suffer? I don't understand it. *Hurt people hurt.* That's what my mom always says. Is it because they're hurting that they want to hurt others, too? That makes them want to keep control, even when facing an entire world of people screaming for change?

Birdie's smile is soft. "Your civilization eventually begins to learn that it's all because of fear. You're living in an exciting time, Lark. An exciting generation. The one that helps create a new era, where you leave behind fear for love."

But maybe I shouldn't get annoyed at my mom. She and countless of our elders and ancestors have dedicated their lives to fighting for a better world. We wouldn't have even progressed to where we are today without their work, their sacrifices, their love for us and dreams of the future. We're their manifestations. Maybe if everyone in the world sits and dreams of a world where we don't harm each other because we're hurt and afraid, we could manifest that, too.

My mom pats my cheek. "Just promise me you'll try to cut the social media down, all right? I don't want you to stress yourself out."

"All right. I promise." Lark the Liar lives on. My mom sighs and rests her chin on the top of my head, and I feel like a little kid. "What were you and Taye talking about earlier? About Kasim, I mean."

My mom just gives a *hmm* and kisses my forehead. "Don't worry about it."

I frown as I walk up the stairs. My mom said not to be worried, but curiosity and concern mix together, and I start to think that something might be really wrong with Kasim, something I haven't noticed is right in front of me.

When I finally sit down at my laptop, I take a deep breath before I open up my web browser. I've been procrastinating even looking at my notifications, because the idea of shifting through thousands of comments makes me freeze, and—

My mouth falls open.

Lark Winters (they/them)
@winterslark

certified enby and wannabe author | they/them (sometimes he/him and she/her but mostly they/them) | 17 | cancer

📍 Philadelphia, Pennsylvania   🎈 Born July 14

1K Following   35K Followers

My follower count has almost *doubled*, holy *shit*, I have 35K followers, what the *fuck*—

I put my hands on the sides of my head, mouth opening and closing. I'm—hold on, where's my phone, okay, calculator app—I'm 15K away from my goal. When I have 50K followers, not only will a ton of agents offer me representation—oh no, not only that—but the ones who rejected me will email me an apology and say that they thought about it more and they realized they were wrong, and they'll all get into an agent battle over me, calling me and telling me why I should go with them, offering to buy me a train ticket to NYC so that they can show me the office and buy me lunch, telling me how much they love me and Birdie and how I'll be the next big author that everyone loves and adores—

"That's what's going to happen?" Birdie asks from my beanbag chair. "Really?"

And Asha was right: From a ton of tags, I see that the thread is getting shared everywhere—on BuzzFeed, Reddit, Mashable, TikTok, people's Insta accounts, all of these sites talking about how it inspired a bunch of people to confess their feelings and tell their own unrequited love stories. The response has been overwhelmingly beautiful. I never would've thought a tweet as simple as the one Kas wrote would inspire so much talk about love.

On the one hand, it's freaking amazing that my profile has basically exploded overnight. On the other, it's kind of crappy that my profile has exploded overnight, because as reality settles in, I realize that I have to figure out how to handle this new online fame thing if I actually want it to work to my advantage.

Birdie squints at me. "Is that the only reason it sucks, though? I'm sure you could think of another one."

I could add onto the thread something new, maybe—a post that goes something like:

But then what if an agent actually *does* hit me up? I would have to sit down and finish Birdie's story in, like, twelve hours.

"Probably not a good idea," they say, nodding.

No. Definitely not.

My phone buzzes me awake. I just went to bed maybe thirty minutes ago after sifting through all of the thread's comments, liking and RT'ing as many as possible, and my wrist legit hurts from clicking nonstop for hours. I groan and roll over, checking the notification. It's 1:23 in the morning, and I have a text message from Kas.

You up?

I plop back down on my back, holding my phone above me, the screen a portal to heaven, light blinding my eyes. I squint and type. **i am now.**

Meet me at our spot?

Caught a vibe—baby, are you coming for the ride? I haven't met with Kas at the courts in over a year. We used to sneak out and meet up every single week, smoking and laughing and talking until the sun started to rise sometimes. And then, toward the end of our friendship, the hours out at the courts got shorter and shorter, and the arguments got longer and longer, until finally one day I realized that Kas hadn't asked me to go to the courts in months.

Kasim's name glares at me on my phone. I could just ignore his text. But I'm pretty curious, too. Why now? **ok. sure.**

I sigh, roll over, and get to my feet. I pull on sweatpants, a sweater, and sneakers before I tiptoe down the hall and the stairs, out the door and into the chilly night.

Chapter Seven

KASIM LIVES THIRTY MINUTES AWAY, BUT HE LIKES TO WALK around when he can't sleep. My mom wouldn't be happy if she ever knew I left my bed in the middle of the night to meet up with him. It's a miracle we did this for over two years and she never found out.

I'm only a few blocks away from the basketball and tennis courts, in the opposite direction of the Commons. The sky is pure black, and there aren't any lights on this particular street, so I use my phone to shine a path on the crosswalk and make sure I'm not about to step in dog poo. I cross the street to the park where the lights shine white, and sitting on a low wall is Kas. He smokes and shivers in his thin hoodie as I hop up beside him. He offers a roll, but I shake my head.

"What's going on?" I ask when he doesn't say anything. "Why'd you ask me to meet you here?"

He doesn't look at me. "I'm sorry about today. With the Twitter thread, I mean. I panicked."

"Okay."

"I shouldn't have let you take the fall just because I was scared." He blows out smoke. "I've been thinking about it all day. It was a bullshit move. I'm always talking about not giving a fuck what anyone thinks, right? And now here I am, too scared to tell the truth."

This is the sort of the thing that he'd say to me when we were still friends. I can't remember when he was last this honest with me about anything. A warm tingling spreads through my chest and over my head, and I feel a little like I've traveled back in time. As much as I hate to admit it, I miss him. I want my best friend back.

I force a shrug. "It wasn't a big deal."

He looks at me for one long second before he snorts, shaking his head.

"What?"

"It's like you're fine arguing with me about bullshit for hours, days, weeks—but when it comes to you actually standing up for yourself, you'll let anything slide."

That's a confusing thing for him to say. "You know what—yeah, let me have a little." He hands over the weed and I breathe in, so long and hard that I begin to cough. He smacks my back. My eyes sting with tears and I suck in a breath.

"Still don't know how to smoke," Kas says with a growing smirk.

I hand the weed back him. "Do you think you did something that I should stand up to?"

He nods, locs falling into his face. "I shouldn't have let fear get in the way of owning up to my mistake. I should've dealt with the consequences. That's why I apologized. I was an asshole."

"I thought you were happy being an asshole."

He grins at me. "I'm happy that I can mess up and be an asshole and still be considered a human being. Same way them white boys get to be assholes and are called *hot* for being abusive. Watching them white girls sleep at night in movies and shit. Fuck. At least let me make a mistake." His grin fades. "I mess up, same as anyone else, but I'm not happy when I actually hurt someone. This has been eating me up all day. I'm really sorry, you know?"

I don't know what to say to that. I swing my feet and stare down at my sneakers. "It's too late now, anyway. I can't say that it was you all along."

"Why not?"

"People will call me a liar."

"Well, to be fair . . . you did lie."

"For *you.*"

"Now," Kasim says, looking away with that little twinge of a smile that lets me know annoyance is beating through him, "that's where you don't get to throw your mistakes off on me. We both fucked up. Yeah, I fucked up first," he says, "and I hurt you in the process. But that doesn't mean you get to blame me for the fact that you went and fucked up, too."

"How did I fuck up?"

"It was still your choice to go along with it. You could've been like, *nah, son, you made your bed* and told the truth from the beginning. But you were worried about what people would think, right? That's literally what you said. So don't pretend you decided to lie just for my sake. You lied for your own benefit."

I hate when he's right. I hate it so much, I feel like my bones are smoldering. "Fine. I'm sorry." There's a long enough silence that I know I could just let it end there, but the fire is getting hotter and hotter until I can't take it anymore. "But I'm not like you. I *do* care what people think. You act like it's a crime, to want to be liked."

"I never said it was a crime."

"And it isn't easy to just come out and say I was lying. People would rip me apart." This could be the end of my Twitter profile, the end of my dream of being published before it's even begun. "I already get treated like trash. Excuse me for wanting a break from that."

After some quiet, Kasim shifts so that he can look me in the eye. "Okay, real talk. Shit's happened between us. I'm not even really sure what. But either way, we're not friends. Not like we used to be."

Yeah. We both know it's true. What's the point in sitting here with Kasim, pretending we're in a different world and a different time?

Kasim goes on. "I guess you started to get mad at me or not like me anymore for not giving a shit about what other people think. Like you get legit mad at me for not caring. But you know what? I also love not needing to convince a single fucking person to like me. I'm just going to be myself. Fuck anyone who decides I'm not worth their respect because of that. I'm over trying to convince anyone to like me. I'm over trying to convince anyone I deserve to exist, too. I'm tired of the fake smiles, trying to show everyone that I'm harmless. You have no fucking idea. When I'm walking down the street, even at school, most people are looking at me like I'm the fucking enemy every god damn day, just because of this body that I'm in, this body that I *love*. You know shit would be different if I looked different. We see that evidence in front of us, everywhere. *Please accept me. Please love me.* Fuck that shit. I don't need other people to love me when I already love my damn self."

No, Kas and I don't always agree, but I also love listening to him when he talks this way, with all the power of poets and pastors, just saying whatever thought comes to him. Plus, I'm a little high. *Fuck that*

shit? God. I really wish I could feel the same way. Maybe I wouldn't be so exhausted, trying to make everyone happy, trying not to think too hard about the question of whether I even like myself, which is definitely a question I try to keep away with a ten-foot pole, yeah, no, I don't want to think about that one at all.

Kas continues. *"Aren't you tired of being so angry?"* Kas says. "Yeah, I'm tired, but it's even more exhausting trying to bend over backwards to be accepted. No. Fuck that, Lark, seriously. It's time to claim what's ours. This is our world. If I let someone in to see me, the real me, it's got to be with the understanding that they're here by invitation only. They're not going to say shit about how I'm allowed to act, how I didn't do enough to kiss their ass and make them feel comfortable with my life, with my body, with my existence. It's time that white people, straight people, cis people start to realize that the world isn't theirs. Never was, never will be. Their opinions and their gaze on me is worth shit. What're *they* going to do to make me feel more comfortable with *their* asses? How're they going to prove to me that they're ready to tear down this society that was built for their success and my death?"

"It's not just white people and straight people and cis people and whoever else that'll wish you weren't so angry," I tell him. "I wish you weren't so angry, too."

"You know what? I'll admit, that hurts."

"I'm just saying. If you weren't so angry, people would probably see things your way more easily. Just stop yelling so much, you know? Don't be so loud and angry about it, and people will actually want to change."

He doesn't look at me. "Don't be so loud and angry?"

When he repeats it with that disgusted tone, it doesn't sound great, but . . . "Well. Yeah."

"So you're trying to tell me what I can and can't say, and how to say it."

"I'm just suggesting—"

"I don't agree with your silent, smiling protest."

"I'm not saying you have to be silent."

"You're trying to tell me to shut the hell up."

"I'm not trying to tell you to shut up!"

"Not with those exact words, but yeah, basically, you are. You're trying to say that I don't get to feel and I don't get to have emotion and I don't get to talk about my traumas with hurt and rage because you're worried about how the rest of the world will view not only me, but you, too, because we're both Black and we're both queer and we're both trans. That's its own kind of trauma, to hear something like that from inside of the community. *Don't be so loud. Shut up. We don't care about your experiences, because you're not hopeful or positive or optimistic enough. Shut up. You can't talk about your pain or your anger, because you're showing too much to the outsiders. Shut the fuck up.*"

I want to fight what he's saying, but I know there's truth in his words. His anger isn't harming me. Him talking about his trauma isn't hurting me. I only want Kasim to stop because I'm afraid of how other people will view me, too. Because they might see his anger, and decide that because we share identities, I'm not the likeable person I've worked so hard to be.

Kasim lowers his voice, eyes hooded as he meets my eye and watches me carefully. "Just doing a call-in."

"I know," I say, my voice hoarse, and not just because I almost choked to death on weed. I take a deep breath. "You're right. I'm sorry. I shouldn't have said that."

"Thank you."

We sit in quiet for a heartbeat. I want to laugh at myself for thinking that Kasim is in love with me. A laugh really does escape, and he gives me that *you're weird* look, but he at least has the *and I'm okay with it* smile to go along with it.

"What?" he says, starting to laugh a little, too.

It's embarrassing to admit out loud, but, well, weed takes away the embarrassment and anxiety and makes it feel like everything is going to be okay, even if it's just for a little while. "Today," I tell him. "When I was trying to figure out who you're in love with."

His smile starts to fall a little. "Yeah?"

Another snort escapes, and I look up at the sky as I laugh. "I can't believe I actually asked if you were talking about me. That's so embarrassing, right?"

I look away from the sky and meet his gaze and my grin instantly drops. Because now Kasim is watching me with that look, that intense-as-hell look, and I believe what so many people say, that we're all made of energy, and emotion is energy, so, yeah, we can feel the emotion of other people, too, and right there, in that second, I can feel it just as much as I can see the answer on his face.

Kasim is in love with me.

He swallows, like he's thinking of saying the words. I look away again, and I'm thinking of just straight up running away, because I really don't know what to do with that information, kind of in the same way that I'm not sure what to do with the information that a shit ton of people believe that parallel universes have been colliding, which would make sense, actually, because that could explain Kasim being in love with me, because it's the wrong Kasim, obviously, from a parallel universe, and I'm starting to think I just imagined it anyway, because it wouldn't make any sense, would it, that *Kasim* from any universe would be in love with *me*, that *I'm* the one he wrote that pining-after thread about—

Birdie does a balancing act as they walk across the wall, arms spread out. "I think it makes perfect sense. Why wouldn't he love you, Lark?"

Kasim nudges my shoulder with his. I'm too afraid to look at him, too afraid of the words that're about to come out of his mouth, but I glance at him out of the corner of my eye and see that he's staring up at the sky, too. "Did you hear that shit about the radio signals?"

I almost sigh in relief. "What radio signals?"

"There're some radio signals traveling through space." He pulls out his phone, scrolling and reading aloud: "*Repeating fast radio bursts are coming from a nearby spiral galaxy about 500 million light years from Earth.* Well, apparently this has been happening all along."

"You're such a nerd."

"Aliens, Lark. It's aliens. You have to admit that's pretty fucking cool."

My breath still shakes when I let it out. "I think it's funny that there're probably a shit ton of super-advanced species out there, but they're too bored with us to even bother trying to make contact," I say. "Or they can see that we're a really young civilization, and we still have a lot to figure out—like, you know, how to stop killing each other and hurting each other and stop destroying our own planet."

He squints up at the sky. God. He's so high. "Pretty sure at least some of the aliens are just us, from the future, or maybe another parallel universe, observing us during the most historic moments in our lifetime."

"Maybe something huge is about to happen, but we just don't know it yet."

"Maybe we're all ETs, but we've had our memories wiped, and we don't remember anything about why we're here or what we're supposed to be doing."

"Thanks, I hate it here."

He laughs, catching my eye and not letting go. Yeah, I've thought that Eli and I have known each other for a thousand years—but if I'm going to be honest with myself, I feel like I've known Kas since the beginning of existence itself. Since the moment there was a burst of energy that exploded into an infinite number of dimensions, and we were split apart, always trying to find each other again and again, throughout the future and into the past, right here and now as we look into each other's eyes and try to remember how to become one. Missing each other so much and wanting to be whole, but getting in our own ways over and over and over, interdimensionally tangled until the end of all time.

Or maybe I'm a little higher than I thought.

His smile fades. For a second it looks like he's got something else to say, but then he jumps down from the wall. "Oh," he says with a half-grin, "have you read the comments? All those people confessing their feelings and shit? Guess we kind of started something."

Lark Winters (they/them) @winterslark

How do I tell them that I love them?

💬 9K   🔁 43K   🖤 108.3K

jj jones @fuckdapolice3000

thx for posting this, nice to know my single ass isn't the only one lonely as fuck lololol

💬 91   🔁 357   🖤 1K

Victoria 🕸 Foster @Spider_Yarrow

hey bestie why you being so emotional and shit you got me feeling things I don't wanna feel pls leave me alone I just wanna be a depressed bisexual in peace ty 🖤

💬 7   🔁 16   🖤 102

bethany (on hiatus) @hexatius

this has me so sad. I know how you feel. I'm so sorry. It sucks to not have the love of your life love you back. I'm tired of adults saying we don't know what love is. we know what love is before we're even born.

💬 0   🔁 0   🖤 0

Lark Winters (they/them) @winterslark

im so blown away by all of the support!! thank you everyone for the love and well wishes. i don't know if ill tell them that i love them, but with so many people rooting for me, who knows? i just might. <3

💬 1.9K   🔁 6.8K   🖤 10.4K

Chapter Eight

Michael Cruz <mcruz@writershome.com>

Dear Lark,

Thank you for reaching out! What a wonderful concept and great first fifty pages. It's so impressive that you're only seventeen. I do love Birdie's character, but I worry that Birdie might be a little too self-aware and "deep" for a teenager. They were a bit difficult to believe because of this, unfortunately.

Also, you should know that a major rule in the writing community is that main characters should not also be writers. It's a little too self-indulgent, if you know what I mean. ;)

Yours truly,

Michael

Why do so many adults assume children and teens can't have any depth? No, seriously—why?! Maybe it's because those adults didn't have any depth when they were younger, so they don't think anyone else can, either. But society evolves with every new generation, right? Sure, not all of us are *deep*, but neither are all adults, and my generation—a shit ton of us have learned from adults' mistakes. We've learned to have empathy and self-awareness and how to communicate what we're thinking and feeling, that it's okay to laugh and cry and think about those big existential questions, like how it is we all got onto this little planet of ours, and why we're here in the first place.

Birdie sighs. "Just another piping hot serving of ageism."

You know what I think? I think that adults don't want us teens to realize that we're powerful and *deep*. They don't want us to question the way things have always been. They don't want us to change the world, when this world is the only one they've ever known. I mean, I guess in that sense, I actually kind of feel sorry for adults. In the end, I think they're just afraid.

I should be writing, but this rejection really punched me in the gut. I don't know. I guess I'm wondering if there's any point in telling a story and showing the world the real, vulnerable me, only to be hated by everyone and told I'm not good enough. Maybe I've got the wrong dream.

This writer's block is the worst. No, literally—it's the worst writer's block I've ever had. Which is ironic, because my profile is exploding and I'm getting closer to being a published author, but I can't actually write a flipping book.

Birdie spread their wings, but no matter how hard they tried, they just couldn't fly.

I can't stop thinking about how these literary agents will react to every word I write. The words of rejection letters ring in my ears *too teen rambling incohesive repetitive exhausting difficult to believe* and it's like I can't do anything to prove that I'm a good writer, can't do

anything to prove that I'm worthy of being published and accepted and loved. On Twitter I always see my favorite authors posting pictures of themselves hanging out, from before the pandemic and now with everyone taking the vaccine and socially distancing, and they all look so freaking cool, so badass, and there're a shit ton of likes and comments about how amazing they all are, and I want to be that, you know? I want to be invited to hang out with amazing authors who I love and who will say that they love me and show off that we're friends to the entire world, because when I do that, I'll be able to prove to every single person who's ever hated me, spat on me, treated me like shit, that they were wrong. I was worthy of being loved, too.

But that's never going to happen if I can't even write another single line. I can imagine Janet Fields now, sitting in her fancy office in New York City, adjusting her glasses as she opens query letter after query letter, until finally she sees one by someone named Lark Winters, oh, what a unique name, and she's intrigued by the subject line and clicks the email open, and she thinks to herself, hmm, this is pretty good, I wonder what the rest of the manuscript is like. And then she requests the manuscript, and I freak out and write the last thirty thousand words in five hours, and after she reads it, she tells me sorry, I can't offer representation because this book is complete trash, because *I'm* trash, and there goes any chance I ever had of being published.

"You're not trash, Lark," Birdie says.

Every three seconds, I sigh and minimize my Word doc to click on my web browser and go to Twitter and scroll, reading through the comments again and again. Better than thinking about Kasim and the fact that he may or may not love me.

I'm running late to class at the Commons, like usual, and everyone's already sitting around the classroom by the time I get there. Eli, shining like the sun, laughs as they talk to Francis. I'm surprised to see Jamal sitting by themselves on the other end of the bench. I give Asha a questioning look, but she just shrugs. Is it self-centered to think Jamal might've moved their seat because of me?

Kasim and Sable are on the couch again. I always wonder what her conversations are like with Kas. How did they figure out that they were in love with each other? I wish I knew the sort of things Sable says. What words she speaks to make her worthy of Kasim's friendship and love.

Kas meets my eye for a quick second before he looks away, ignoring my existence as he usually does whenever he's with any of his friends. Fine. I'll pretend we didn't meet up in the middle of the night to smoke weed and talk about aliens, too. Micah and Patch sit on the end of the bench close to them. Micah has medium brown skin, thick curls with the sides cut short. He's probably the weebiest of everyone in Kas's group. He rocks old-school anime T-shirts like *Afro Samurai* and talks about D&D and RPGs. Funny thing is, if Micah didn't hate me so much, I'm pretty sure we could be friends.

And, I don't know—maybe he's just bored or something, because the second I walk in, Micah smirks at Patch. "Oh, look—it's the racist-lover."

I pause. Everyone else does, too, and they all look at Micah and then at me. Eli's brows are raised. Asha frowns. Fight or flight is real,

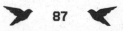

but I've been learning online that there're other trauma responses like freeze and fawn, and, well—yeah. My body is in full-on freeze mode. It's like everything shuts down. Thought. Emotion. My body doesn't move, and I can't even breathe. For a full five seconds, I just stand there. I feel like I've walked into my classroom in Brooklyn. I learned a lot about how bullying works while I was there. How people group together against one person just to make that group stronger, so they can all talk about how much they hate that one person and form bonds and friendships at that person's expense. How, after a while, it doesn't matter what you do or say—everyone will hate everything that comes out of your mouth. How, after a few years of being hated by everyone around you day after day, your brain starts to become desperate for a way out, and I considered it, yeah, I considered suicide for a few months until I told my mom what was going on, and she hugged me and cried and said she was so sorry, she didn't realize that the bullying was so bad, and that was it. We left Brooklyn. I met Kasim. I learned how to feel happy.

I haven't had to deal with bullying since then. People get annoyed with me, sure, but this—I can feel the shift in the room. It's too famil-iar. I know how easily Micah's and Patch's smirks and comments and energy could spread. Even Asha and Jamal and Eli might start to think that I'm a little more annoying than usual, and they can't put up with me anymore, and why did they ever think they liked me enough to smile at me and have conversations with me in the first place? They could start making snide, sarcastic comments, and the attacks could grow and grow until I'm being spat on again, shoved into lockers, punched in the face. And I don't want to go back. God, I really don't want to go back to being hated by everyone, trapped in a room with people who don't want me to exist, until one day I agree, and I don't want to exist anymore either.

I meet Kasim's eye, but he frowns as he looks away and scrolls on his phone. I sit on the bench, ducking my head, and I take a deep breath. My words finally find me. "I didn't say that I love racists. I never said that."

Patch laughs. "Yeah, you did. You said that you love racism."

"I didn't!"

Patch grins. "I wonder what all of your amazing fans will think if they ever found out you hate Black people."

Asha smacks the bench's top. "Patch, *stop* it. Lark never said that."

"But racists are good people, right? I mean, according to Lark they are."

Eli leans forward to look at Patch and Micah. "Why're you attacking Lark?"

"They're jealous," Asha says loudly.

This grabs Micah's attention. "Jealous?" he repeats. Kasim just glares harder at his phone. Why doesn't he ever say anything when Patch and Micah start in on me? "Why would we be jealous of Lark?"

"I don't know. Why don't you tell us?" Asha demands.

"It does kind of seem like you're bullying them," Eli says.

"First of all," Micah says, his voice rising, "who the hell are you?"

"Micah, you know who Eli is."

He ignores Asha. "You don't know me. This is—what, our third conversation? You don't fucking know me."

Eli shrugs, hands up. "Fine. Okay."

"Second of all," Micah says, "I'm allowed to use my voice to say when someone is being harmful. Lark is harmful as fuck for the shit

they said. Good and bad people? That's what the Cheeto said about those racists. Good and bad people on both sides. Are you fucking kidding me?"

"But I didn't mean it that way," I say. "You're putting words in my mouth."

Micah ignores me, sitting straighter in his seat. "It's our right to challenge them."

It hurts, of course it hurts, to hear Micah say all of this. And that hurt part of me wants to be pissed at Kasim. Why is he pretending his friends aren't attacking me the day after I saved his ass? And after we had our real conversation for the first time in over a year, too—the way he looked at me, like he might actually be in love with me . . .

I wish I didn't care so much about what people thought of me. I wish I could say fuck it, like Kasim does. Be myself, no matter what. But I guess I've really, truly, always believed that every single human being is meant to love each other. It feels like a slap in the face whenever I realize another person doesn't love me.

"We should call shit out when we see someone toxic, right?" Micah says. "Lark is toxic. I'm allowed to say that. Doesn't mean I'm *bullying* them."

Jamal's been ignoring the entire conversation, like they usually do whenever there's a fight—but at this, they glance up at me from the book they're reading. They might be thinking Micah is right. I'm lying to everyone about this thread, aren't I?

"They're well-known and well-liked for their social media presence," Asha says, head high. "While you have . . . what, ten followers?"

"Lark is well-known and well-liked because they're fake as fuck," Patch says.

"That shit is just a fucking popularity contest," Micah says. "That's all Lark cares about. They only care if they're getting enough likes. All they do is talk. Okay, and? Where's the action? I actually give a shit about this neighborhood, right? I'm actually from here. My family's been in West for six fucking generations. I don't need some New York City gentrifier coming in and pretending to be peaceful and care about shit. Meanwhile, I know people who're hungry and don't have a place to stay."

There's a long, unbearably painful silence.

"This is really awkward," Eli says.

Micah's smile grows. "Yeah. Well. Calling people out on their shit is usually uncomfortable. If you want to say I'm a bully to make yourselves feel better, then fine. Go for it. But Lark knows I'm right. They know they're fucked up. That's what makes them toxic."

Asha tells me that she's sorry, they're assholes. Jamal is quiet. So is Kasim.

And I just don't know what to think or feel.

Is Micah right about me?

Maybe I really am toxic. So toxic I've even tricked myself.

When Mr. Samuels walks in, it's like he can sense the energy of the room or something, and he figures out that a class discussion isn't the right way to go. He tells us today will be a silent writing day and asks for volunteers to start getting critiqued.

"Oh, and Lark," Mr. S says. "I saw you went viral again."

Kasim's head snaps up from his spot on the couch. This isn't the first time that Mr. Samuels has mentioned my Twitter account. I think

that the center's elders like that one of their students is a sort-of famous voice online. Mr. S has showcased a few of my most popular
tweets alongside awkward pictures of me in the Commons' online
newsletter, which is usually a collection of poems from students and
photos of classes and updates about the center. But this thread isn't
about a serious topic or anything the center would be excited about.

"I was surprised that it was your post," he says.

Patch mutters as they play with a lighter, clicking the fire on
and off, on and off. "I'm so fucking over hearing about this fucking
stupid-ass thread."

"Surprised?" Nerves twinge through me. "Why?"

"The voice isn't the same as your usual writing," he says.

Everyone's eyes are on me. I try not to blink. "I guess because I
was feeling more—uh—emotional . . ."

He leans against the table in that favorite teacher pose. "It's a wonderful series of—what do you call it again? Twitters? Tweets?"

Fran helps out. "Tweets."

"Right. Beautifully written. It almost felt like poetry. I wondered if
you might consider letting us use the twitters in the newsletter."

Kasim's *oh, shit* expression probably mirrors mine. "Really? You
want to use my unrequited love thread?"

"And an interview, too, if you're up for it."

"An interview?"

"Only if you're comfortable."

I'm not even sure if I know what *comfortable* feels like. I'm never
really comfortable. I'm always on the defense, thinking about how
people will react to me, if someone will attack me, especially now. It's
always confused the heck out of me, why people hurt other people.

Mr. S shrugs. "I thought—eh, maybe we could switch things up. Make the newsletter more of an online newspaper. An interview would give a new spark of life, don't you think?"

Why do people even decide that they don't like others? I really believe, at the core of it all, we're only made of love—that we're all able to love everyone else around us unconditionally, if we chose to. I try my best to love everyone around me. Even Micah and Patch.

"And it serves as a reminder, too," Mr. S says. "We have feelings. We laugh. We cry. We fall in love."

Yeah, they really hurt my feelings—yeah, I'm angry and upset—but beneath all of that, I'm scared.

I've been hearing a lot about forgiveness lately. Most people, they don't like the idea of forgiveness—but I don't think forgiving someone is really for the person that hurt me. I think it's for me. Because if I can forgive Micah and Patch right here, right now, then I can also let go of all of that energy that's buzzing around in my chest, making my shoulders and back ache, growing more and more in anger, until I know all I'll ever be able to do is think about them and how much they hurt me. I can forgive them for me, and even love them, because they're human beings who make mistakes and who hurt other human beings, the same way that I do, and because we're all trying to figure this out, this thing called life. We're all trying our best. I really do believe that. And I think that if they're hurting me, it might just be because they're hurting, too. I forgive them because I want to.

The weird part about it all, I guess, is that I can forgive Micah and Patch—but I've never really been able to forgive Kasim. Believe me, I've tried. I've tried to let him go, to say that I forgive him, but that's the thing about energy: I can say the words, but I can't ignore the truth

beneath it all, the hurt and anger and fear that buzzes around and around and around again.

Mr. S smiles as he watches me, and I begin to feel hot with everyone's eyes on me and I realized I spaced out again.

"You don't mind, do you?" he says. "If you're interviewed today, we could have it for this week's newsletter. Something different for our summer theme."

I don't want to put the thread in the newsletter or do the interview, digging myself even deeper into this grave, tombstone reading *Here Lies Lark the Liar*. But I also don't want to upset Mr. Samuels by turning him down. Besides, attention spans don't last very long, right? The thread is getting a lot of attention now, but so are hundreds of thousands of other threads. Everyone's probably going to forget about Kasim's before the week is even up.

Birdie gives me a skeptical look. "Whatever you say, Lark."

"Sure," I tell him, staring at anywhere but Kasim, whose gaze feels like a laser burning right into the side of my neck. "I mean. No, I don't mind."

"Great. Then we need a volunteer to interview them. Any takers?"

There's one long beat of silence, filled in by my daydream of Eli saying they'd be happy to do it—and burst by a hand going up lazily to my left.

Patch shrugs. "I'll interview them."

Oh, sweet Jesus. This is the definition of *not good*. Why the hell would Patch want to do the interview?

Mr. S doesn't notice my internal panic as he thanks Patch.

Maybe they want to do an ironic piece, to question the importance of social media and online celebrity worship.

"There're no topics or prompts today," Mr. S says. "Let your imagination run wild. But remember: Vulnerability and honesty is key. Even—no, especially—the parts that aren't pretty. That's how your character becomes real."

Maybe Patch is just bored and doesn't have anything else to write about today, and this is an easy out. Yeah. That's the reason I'm going to stick with.

Birdie winces. "Sure, Lark. If that's what you want to believe."

Chapter Nine

PATCH GESTURES AT ME TO TAKE A WALK WITH THEM. IT'D BE easier to do an interview that isn't in front of everyone, and I'm relieved we'll have more privacy, too. Now I don't have to be humiliated in front of the entire class, Eli included. A few rooms are empty, so it's easy to open a door and grab seats at a bench, sitting opposite each other.

Patch has a shaved head and gauged ears and light brown skin. They fiddle with their phone for a second, going to a voice recording app.

"So—um—thanks for volunteering," I say as brightly as I can.

They glance up at me from the phone with the twitch of a smile. *Definitely* not a good sign. Patch has always been just a little more chaotic for the hell of it—wanting to burn down the system, not just because they want liberation for all, but because they enjoy looking at fire.

"Of course, Lark," they say, their voice an attempt at sounding serene, but just makes the hairs on my arms stand up. Maybe it isn't too late to back out of this.

"So, first question," Patch says. "What made you want to post such a—uh—*heartfelt* thread?"

What's that thing people always say about lying? It's better to stick as close to the truth as possible. "It was an accident. I meant to post it on a private Twitter account, but I didn't realize I was still logged into my public one, and when it was morning, it was too late, because so many people had already seen it, and—"

They cut me off. "How does it feel to know that your post has inspired so many people?"

They couldn't sound more sarcastic if they tried. Still, this isn't the horror I'd begun to write out in my head. Which is a good thing, because I'm not great with horror. "Well, it feels weird. It sucks that so many people are struggling with the same thing."

Patch fakes a smile. "This is really wonderful information, Lark. Thank you for sharing. Just one more question: You've already posted about the love of your life. Why don't you take it a step further and say who you'd been writing about in your thread?"

And—ah, yes. There it is. Patch's smile doesn't falter. My throat starts to close up. "I—um, I don't know if I'm comfortable with doing that."

Patch frowns, tilting their head. "Oh. Really? Why not?"

"I mean. You know." I swallow and nod. "I meant it to be private."

"How do you feel about allegations that you posted the thread for attention?"

"What?"

"Some people are saying that this is exactly the sort of thing you would say to gain more attention and followers."

"Come on, Patch, why would I do that?" I shift in my seat, uncomfortable that they aren't that far from the truth. I didn't post the thread, but I didn't take it down, either.

"I looked at your other recent threads. They weren't getting as many likes and retweets as usual."

I shrug. "What's that got to do with anything?" And why're they stalking my Twitter account anyway?

"Would it really be so off to say that you did this just for the profile boost? Hoping people would feel sorry for you?"

Okay, I try to be as peaceful and loving as possible, but it would feel good—so, so good—to explode at Patch right about now and say that I lied about the whole thing to cover *their* friend's ass. Kasim's in love with someone who doesn't love him back. Maybe it's Patch. They'd suit Kasim perfectly, actually. The two of them could burn down the world together.

"I didn't even mean to post it to my profile," I tell them. "I had no idea it would go viral."

"To shut down everyone who thinks you're lying," Patch says slowly, scribbling a doodle in their notebook, "why don't you just tell us who it is?"

Here's one thing I kind of hate about all of this: My brain instantly begins to track what would happen if I gave Patch a name. It'd end up in the newsletter, and someone would probably screenshot it and post it to Twitter, the original thread gaining even more attention, and my followers—the number could explode, maybe even past 50K. Agents would recognize my name. The story would be seen as an unfolding romance. A rom-com in the making. Someone would *have* to offer me representation then, right? I could say that I was too afraid to declare my love in the Twitter thread, but now that I've seen the amount of support and people rooting for me, I've decided to give love a chance, and . . .

Patch waits for one long moment. Long enough that I can feel the silence itching through me. This is something we were taught by Mr. S a few semesters ago, when we had a couple of classes on journalism. Get comfortable with silence. Let the interviewee fill up the quiet with enough words that the truth slips out. I try not to let Mr. S's advice work. "I—uh—I don't know—"

"So, then, I'll just go ahead and give my opinion on everything that's happened here," they say, and if they had glasses, they'd probably adjust them. "You're obviously lying about being in love with someone."

"I'm not lying!"

"You kinda are," Birdie says.

"You went up onto Twitter, giving your oh-woe-is-me bullshit."

"I *don't* want anyone to feel sorry for me."

"But you kinda do," Birdie says.

"You've refused to respond to people who've called you out."

"I didn't even know people were calling me out!" I say, voice loud now. "There're so many comments, I haven't been able to read through all of them."

"That's true, at least," Birdie says, nodding.

Patch ignores me. "You're unable to come up with a name because you're a lying attention whore who's obsessed with fame. Is that about right? Did I miss anything?"

Patch might be even crueler than all of Kasim's friends combined. Do they really hate me this much just because they think I'm annoying? Why do they want to hurt me so badly? "You have no reason to think any of that."

"You stuttered and stammered your way through this interview, giving bullshit answers, trying to keep up the lie but refusing to give a name. I think that's enough of a reason."

Would it really hurt to say someone, anyone, just to get Patch to shut up?

Patch taps the bench surface with their pen. *Your move*, their smile says.

I'm tired, and I just want this interview to be over with already, and . . . I don't know. Maybe it doesn't really matter.

I scan my brain before I land on the obvious answer. "Eli."

Patch's smile freezes, along with their tapping pen. "Eli?"

"Yes. I'm in love with Eli."

There's another long pause, just long enough for a bad-tasting mixture of dread and regret to pulse through me. Oh, that was a big mistake. A big, big, *big* mistake. It's like, for that one second, I forgot that yeah, sure, everyone online will see this. Eli included.

But I can't take it back now. That'd look even more suspicious. And besides, Patch doesn't look as smug as they did a few moments ago. They have to admit defeat, now that I've given a name.

"Satisfied?" I ask.

Their annoyed silence feels pretty good, I've gotta admit. "Yeah. Sure." They scrape their chair back and grab their phone, getting up to leave me behind. "Whatever you say."

I volunteer at a charity bookstore on Baltimore Avenue called Book Spells. There isn't a set schedule—I just sign up when I want to come in and work the register, and I usually do it when I need to get out of the house because I feel like I'm crawling out my skin, and right now, it's hard to ignore the panic that fills my bones whenever I think of that interview and the fact that Patch is going to tell the entire world that I said I'm in love with Eli. I want to be surrounded by books, which, when you think about it, are collections of people's thoughts and dreams, their love and their passions, so whenever I'm in a bookstore, I feel like I'm being embraced by thousands of different human beings, humans who don't even know me and who love me, just for the simple fact that we're all on this little Earth together.

I had to stop volunteering for a while with the pandemic and everything, but now that there have been vaccines and pretty much everyone in the area is in agreement that we should all be socially distancing and wearing masks, my mom said that it's okay for me to go back to volunteering, as long as I'm super careful. It's fine, because the bookstore only lets one customer in at a time now, on account of the fact that the store itself is actually kind of small, with big shelves in the middle of the room like a maze and cramped corners and books falling to the ground if you brush too close to them or even look at them the wrong way.

The store tends to be quiet in the middle of the day, so after class at the Commons, I head over and unlock the door with the key the owner, Jim, gave me—then pause. There's a flyer on the door.

BIG RED RALLY

I grimace, then rip it off, leaving pieces of paper behind, and crumple the flyer up into a ball. When I open the door and flip on the lights, dust flies everywhere as I toss the flyer into the trash. Big Red is a new group that's popped up—they say that they're only a pro patriarchy group, which is *blech* enough on its own, but, of course, any group that is pro-patriarchy is also racist and anti-trans and anti-queer and ableist and basically any sort of hate because its members want to be considered more worthy of love than another group of people. And,

according to the flyer, they are coming here, to my neighborhood, to march around the Dog Bowl in early July, which sucks extra hard, because the Pride march at the end of June was canceled again this year, and it feels like this hate group is taking its place.

I try to shake off the grossness of the flyer and sit at the register and listen to music on Spotify and sing as I read. I'm almost at the end of *Every Body Looking* by Candice Iloh, and as much as I want to keep reading, I also don't want it to end. That feeling when you read the last line of a book that you love? I can't think of a lonelier feeling in the world. It's like that story's characters became your friends, the best friends you could ever ask for, because you were living in their heads and understood them and they understood you and you shared all these experiences and maybe even fell in love, and you felt like you really belonged somewhere, just for one second, just this once. And then the book ends, and you remember—oh, yeah. None of it was real. Even sadder, I guess, to realize that you're so lonely that your only friends are imaginary. Loneliness is embarrassing, right? Like I bet people are wondering, *What's wrong with you? Something must be wrong with you, to not have any friends.*

Will somebody wear me to the fair? The bell above the door rings while I'm mid–high note. I swallow and cough as I turn to welcome the customer, then leave my body and float overhead and take a moment to decide if I want to go into the white light as I watch Eli walk in with a smile.

"Hey," they say, hand up. "I didn't know you worked here."

I go back to my body and force on a neutral expression that I hope doesn't look overly excited or too weird. "Yep."

"Was that you singing?"

I should've gone into the white light. "You heard?" I ask, wincing.

Their smile softens. "Your voice is beautiful."

I rub the back of my neck. "Thanks."

Maybe I should take this moment as a blessing. The last chance I have to be with Eli before the newsletter drops and I can no longer be anywhere near their vicinity. They look at the shelves for a second, and I wonder if I should just leave them alone, or if I should ask if they want any help, or—

They look over their shoulder at me, book in their hand. It's a collection of essays by James Baldwin. "I'm sorry about what happened in class today," they say.

My face is hot. "Oh. Thanks." I pause, and then blurt out, "When I said people are only people, not good or bad, I didn't mean that racists are good." I say this as if Micah and Patch are right in front of me, not Eli, and I have the chance to explain myself. "I just meant that people are inherently good, right? We're all made of love. People are taught to be racist or misogynistic or transphobic or anti-queer or anything else that's harmful, and they usually do it because they feel like they need to be more powerful than another person because they don't realize they've got all the power they need inside of themselves, and because they're hurting and they're scared. I mean, if I didn't believe that, then wouldn't I have to believe that people are born racist and misogynistic and all that? That would mean people are inherently cruel to other people. But I don't think that's true at all. Babies don't look at another human being like they think that person is beneath them and unworthy of love and like they're thinking of hurting them and destroying another person's life. We're taught how to hurt other people, right? I think people are born loving, and a part of life is figuring out how

103

to get back to that place of love, and that some people—yeah, they're really harmful, more harmful than others, but they're not excluded in that. We're all still capable of love."

My Spotify is on an old-school playlist and Nina Simone starts to sing. *Oh, Lord—please don't let me be misunderstood.* Isn't it funny the way the perfect songs always play at just the right moment?

Eli's gaze is thoughtful, careful, watching. "You talk about love a lot."

My heart starts to stampede in my chest. "Yeah, I guess I do."

"Why?"

This might just be my last chance to have a semi-normal conversation with Eli, so I should just go for it, right? "Well, so—okay. I think we all have the ability to love every single other human being unconditionally, and—I don't know, something about that excites me," I tell them. I blush and look away. "When I was a kid, I remember writing in my journals that we could all save the world just by figuring out how to love to everyone else, no matter what. I even wrote that I thought world peace was possible."

Birdie leans out from behind a shelf. "You still think world peace is possible."

"Do you still think world peace is possible?" Eli asks me.

I hesitate. "Um—yeah, kind of," I say, embarrassed. "If every single person in the world loved each other, then it would be possible. I guess the question is how. How do we love each other, when there's so much hurt, too?" I shrug. "I know. I sound like a pageant queen, right?"

But they shake their head. "I don't think so."

We stand there for a second, staring at each other, and it looks like they're thinking a thousand thoughts and maybe seeing me in a

new way, different from just that weird kid in class, and the heat and pressure builds in me until I take a deep breath. "Do you want to buy that?" I ask, gesturing at the book in their hand.

They look at the book like they forgot they were holding it and offer me a grin. "No, sorry—I was just taking a walk and decided to stop in here." They turn and slide the book back into its spot on the shelf. "I'm glad I did."

I manage to keep on a polite smile and wave goodbye as they turn to leave, door closing behind them with another ring.

Chapter Ten | I

COMMON GROUND COMMUNITY CENTER NEWSLETTER

An Interview with Lark Winters

by Patch Kelly

(interview continued)

When I asked Lark if they were ready to tell the world the name of the person they loved, they were enormously hesitant (strange, I believe, for someone who is usually so open, especially if they will be rewarded with attention) but in the end, they decided that love was worth risking everything for. "Yes," they said. "I'm in love with a senior named Eli."

Lila Flowers @lilainautumn

@winterslark omg Lark ahhh I'm rooting for you!!!!!!

💬 0   🔁 0   🖤 0

Jennifer @jennyflinch

@winterslark I'm CRYINGGG this is so amazing! I hope they love you too and this is the cutest romance ever!

💬 0   🔁 0   🖤 0

I feel like a little kid again, hiding under my covers and pretending to be sick so that I don't have to go to school. Except now, I'm pretty sure I might actually *be* sick. And—yeah, yep, there's some bile in my mouth.

Birdie groans. "That's disgusting."

I swallow it back down. "It is what it is."

The notifications aren't as much of a frenzy as they might've been even just yesterday—people move on quickly, memories short and new viral stories springing up every few minutes—but I'm still getting a shit ton of tags and DMs, so many that it's hard to keep up with as I scroll through my phone in bed.

Randy @WHYRANDY

@winterslark Good for you!! I hope they return your feelings and y'all get your own happily ever after 🖤

💬 0   🔁 0   🖤 3

Jason Sorton @Amiilao

@winterslark Hi Lark, I really hope that this works out . I need to see a win for a nonbinary person in love !

💬 0   🔁 0   🖤 1

Sabrina Molly @CaptainSabrina23

@winterslark wow this made me cry lol I'm so excited for you. I never see people like us get to be in love so I really hope they're in love with you also.

💬 0   🔁 0   🤍 0

And, well, there are the other notifications that pop up into my comments, too.

um chile anyways so @huhbigboobs

god damn this kid is so annoying lmao, who gives a fuck??

💬 5   🔁 3   🤍 13

alex uwu <3 @alexwawa

can we talk about ppl's obsession with this CHILD'S love life? it's WEIRD.

💬 9   🔁 16   🤍 37

Jasmine @jasoflove

@alexwawa they're sharing the news. It's not like we're getting into their business w/o their consent. we're celebrating their happiness.

💬 6   🔁 7   🤍 15

N. Kay @nkay95

I'm uncomfortable with the fact that it does seem like a certain teenager is, at this point, sharing inappropriate news about their love life in an attempt to continue to boost their profile.

💬 26   🔁 51   🤍 103

Jesus. This drama alone would be enough to make me want to hide in a hole, but just the thought of seeing Eli makes my stomach implode.

"But what did you think was going to happen?" my mom asks when I tell her why I can't go to the Commons anymore. Like, ever. She's on the impatient side today.

"Patch just kept badgering me about it. They wouldn't stop."

"Hiding isn't going to change anything."

And with that, she practically yanks me out of bed, throws a pile of clothes at me, and shoves me out the front door. I drag my feet, my heart thudding slowly like it's trying to help me by making me pass out so that I won't have to face Eli. Maybe I can try to laugh it off. Say that I didn't really mean it, Patch just needed any name and Eli's was the first that popped up into my head, haha, isn't that funny? Maybe I can just pretend it was a completely different Eli I happen to know, from another school and state and country and universe. Maybe I can just drop to the ground and play dead as soon as they see me so that I don't have to deal with what is going to be one of the most awkward conversations in human history.

Everyone will want to see. They'll stare at us with freshly popped bags of popcorn to watch Eli reject me on center stage. Whomp, whomp. What was supposed to be a romance just turns out to be a tragedy.

I get to the Commons. I take a deep, *deep* breath. And I push open the front doors.

I'm expecting to be descended on by a pack of hungry gossipers, but when I walk inside, no one even looks at me. I'm unusually early today. Only a few people hang out on the sofas, and they barely glance up. I see Kasim sitting with Sable, her legs across his lap with her clunky black combat boots, so deep in their conversation that they don't even see me. Maybe this is one of those moments where I really do feel like I'm the center of the universe, but in reality, no one gives a shit.

I'm thinking I'll try to sneak up to the classrooms when I hear my name.

I turn.

And Eli is in front of me.

I don't know how I missed them. They're at a table with a couple of other seniors, half-standing and waving at me. I must have subconsciously seen them, but in my desperation for survival, my brain refused to register their existence. Even if no one else around really cares to see, I can tell that Eli's two friends are listening closely as they stare very intently at their phones.

"Hey," Eli says slowly, hesitantly, like they're approaching a rabid dog. "I wanted to—uh—talk to you, if that's okay?"

I wish I could melt into the floor. I wish I could be snapped out of existence. Thanos, help an enby out. "Sure!" I say, and try not to wince at how overly chipper I sound.

We walk toward the staircase. No one else is around, so it should be fine to speak here without being overheard, but I wish we could continue walking up the stairs to find more privacy in the classrooms. I feel like we're on a stage.

"So," Eli says, smile growing. God. Even with everything that's going on, their smile still feels like a hand reaching into my chest and slapping my heart. "I saw the newsletter."

"You did?" I say, gripping one arm to my side. How corny. Yes, of course they did.

"Yep," Eli says, leaning against a railing, looking relaxed and mature. "I also saw that the Twitter thread was originally—um—about me?"

My brain glitches. I try to remember words of the English language, but I'm coming up short. I'm only able to make a low, gurgling sound that is somehow both a laugh and a strangled cry for help.

"Is it true?" they ask, pitying me enough to pretend I didn't summon a sound from the pits of hell.

"Is what true?"

"Are you really in love with me?"

Love is confusing. Yes, I love them. I love everyone, because I truly do believe that's what we can do as human beings: love each and every single person, come together to form unity, to remember that we're one consciousness, that we're all the same threads of the universe, that we have all lived an infinite number of lives, but we managed to come here to this time and place, and that's a miracle, really, when you think about it, a miracle we've created together—that any of us were ever able to cross paths, much less meet and speak and smile and laugh. I love Eli, in the way that I love everyone on this planet. So what's the difference between loving a person, and being in love with them? I have a massive crush on them. But am I in love with them? I honestly don't know.

I realize that I've been quiet for too long, and Eli's smile has begun to fade. There's an uncertainty in their eyes I hadn't noticed before, like they're afraid this might all be one big prank. I try to gather some courage.

"Yes," I say. "I mean—yeah, um—I'm in love with you."

They're like the sun, they really are, shining so brightly I have to squint into their light. That's all that I can hang on to in that moment. Their light. I'm too scared to think about anything else, like how

they're about to gently, politely, kindly tell me that they don't feel the same way, right here and now . . .

"No one's ever been in love with me before," they tell me. "I don't know what to say."

I stumble over my words. "You don't have to say anything." I don't expect them to return the feelings. "I didn't even really mean for you to know—it was just an accident, the thread I mean, and then Patch was asking for a name, and I told them yours without thinking, and we can just pretend this never happened. I'd prefer that, actually."

I try to run away, to race up the stairs where I can officially hide, already starting to cry, thinking about how the rest of this summer will be painful as I do everything in my power to avoid Eli—when there's a touch on my wrist. They've reached out, fingers against my hand, a small enough gesture to make my entire world stop.

"I don't know if I'm in love with you," they say, still looking at their hand and mine, where their fingers turn my hand over to let their thumb press into my palm, my lifeline. "But I do like you a lot."

"Really? Me? Are you sure about that?" My words moved faster than my brain, which is still trying to catch up.

They look like they want to laugh, hopefully *with* me and not *at* me. "Yeah, you. I never said anything because . . . I don't know, I was afraid you wouldn't feel the same way."

"Me too." My voice is hoarse. I'm starting to realize why all those clichés in books and movies repeat themselves again and again. I feel like I can't breathe, and my brain is starting to catch up now, starting to process what seems like the impossible.

They give a half-shrug, still watching me with that smile. "Should we try . . . I don't know, going on a date or something?"

"Yeah. Yes. Please. Definitely. I'd like that. No. I'd love that."

I'm pretty sure they're laughing *at* me this time, but at least it's in a *you're cute* way. "I'd love that, too."

I'm higher than I've ever been in my entire life. It might just be a high I'll chase for the rest of my days. I've known what it's like to have a crush and keep it a secret and never think, not once, that I would ever actually be the main character in a romance. That I would deserve that kind of happiness. But now I know I deserve it, because I see that evidence right there in front of me: Someone has actually said that they like me. Someone has actually said that they want to go on a date with me. No one can say I'm unworthy of love. I've got the proof that I'm enough.

Birdie walks beside me, stretching out their wings. "Would you have been enough whether Eli asked you out or not?"

And then I turn the corner and run right into Kasim.

I startle back before I can touch him while he holds his ground. He's alone, which is rare. If he'd been with one of his friends, he probably would've brushed past me in annoyance, but now he pauses and stares.

"What?"

"I saw the newsletter," he says with a nonchalant shrug.

"What about it?"

"Eli?" he says, grin growing. Not the friendly kind. "Really?"

"Yeah, really," I answer. "I've had a crush on them for a while. So what?"

"You—" He pauses, like he's really confused, staring at me in amazement and looking like he's seconds away from laughing. "You didn't write the Twitter thread, Lark."

"I *know that*, Kasim."

He makes a *tsk* sound, hands stuffed in his pockets. He's so annoyed. More annoyed than usual. Why would he even care about the interview, anyway? A memory flashes: standing in the classroom the first day back, laughing at the idea that Kasim had written the post about me, Kas staring for a heartbeat too long, the same exact way he stared at me in the park, the same way he's staring at me now . . .

I've got to fill the silence. "We're going on a date," I blurt out. I don't know what else to say. "Me and Eli, I mean."

Something shutters in Kasim's eyes. He blinks and looks away again with a shrug. "Have a good time, I guess."

And before I can even answer, he's already gone, sweeping past me and down the hall.

I'm not feeling so high anymore as class begins. I barely pay attention to Mr. S and the discussion—I can't anyway, with Eli sitting just a few feet away, smiling at me whenever they catch me staring—and when we start to write, I stare blankly at my screen as I make a list in my head:

REASONS THAT KASIM COULD BE IN LOVE WITH ME:
1. He just acted like he was jealous??
2. He won't stop giving me that super intense stare
3. He's always coming over to my house, maybe it's not just to eat my mom's food
4. That thread—he said he's afraid the person he loves might hate him, so it can't be Patch, and I don't know anyone else who uses my pronouns and is close enough to Kasim for him to have feelings for

REASONS THAT KASIM IS NOT IN LOVE WITH ME:

1.   He hates me

That's the story I've been telling myself for the past year, anyway. But what if I got it all wrong? Because, as much as the thought just makes me want to roll myself up into a ball and hurl myself into the sun because it's too impossible to deal with, nope, no thanks, I really can't handle my-former-best-friend-and-now-currently-number-one-enemy loving me . . . I think it might be true. God. I really think Kasim might be in love with me.

Birdie shrugs like it's obvious. "Yeah, well. Now what're you going to do about it?"

The Commons gives free lunch. There's a cafeteria on the third floor, but most people grab a meal and leave to sit somewhere else with friends. I usually go straight home to eat there, but I don't want to be boxed in my room with so many thoughts racing through my head right now. That's usually a first-class ticket to anxiety. I'm grabbing a salad when I see Jamal, sitting in a corner by themselves, leaning over a book.

It's kind of amazing to me that Jamal never makes an effort to fit in with anyone. How can they be so comfortable with being alone? Why don't they want any other friends besides me and Asha? They told me once that they'd rather be themselves by themselves than be someone else with someone else. And, I mean . . . I get that.

I think.

But I can't feel the same way. Anxiety bulldozes through me at just the thought. After Kas stopped talking to me, I was scared people would start to bully me again. *See, Lark? There's a reason no one likes you.* I guess I'm still the same awkward, scared, shy kid I've always been.

Things are weird between us. Me and Jamal, I mean. They haven't answered my texts. They ignored me when I sat beside them in class today. It's the little things you start to pick up on, same little things that started to separate me and Kasim. Jamal can't be that mad at me for lying about the thread, can they? I hesitate, then head in their direction. They barely glance up when I sit down opposite them, brightest smile I can force on my face.

"Hey," I say, smile faltering a little when they don't say anything and look back down at their book again. "Um. Everything okay?"

They give a half-hearted shrug. "Why do you ask?"

"I don't know. You're in here by yourself, and . . ." I take a breath. "I guess things have been weird between us. And I wasn't sure if you're trying to avoid talking to me."

"Not everything revolves around you, Lark."

Harsh. But okay. "Things *have* been weird between us, though, right?"

"Yeah, pretty weird," they agree.

"Why is that?"

"You're lying to everyone about this thread."

Not a big surprise. I thought that might be the problem. But. "It's just a white lie."

They stare hard at the book in front of them, but I can feel the lightning strike of rage that pulses through them. "I hate that term. White lie. *White*, a word our society has decided means *pure*, so that even when a white person commits a crime, they're innocent of the harm they've caused. Lies are inherently hurtful. Putting the word *white* in front of a lie doesn't make it innocent. I don't care about the reason. If you're a liar, Lark, then I can't trust you."

I feel like they've reached over the table and slapped me across the face. I've never seen them this angry before, ever. "Okay, yes, I did lie, but I was just trying to help Kasim."

"Help *Kasim*?" they repeat.

"It was their post. They—I mean, sorry—*he* didn't want anyone to know. I was just trying to help him out."

"I don't care about the reason," Jamal says again. "A lie is a lie. I don't trust liars. What else have you been lying about? What other *little white lies* did you think were necessary?" They take a breath and close their eyes. "It's important for me to trust the people I'm around. It might not seem like a big deal to you, but this is the kind of shit that triggers me."

I'm breathless. "I'm sorry. I didn't know."

They rub the corner of their eye. "It's fucked up, Lark, that you're lying to so many people and you won't stop. Why're you doing it? Are you afraid of what they're going to say? What they're going to think? I don't know. It doesn't matter, I guess. I could use space from you right now. Until you figure out how to be honest."

Jamal doesn't look at me again as they pick up their book and half-eaten pasta bowl, leaving me at the table alone with just the echo of their words.

It's Time for a Revolution

Essay by Kasim Youngblood

Many white people happily believe their racist thoughts to excuse themselves for their oppression of others, so that they don't have to feel bad about themselves or their ancestors. However, many white people don't even realize they're doing it. They don't realize they look at a Black person differently, even "allies." Except "allies" are even harder to deal with, because they've convinced themselves they're not racist because they don't wear white sheets. The fact is, every single white person in this country is racist. They're all participating in the collective system that upholds their white supremacy: capitalism.

Capitalism and corporations are the root of slavery and most of the evil in this country, the bloodline of racism. Plantations using slavery were essentially early day corps. Capitalism still teaches us today to use and mistreat others, to pay them little or nothing at all for the greatest profit possible. To feel better about ourselves when we own something expensive, and to think we are better than other human beings because they live on the streets. Even Black people have bought into this mindset, wanting to show they are rich to imply they are worth more than another human. We are long overdue for a revolution.

Comments:

Richard Samuels: This is well thought out, Kasim. My only suggestion is to find a place of vulnerability. What is the role

you have played in capitalism, and where do you seek internal change?

Sable Lewis: Strong points are made throughout, but I thought that the beginning was choppy and that you could work on the sentence structure more.

Jamal Moore: What are the sources?

Micah Brown: Fuck sources. This is fucking amazing. I want you to talk more about white performative "allies."

Patch Kelly: YES. Tell us about your ideas for revolution.

Eli Miller: I don't think that you can just say "fuck sources"? This is nonfiction. Sources are required, right?

Asha Williams: No comment.

Francis Bailey: Sorry I didn't have a chance to read.

Lark Winters: I've always loved your writing, Kasim.

Chapter Eleven

ELI DECIDES ON ETHIOPIAN, SO ON FRIDAY NIGHT, WE MEET UP IN the backyard of Nora where benches and menus are set up. I'm on the edge of hyperventilation. I feel like I'm shutting down, brain blank, and I'm not sure I'm even in my own body anymore, because I'm so afraid, so freaking afraid to even *breathe* too loudly and make Eli realize that they shouldn't have asked me out, what were they thinking, they don't like me at all. I'm weird and loud and annoying and way too self-conscious and exhausting to be around and why, *why*, would anyone ever like me?

Birdie is thoughtful as they sit beside me. "I always forget that humans haven't learned to accept and love other human beings for who they are yet."

There's a chain-link fence surrounding the backyard and potted plants blooming everywhere. The benches are usually packed with people, but with the virus and everything, right now there's only an older person sitting off in the corner, smoking a cigarette. After we order injera and okra wat, we sit quietly, Eli smiling at me as they pick up their hot tea with both hands, blowing on the steam. I tried to think of dates in books I've read to figure out how the main characters handled them. How do you play it cool? Not too thirsty? But still thirsty enough that it's not like you're *uninterested*, just not *desperate*, while also managing to be cute?

"You're quieter than usual," Eli says.

I feel like a shell of myself. "Ha. Sorry."

"Nothing to be sorry about. It's just surprising."

"Oh. Okay."

God. I'm so fucking awkward. Eli takes a sip of their tea. I stare at my hands in my lap. It's a little chillier tonight. I wish I'd worn a thicker sweater.

"I was surprised when you said that you were in love with me," Eli says.

I struggle to meet their eye. I *love* them, just like I love everyone, but I don't know if I'm actually *in* love with them, because I don't even know what that really means, I guess, or if there's a difference between being in love with Eli and just loving them, and since I haven't figured that out for myself, maybe that's another lie I've found myself in. Lark the Liar strikes again. Jamal might've had a point. I haven't been honest about a lot lately.

"What do you love about me?" Eli asks.

"Um—well." *You're beautiful.* "You're always kind to everyone." *Your smile reminds me of the sun.* "And—um—you're super grounded, I guess. You don't really care about what anyone thinks." *Your dimples. I freaking love your dimples.* "I admire that. A lot."

Their smile flickers. "I don't care what anyone thinks?"

"I don't know. You just seem really confident."

They sip their water, and I have no idea what their silence means, and now I'm freaking out, because I might've just insulted them without even realizing it—

"You know," they say, "the other day in the bookstore—I've thought about that conversation a lot. Do you really think it's possible to love every single person in the world unconditionally?"

I blink rapidly. "Yeah—yes, I do."

"I guess that means you're polyamorous," Eli says, grinning.

I nod. "Yeah, I am."

"I was just joking."

"Oh."

"But I am, too," Eli says. They play with a petal that's drifted onto the table. "My partner and I—we broke up a few months ago. Well, they broke up with me."

Ah—so that's why Eli related to the unrequited love thread. "I'm really sorry, Eli."

They shrug. "It's okay. It happens, right?" They let out a big sigh. "So, if you love everyone in the world, do you also love people you don't even know?" Their smile is more on the skeptical side.

"Yes. I really do. I mean, when you think about it, every human being is made of the same stuff, right? The same energy or atoms or whatever you want to call it. And that means we're all energy, we're all connected, even the people who do really horrible things, and yes, I love them, too, because they're not the horrible shit they did, not really, because we're made of the same infinite light of love, right? And my light loves their light, and their light loves my light, and we forget about that, I think, the way we all love each other underneath all the layers of hurt."

"Infinite light of love," Eli repeats, that dimpled smile on their face.

I blush. "That's what I really believe. I mean, I can *feel* it. That light inside. That love. Can't you?"

They nod. "Yeah. I can feel it, too."

There's something about their smile that makes me feel a blast of joy. I'm saying weird shit to Eli, the kind of thing that people usually

reject without another thought, and they're really listening. It's like their smile is thawing me, and I feel like I'm getting closer to myself again. "It's kind of like looking up at the sky and thinking that the gray clouds are the sky. The mistakes people make, the horrible things humans do, it's all the gray clouds, but behind that is the sun and the blue sky, and if we could figure out how to remember that we're the sun and the blue sky, we might figure out how to be in a better place. The whole world, I mean."

"World peace," they say. "Right?"

"Do you think I'm completely ridiculous?"

They laugh. "No, Lark—I don't think you're ridiculous. I just—I don't know, I don't think a whole lot of people would agree with you."

"Yeah. I know. You're right."

"It doesn't mean you're wrong," they add. "But there're also a ton of people who do some really evil shit."

I nod. "Yeah. That's true. I don't know. I'm not trying to say we should just forget about all the bad stuff that happens. I just think— maybe we like to focus on other people a lot, you know? We like to say that everyone else is the villain and only we are the heroes, without wanting to look at the ways we hurt other people, too, because that's kind of the problem all around, isn't it? No one wants to be the villains, so we don't look at the mistakes we make." (I don't want to be the villain, so I don't want to think about how much my lying might be hurtful, too, but let's just push that back down into the shadows, shall we?) "And besides, usually the things we say we hate about other people are actually the things we hate about ourselves, and we forget that we're all worthy of unconditional love."

"Do you love yourself unconditionally, too?"

I just spoke for maybe a minute straight, but now, my mouth opens and closes and not a single sound can escape. They really know how to go in for the kill, huh?

There's a look of panic on their face at my silence. "I'm sorry—shit, I didn't mean to get so personal."

"No. That's—ha, that's actually a question I ask myself a lot. I wish I had an answer that didn't make me sound like a hypocrite." I sip my water.

They offer a small smile. "It's hard for me to love myself, too."

What? Really? "Why?"

"I don't know." They take a deep breath. "Like, when you said I seem confident? I try so hard to *be* confident, and to look like I love myself so that other people won't know that I don't, but I feel like I don't even know myself. How can I love myself if I don't know myself? I feel like I'm always on stage, giving people the act that they want to see. And we're all performing, aren't we? We're all putting on masks. Deciding who we want to be."

Yeah. "I guess that's true."

"I keep trying on a million different masks, and I don't know which ones are real. It's like I'm a chameleon. I just do what everyone else wants, follow along with what everyone else thinks. And I look at you, and—well," they say, and give me a grin, "you're so weird, Lark. You don't care about the mask. You're so loud and funny and you seem so free."

"Me? Free?" I shake my head quickly. "No, you've got it wrong. I'm trapped in my head. It's just because I don't think before I speak that it looks like I don't care, but then I spend the rest of my life regretting that one thing I said like five years ago."

They laugh. "You're not alone on that one."

"Speaking of regret," I say before I can second-guess myself. "The first day at the Commons. When I laughed while you were telling me what the thread meant to you." I wince. "I'm really sorry. I don't know why I did that. I think I was just feeling awkward and I didn't know what to say."

"It's okay," they say. "I also felt super awkward. Like maybe I'd overshared."

"No, no! I was happy to hear that you related to the thread. Well, not *happy*, shit."

They're giving me that smile that I'm more used to seeing from them now, that *I think you're cute* smile that makes me want to blush and hide and never show my face again. I hold my hands up over my face so that they won't see me. "I was surprised to hear you'd dealt with unrequited love, too," I say, voice muffled. "I mean, I think you're amazing and really—um, really attractive—so, obviously, anyone would be so effing happy to find out you had feelings for them."

I can't believe I said any of that, and now I'm too afraid to even look at them. Their voice is low. "Thanks, Lark." Something touches my hand, and I chance a peek at them as they offer theirs. I take it, and they smile as they look at our fingers, also blushing. "I think you're really cute, too. Anyone would be lucky to be with you."

The silence is more comfortable now, at least, even if it's filled with that buzzing kind of tension where I wouldn't be able to speak without my voice cracking, and there should probably be some romantic music playing, right? *Can't take my eyes off of you.* Lauryn Hill version, though. We just sit there and smile at each other and blush and I think to myself, yeah, we're pretty corny and cute right now. But it's okay to be corny and cute, right? Especially when I never get to be, and I never see anyone like me being corny and cute in books or on TV. This feels amazing.

"Uh—so," Eli says, suddenly sitting straighter and looking more uncomfortable as they play with my hand. "What do you want?"

Huh? "Want?"

They nod. "When you said that you're in love with me, what were you hoping would happen?"

My eyes widen. "Oh—um, I mean, I didn't really have a mission. I didn't even think I'd be lucky enough to go on a date with you. It's not like I was hoping I'd get to kiss you or anything like that." I bite my lip and close my eyes, silently cursing myself to hell.

Birdie snorts. "Smooth."

"I mean—not that I don't want to kiss you," I say, then wince.

Birdie whispers, "You should probably quit while you're ahead."

Eli just laughs. "I kind of want to kiss you, too," they say, then shake their head. "Not kind of. I've been wanting to all night."

This isn't my first kiss. I've kissed a lot of people, actually. When we're queer and Black and beautiful as hell and feeling happy and free (i.e.: super high), kissing just happens naturally, like a conversation that's an exchange of energy. I've kissed Asha. I've kissed Fran. I even kissed Jamal, once, though the second that happened we both looked at each other and immediately knew that was something that should never, ever happen again.

So why am I hesitating now? What am I afraid of? Eli's smile starts to fade, and I don't want them to stop smiling, so I swallow as I nod. "Yeah. I'd really like that."

Their face lights up again as they lean in. Their smile is gentle, eyelashes closing. There's one eyelash—there, right on the corner of their cheek. They wait for me to lean in, too. Their lips are soft. They remind me of Eli's voice, gentle and calm and warm. We only kiss for, like, three seconds, but my heart races in my chest like it has zero plans to ever slow down again. And I want to cry, too. I've been so lonely, missing Kasim, wishing I could have a best friend again, and now I'm here with Eli, living a dream I never would've thought was possible even just a week ago. God. I was afraid I was going to be alone forever.

When they pull away, they stay close enough to kiss me again, letting out a small laugh. "That was nice," they say, voice soft, still looking at my mouth.

I nod, and nod, and nod some more, because that's all I can manage to do.

They rub a thumb over my hand. "Do you think we should— I don't know," they say.

"What?" I'm so breathless it's embarrassing.

"Do you think we should try becoming official?"

I manage to suck in a breath now. "You mean—like, partners?"

Birdie frowns. "Isn't that kind of fast?"

Eli nods. "Yeah, I know. It might be too fast. I just—I don't know," they say again. "I like you a lot, and you love me, right? And I think it could be really good, the two of us. I think we could be good together."

I hesitate. This should be a dream come true, hearing these words from Eli of all people—I mean, come on, *Eli Miller* is telling me they want me to be their partner—so why does it feel so off, so weird, so like that moment when Anna and Hans decided to get married

after knowing each other for five minutes because they could finish each other's sandwiches? Readers online complain about instalove in books, and now I know how it feels firsthand. Sure, I'd love to be Eli's partner, but I haven't even had a chance to go home and daydream about them asking me to be their partner yet.

"Plus," Birdie reminds me, "you didn't actually write that thread."

Eli's expression starts to fall. They nod. "I get it. It's too soon."

But maybe I'm just overanalyzing. Maybe I'm ruining a good thing before it's even had a chance because I'm too scared. Sure, I didn't write the thread, but that doesn't mean I don't love them. I want to be their partner, too—so why not?

"Yes," I say.

They look up, eyes wide. "Yes?"

"Yes, yes—God, yes, I'd love to."

Eli grins as they lean in and kiss me again, longer this time, even more slowly, and I really might just melt into a puddle right here and now. They hold up their phone, snapping a picture of us. I look cold but cute, and they look so happy beside me, eyes shining. We look great together, like a couple that's in love.

Eli Miller @EliLovesYou17

@winterslark was talking about me?! I'm beyond lucky.
Let's give love a shot ♥

💬 0   🔁 0   ♥ 0

Eli's tweet has almost three thousand likes by the time we're ready to leave.

Chapter Twelve

ASHA MEETS UP WITH ME AT THE COFFEESHOP THAT'S ACROSS from the Dog Bowl the next afternoon. We grab iced teas and sit at a table outside. The flea market's returned for the first time since the pandemic began, and across the street there are tables of books and folded clothes and candles and flowers, and kids are running around and dogs are barking and couples are holding hands and it's almost easy to pretend that things are back to normal again. Almost.

"I'm so excited for you," Asha tells me. "This is the kind of thing people daydream about happening to them."

I swirl my iced tea around and grin. "We stayed up texting all night." Okay, so I might be bragging a little, but don't I deserve to also?

She scrolls on her phone and turns the screen to me. "Have you seen these comments?"

Lark Winters (they/them) @winterslark
when I posted that thread i never ever thought id
actually end up with the person i fell in love with!!!!
@EliLovesYou17 thank you for giving me a chance
💬1.1K   😂4.3K   ♥11.6K

Eli Miller @EliLovesYou17

Never knew someone could make me so happy. @winterslark is everything to me

💬 603   🔁 1.3K   ❤️ 5.3K

Lila Flowers @lilainautumn

ENBY LOVE FOR THE WINNNNNNNNNN

💬 4   🔁 7   ❤️ 34

Jennifer @jennyflinch

Ahhhhhhhh I can't stop crying!!!!!! This is the best news ever!!!! T_T

💬 0   🔁 2   ❤️ 9

Randy @WHYRANDY

@winterslark Congratulations, Lark! You got the happy ever after you deserve.

💬 0   🔁 0   ❤️ 3

Jason Sorton @Amiilao

Hi Lark, I feel like I never belong or will never be loved bc I'm nonbinary and ND . Thank you for sharing your story and giving me hope .

💬 0   🔁 0   ❤️ 0

"People are so happy for you." Asha puts a hand to her chest and looks genuinely emotional for a second, which makes me emotional, so we sit there and smile with our eyes shining with tears for a good few seconds, and that's the thing I love about Asha, the one thing I think really connects us—neither of us think it's embarrassing to cry, especially when they're happy tears like this.

I wipe mine away with the palm of my hand. "There's almost a—I don't know, a weird pressure?"

She frowns. "What sort of pressure?"

"I mean, like, there're all these people saying they've never even seen two nonbinary people together and happy and in love before and we give them hope, and—God, I don't know, what if it doesn't work out?"

Asha gives a dramatic gasp. "Lark, are you being *pessimistic*?"

I laugh, I can't help it. "Maybe a little?"

"I think you're just scared," she says. "And that's natural. This is your first relationship, isn't it?"

I nod. "Yep. Yeah. The first. Hopefully it won't end in a week and be my last."

She rolls her eyes, grinning. "Let's just ask the cards. How will Lark's relationship with Eli work out?"

I watch as she pulls out her deck and begins to shuffle them. Her other friends must really hate her readings if Asha wants to hang out with me in the first place. "Have you seen Jamal at all?"

She tilts her head to the side, sucking in a quick breath. "Not outside of the Commons." She glances up at me. "What's going on between you two?"

I wince. "You've noticed shit's weird, then?"

"Who *wouldn't* notice?" she asks. "They won't speak to you, won't sit down next to you, won't even look at you. Did something happen?"

I don't want to admit the truth to Asha. I'm sucked way too far into this lie now, and she might be just as angry as Jamal. I'm not sure I could take that, the only two sort-of friends I have hating me, maybe even joining leagues with Micah and Patch. I shake my head quickly. "I'm not sure."

She frowns thoughtfully as she pulls a card. "You need to let yourself shine and be your truest self, for when you shine brightly, you give others permission to shine, too."

"That's good advice."

"Doesn't say how your relationship with Eli will go, though."

"Not really, no." I sip my iced tea and watch as she continues to shuffle for a while, then say, "Can I tell you something weird?"

"You always tell me weird things," she says, still shuffling.

"It's kind of a secret."

"I won't tell anyone."

"I'm serious," I say, and even nod and force my face into a frown for good measure. "You can't tell anyone, Asha."

"You're scaring me," she says. "Just say it already."

I bite my lip for a second. "I—um—I kind of think that Kasim might be in love with me."

She stops shuffling. She looks up at me, and she stares at me for one, two, three seconds before she blinks. "*That's* the big secret?"

I nod solemnly.

Asha snorts, then laughs, then laughs so hard that someone walking by jumps, and Asha has to hold up a hand and say that she's sorry, she didn't mean to scare them, and even then she's still laughing. So many jokes fly right over my head that they've got their own airspace, so I'm used to it, but this time I can't for the life of me figure out what the hell is so funny.

"Lark," she finally says, gasping, wiping a tear from her eye. "*Everyone and their mama* knows that Kasim is in love with you."

My mouth falls open. "*What?* What're you talking about?"

"I've told you that Kasim is in love with you before!"

"I thought you were just joking!"

She sighs and shakes her head, as if to say *oh, Lark*. "If you don't know that Kasim is in love with you, then it's because you didn't *want* to know," she says, looking away as she pulls out cards from the deck. "It's so obvious. He's constantly staring at you with that *look* in his eyes."

"What *look*?"

"That *look*, Lark—that pining, pitiful, lost look, like you broke his heart and tore it up into a million pieces. And everyone knows that you're in love with him, too."

Okay, now she's *officially* taken things too far. "No, I'm *not*," I tell her. She raises a skeptical eyebrow. "I'm serious! I'm not in love with Kasim!"

She gives a wicked smile. "Defensive much?"

"Defensive of *what*?" I demand, and I really can't understand why I'm angry at all. I'm almost never mad. The only person who ever upsets me is Kasim. He's pissing me off and he isn't even here.

She flips one card, and then the next. "It's nothing to be embarrassed about," she says. "I mean, Kasim isn't exactly my taste, since I'm not really into assholes, but I can see how friendship can turn romantic—"

"We're not romantic," I say, voice growing louder. "We're not even friends! Kasim, he—he—"

Birdie raises their eyebrows. "He . . . ?"

"I mean, I love everyone," I tell Asha, nodding.

She looks like she's about to burst out laughing. "Okay."

"But I don't love Kasim in *that way*. And, I mean, even if we did love each other, which I'm not saying we do, we would be horrible

together, the worst couple ever. We'd only fight every other second, just like we do right now. Nothing would change."

Asha is thoughtful. "What do you think makes a good relationship, anyway?"

I shrug. "I don't know. Maybe it's two people who need something the other person has, and they come together and make each other whole."

Birdie frowns. "You're already whole, Lark."

Asha raises her glass at me. "I have an idea. Why don't you ask Kasim?"

"What?" I say, and then, for good measure, I say again, *"What?"*

"Just ask him if he's in love with you," she says, nodding. "What's the worst that could happen?"

"Um, you could be wrong, and he could laugh at me, and I would never be able to show my face around him again?"

"Or I could be right," Asha says. "And something tells me that's even scarier for you."

There's a second of quiet. Asha gestures to the cards. "You're on the right track, according to this."

"On the right track for what?"

"I don't know," she admits. She picks up the cards and starts to shuffle again.

I groan and rub a hand over my face. "I'm really not in love with him," I say. "I swear, I'm not." *No chance, no way, I won't say it—no, no.*

Asha nods slowly, and I can tell that she doesn't believe me at all. "Okay. If you say so."

Eli and I text all night, me hidden beneath my covers and laughing at my phone, grinning, trying not to be *too* happy, because happiness is scary, right? Like, the second you get really happy, there's a possibility that the happiness is going to be taken away.

happy 24 hour anniversary my love, Eli says.

we should celebrate!!

okay, how do you want to celebrate?

i have a couple of ideas

does it involving kissing? bc I would really, really like to kiss you again

I could die of embarrassment, I seriously could. I squirm under my sheets. **id really like to also *blush***

tbh i'd like to kiss you,,,,,, and maybe a little more

I sit up in my bed. **um are we officially sexting?**

lmao no lark, if we were sexting you would know

oh. okay.

are you disappointed?

maybe a little? i wanted to be able to say ive officially sexted

lark lmao you're so funny. you can say that we've sexted if you want to.

I bite my lip, then force myself to type and hit send before I can chicken out and stop myself. **no i think ill wait until weve actually done that. and;;;; maybe other things too**

oh? are you saying you're open to other things?

im saying im curious about other things? I hesitate, then type out another message. **have you done other things?**

yep. but there's no pressure to go fast you know? i like getting to know you.

i like getting to know you too

besides it is more intense and feels rly good when you know the person well. but if that's something you want to try, we can always plan for it,,,,

I flop back onto my bed, holding my phone to my chest and trying not to freak out. *Other things* was always on the back burner, something I've thought about more than once, okay, fine, practically every night, and—well, something I've *dreamed* about, too—but I never thought it would actually happen any time soon, because I never thought I would have a partner any time soon. It's embarrassing as all hell, it really is, but I feel like I'm on fire at just the thought of doing anything more than kissing Eli.

um. okay. i would really like that.

The next afternoon, after I stayed up until four in the morning texting with Eli, I'm still thinking about the conversation I had with Asha, my mind going around and around in circles—*why* did I even get so angry at Asha, and why the hell does she think I'm in love with *Kasim*?—when my mom calls my name. I hop to my feet and thud down the stairs.

She's tying together the handles of a tote bag in the kitchen. "Lark, baby, bring this meal over to Kasim's house."

My heart goes supernova. "What? Right now?"

"Yes, right now. I called Taye and he said Kasim is home."

I've barely spoken to Kas since that night on the courts (for a real conversation, anyway, not that twenty-second fight in the hallway), and I haven't been able to look him in the eye when I'm about eighty-five percent sure that he's in love with me, which is eighty-five percentage points too many.

"Taye just got a fourth job," my mom says. "He's too busy to cook for anyone." When I try to argue, she gives me *the look*. "Have some empathy."

My mom really knows how to give the cold, harsh truth when she wants to. I mumble an apology, and she says it's all right. We all get a little caught up in ourselves sometimes. She hands me the tote bag filled with Tupperware, and after throwing on my sneakers and shorts and a graphic tee, I get started on the walk.

Lark Winters (they/them) @winterslark

when I posted that thread i never ever thought id actually end up with the person i fell in love with!!!! @EliLovesYou17 thank you for giving me a chance

💬 7K   🔁 12.3K   ♥ 39.6K

Lovely Jean @JeanGraced

@winterslark @elilovesyou17 I'm so happy for both of you. Congratulations.

💬 0   🔁 0   ♥ 2

trans spider man @kilometersmorales

@winterslark AHHHHHH this is so awesome, we love to see it!!!

💬 0   🔁 0   ♥ 0

um chile anyways so @huhbigboobs

so can anyone explain to me why @winterslark is always on my TL, this shit is annoying

💬 8   🔁 4   ♥ 19

alex uwu <3 @alexwawa

LOL they really think we give a fuck about them and who they're going out with

💬 17   🔁 23   ♥ 63

N. Kay @nkay95

There needs to be a conversation about the appropriateness level of an underage child sharing news about their love life for the sake of fame.

💬 51   🔁 71   ♥ 201

Chapter Thirteen

KASIM AND TAYE LIVE ABOUT THIRTY MINUTES AWAY NEAR
Malcolm X Park. Kas never liked me visiting, even when we were still
friends. He'd always suggest we sit in the grass at the park instead. I walk
up the townhouse's front steps and take a deep breath before I knock.

There's some slamming inside, and the door bursts open. Kasim
frowns down at me. "Oh. Hey." He glances over his shoulder inside.
"What're you doing here?"

I hold up the tote bag. "My mom cooked for you."

He hesitates.

"Just take it."

He bites his lip, then reaches for the bag. "Thanks. Tell your mom—"

"Yeah, I know." I'm already turning away, hand up to say goodbye.

"Do you want to come inside?"

I pause, then slowly turn. Kasim is looking in the tote, like he
couldn't care less about what my answer will be.

I narrow my eyes suspiciously. "You want me to come inside? Why?"

He shrugs. "You don't have to if you don't want to."

"I'm just surprised you invited me in."

"You're acting like you're a fucking vampire or something."

I bare my teeth at him, and he snorts and shakes his head. "Sable's
asleep, though, so we just have to keep it down."

I swallow. "Sable's here?"

"She's asleep in my room."

I don't want to think about what they might've been doing in Kas's room.

"It's fine if you don't want to," Kasim says with a half-shrug.

I squint at him, as if I'll be able to read his mind if I stare at him hard enough, which would be a big help, actually, to figuring out the enigma that is Kasim Youngblood. Pissed at me one second, inviting me into his house the next. Acting holier than thou one moment, staring at me like he's in love with me within the same breath. Going inside is a very bad idea, right?

Meh, whatever. "Yeah, okay."

He steps aside to let me in. I walk into the shadowed foyer, a jumble of sneakers and boots at the door. The kitchen and living room share the same space, dirty dishes piled on the counter and in the sink. The TV has some anime playing.

"What's that?"

Kasim has a slow smile, one I know better than to trust. "It's called *The Promised Neverland*. Wanna watch?"

"Mmmm—no, thanks, I'll pass. Knowing you, it's probably something that'll give me nightmares for a year straight."

Kas fiddles around in the kitchen, putting the Tupperware in the fridge. "Why're you such a punk?"

I hover near the sofa and only sit when Kasim drops onto a worn spot. "Excuse me for not wanting to watch giant man-babies eat people."

He rolls his eyes. "*Attack on Titan* isn't even that scary."

And then the silence. The unbearable, awkward silence.

"How're things going with Eli?" Kasim asks.

I narrow my eyes at him. He wouldn't ask unless it was to mess with me, right? "Why do you want to know?"

He shrugs, still not meeting my eye. "Just curious. Looks like you two are happy. From what you posted on social, anyway."

I ignore the flinch in my gut, the memory of seeing the not-so-kind comments that have been cropping up more and more. "Yeah. We are happy."

"Do they know?" he asks. "That you hadn't originally posted the thread?"

Maybe he's trying to imply something—that we can't actually be happy, not really, if our relationship is based on a lie.

Birdie turns and stares into the camera as it slowly zooms in.

"No," I say, "they don't."

Kasim rubs his mouth with his hand, like he's literally trying to force the words back down, and I can tell he's just dying to speak, so I sigh and tell him, "Just say it already."

Kas looks up, surprised, then clenches his jaw. "I don't know. Don't you think it's weird?"

"What's weird?"

"That you and Eli are already partners?"

"So you're going to be judgmental of that, too?"

"I'm not trying to be judgmental, Lark—I'm just saying. You two literally went on one date."

He's acting like he's jealous. Not that I'd actually say that out loud and wade into that particular *Kasim loves Lark* territory. "So what?"

"I'm just saying."

"Just saying *what*?"

"I don't know! Jesus, I just think it's weird." He lets out a heavy breath. "I'm sorry, all right? I really wasn't trying to get into a fight with you about it. Congratulations."

"Yeah. I'm sure you mean that."

"I do," he says. The usual fire that sparks through Kas is gone, and it's a little funny, isn't it? A little funny that I kind of miss it. "My opinion on your relationship doesn't matter. As long as you're happy."

The silence returns, and I can't focus on anything but the heat of the awkwardness between us. I remember Kasim's stare, and Asha was right—Kasim stares at me a lot, like all of the time, in the middle of class and in the hall, always looking away the second I catch him.

"I guess you have a point," I say. "The roots aren't real, even if other feelings are."

"It's really none of my business."

Asha suggested that I ask him, but I don't need to ask. I already know. Yes. Hasn't it been obvious? I've always known, even if I don't want to admit it. When we were best friends, that shine in his eyes when he met my gaze with a smile, the way his hugs lingered, the way he always waited for me even if everyone else had already left, the way I'd catch him staring at me like he'd just witnessed a miracle. Getting looked at like that is freaking terrifying. What if I let myself love him, too—let myself be vulnerable, let my guard down and trust him enough not to hurt me—just for him to realize I'm not actually worth his love or anyone else's? I don't think I would survive that.

"None of your business," I repeat. I don't really know why I'm so angry all of a sudden, like the anger was sucked out of Kasim and injected into me instead. "Maybe you could pass the message on."

He narrows his eyes. "What?"

"Micah, Patch," I tell him. "Sable. They won't leave me alone. They treat me like shit every chance they get."

"Where the fuck is this coming from?" he says. There's that fire I missed. "You've got a problem with Micah and Patch holding you accountable for the shit you say—then yeah, fine, you're angry at them. But don't bring Sable into this. She hasn't done or said anything to you."

It makes sense he'd want to stick up for his girlfriend. "And what are Micah and Patch even holding me accountable for?"

He looks up at the ceiling in frustration. "You know. Yeah, I mean, I don't always agree with the way they do it. But we have to be able to hold people accountable. Even people in our own community."

"They're fucking bullies, Kasim."

He still won't meet my eye. "I—fuck, I don't know, all right? That's the same shit people always say when they're being held accountable. *You're bullying me. You're a part of the woke police.* All that bullshit gaslighting."

Frustration rips through me. But that's the one thing that's scared me, too—that I'm the narcissistic villain in all of this, gaslighting everyone else and even fooling myself. And what sucks the most is that I do have to admit that I'm wrong about at least one thing.

"It's too late," I tell him. His brows pinch together in confusion. "The thread, I mean. It's too late to come out and tell everyone the truth about it."

"Why?"

"Kasim—seriously, you should see all of these comments I'm getting, all of these people who're messaging just to say that my

relationship with Eli is giving them hope, that they've never even seen two nonbinary people in love, and—"

"It's never too late to just say the truth."

"At what point would telling the truth cause more harm than good?"

"You're just trying to convince yourself that you shouldn't do what's right."

I want to ask him why he's in love with me. Why would he, when I'm someone who is willing to lie to hundreds of thousands of people? Why would he love me, when I don't want to take accountability for something I've done? Why would Kas love me, when I'm not even sure I love myself?

Birdie's smile seems sad to me. "Oh, Lark," they say. "Does another person need to love you for you to be worthy of love?"

There's thudding on the stairs, and when I turn around, Sable is standing behind the couch, wearing a crop top and sweatpants. She has no makeup on, and it's my first time not seeing her in her black combat boots, but even then she's still stunning and intimidating and I can see why Kasim would be drawn to her in the first place. Surprise lights her eyes as she pauses, but she doesn't speak as she looks from me and over to Kasim. They watch each other like they're communicating telepathically and, I mean, I don't know, maybe they are.

"I'll head home," Sable says. She so rarely speaks that these are the first words I've heard her say since classes at the Commons started, but her voice has so much finality to it, so much unapologetic certainty, that she could say the sky is green and I might just believe her.

"No," I say. Shit was getting awkward anyway. "I'll go."

Kasim's practically laughing at us, but I think he might be laughing at himself, too, and how we're all acting, like we don't sit next to

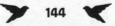

each other at the Commons every day. "You know that you can both stay, right?"

Sable eyes Kas. Kasim just shrugs. She nods an okay and sits down on the couch in between us. I notice she isn't right beside him like usual, fingers intertwined. Did they have a fight? She sits on the couch like she's used to hanging out in total silence. She looks from me to Kasim and back to me with confidence and power and . . . I envy her. I almost want to ask: *How do you know, without a single doubt, that you belong?*

I desperately rack my brain for something to say, anything at all, because I'm not like Kasim and Sable—I'm not cool enough to just sit here in silence. "So, um," I start, just to make a sound, I don't even have a question yet—but it doesn't matter. Sable interrupts.

"I don't like small talk."

I snap my mouth shut. I look at Kasim, who laughs a little, scratching his cheek.

"No offense," Sable says, "but small talk bores me."

I swallow. "I'm sorry. I don't mean to be boring."

Sable frowns. "I didn't say that *you* are boring. I said that *small talk* is boring. I actually find you pretty interesting."

Now that's *very* surprising. "Really? Why?"

"I can feel energy," Sable says, "and your energy is beautiful."

My neck and face get hot. I don't think anyone's ever said my energy is beautiful before. "Thank you," I say. "That's—um—that's really kind."

Sable doesn't answer me. She only looks at Kasim, who clears his throat. "Hating small talk," he says quickly. "That's an ND thing, right?"

Sable gives one short nod.

Excitement zaps through me. "I'm neurodivergent, too," I say, more loudly than I probably should. "I mean, I think I am. I might have ADHD, or autism, or both."

"I was misdiagnosed with ADHD when I was younger," Sable says. "But Black autistic people tend to be underdiagnosed or misdiagnosed because we're only used to seeing white autistic people, and Black autistic people tend to be reprimanded for misbehaving or for being annoying while white autistic people are given compassion and a diagnosis, and also because we're forced to mask ourselves more in a society that already hates us so much for being Black. Can't be crazy on top of that, too, right?" She gives a quick smile.

This is the most I've heard Sable speak. Ever. In all the three-ish years that I've known her. And as she spoke, her voice was fluid, intense, and reminded me of a panther moving through the shadows at night, eyes glowing yellow—

Birdie groans. "Oh, no. Not the bad metaphors again."

I blink. I can see why Kasim fell for her. "I—I mean. Yeah."

Sable's smile falls. "How did you figure out you have autism or ADHD or both?"

"All of the thoughts," I say. "Not that they're a bad thing. Just—I have so many thoughts—and plus I was bullied a lot, and I found out that's a thing for people who have autism." My voice gets quieter. "The bullying, I mean." I shift uncomfortably. "What about you?"

"I don't know how to connect with people."

I look from her to Kasim and back to her. "Is that true? I mean—sorry, I don't want to invalidate what you're saying."

"I didn't know how to connect with people in the way that society expected me to," Sable says. "No oversharing. Force emotion into

my voice and my face to make other people comfortable. If someone comes to me with a problem, I should only listen and nod and then say something like, *How would you like me to help?* I should never respond with an anecdote of my own, because then it seems like I don't really care, and I'm only making everything about me." She shrugs. "Those were the observations I made, anyway."

Kas lets out a low, lingering laugh. "I hate that question. *How would you like me to help?* It always sounds a little like, *Stop complaining, I don't give a fuck, why're you telling me this?*"

I laugh, too. He's so right. "I actually prefer to hear anecdotes."

"Same," Sable says. "It lets me know that you truly understand what I'm trying to communicate, because you've experienced the same thing. I'm tired of suppressing myself for neurotypical people, so I just don't talk to them anymore."

"Is that why you're talking to me now?" I say. "Because you found out I'm ND, too?"

She seems confused by the question for a second—then lets out a surprised laugh. "I didn't know you were funny."

Kasim grins. "Lark can be funny when they want to be."

I blush. "I wasn't trying to be funny."

Kasim's eyes shine when he looks at me. I hold his gaze for a second, heat growing—then bite my lip and look away, only to catch Sable watching me closely, and she doesn't seem to care that I caught her staring, probably feeling my energy, which she thinks is beautiful, and which is telling her at this exact moment that I know Kasim is in love with me. When I started the day, sitting with Kasim who loves me as I talk to his girlfriend who I know he also loves was not on the planner.

"I like getting a chance to speak with you," Sable tells me. "I never talk to you at school. It's difficult to, since Micah and Patch hate you."

Wow. Holy shit. Okay. Sable takes my breath away with the straightforwardness. But I also admire it. I really do. Why try to pad and be gentle? It's the truth, isn't it?

Kasim seems more uncomfortable. "I don't think—no. They're just—I don't know." He doesn't say anything else.

"They have very little respect for you," Sable amends. Okay, so she's willing to pad for Kasim's sake. "But I know that you mean a lot to Kasim."

You mean a lot to Kasim. Kas stares at the floor and works his lower jaw back and forth, eyebrows pinched together like he's lost in thought.

And I get the hell away from *that* topic. "Do you know why Micah and Patch hate me so much?" I ask her.

"It's none of my business," Sable says. "That's a conversation you should have with them." She looks at Kasim pointedly. Something's definitely up, right?

I nod slowly. It's weird, but after speaking to Sable for approximately five minutes, I feel like I know her just as well as I know Kasim and Asha and Jamal and Eli, like I trust her, this neurodivergent, queer, Black human being who is so calm, so steady, so powerful. I'm almost afraid to ask her my next question. "So—do you know about the thread?"

Sable nods. "Yes. I know that Kasim originally wrote the thread, and that you took the credit for it."

What's funny is that I don't actually feel like Sable is trying to make me feel bad or is judging me for what happened. She's only telling the

simple, plain, straightforward truth. And the bubbling of shame that catches me, forcing my gaze to the floor—that's my shame, my embarrassment, mine to handle.

Kasim sighs. "I don't know, Lark—maybe you should tell Eli, at least, that it wasn't originally you."

He might as well have suggested that I leap into a pit of fire. "We just became partners," I say. "If they find out—that'll just hurt them, won't it?"

"Are you afraid of hurting them, or are you afraid that they're not going to react well?" Sable asks me.

I hesitate. "A little bit of both?"

"If you really love Eli, then you need to respect them enough to tell them," Kasim says. "They deserve to know."

Hearing the truth isn't always easy, but especially for something like this. I hate that I know Kasim is right, and that I'm just too afraid to do what I need to.

Kasim nods his head at the TV screen. "You sure you don't want to watch some?"

I nod. "I should probably get going."

"Yeah. All right."

I wave goodbye to Sable, who is now scrolling through her phone and barely glances up. Kas walks me to the door. I think the most painful thing about our relationship is everything that's unsaid, everything that I'm too afraid to say. Maybe it's my imagination, but his smile seems sad to me. Maybe he's thinking the exact same thing.

"See you, Lark."

"Okay. See you, Kasim."

On the walk home, I can't stop thinking about Kasim and Sable. They're alone, so they're probably holding hands again, or—God, something else that I probably shouldn't be thinking about. Sable said she was curious. She said that my energy was beautiful. I always thought she silently hated me, judged me, thought I wasn't good enough for her attention. And now . . .

Birdie raises an eyebrow. "And now?"

Birdie Takes Flight

By Lark Winters

Birdie remembered the future. They remembered the buildings of white with plants that grew on the walls and jungles on the rooftops, the pathways where people sometimes walked but would mostly fly, flapping their wings up into the air, over the ancient ruins of cities, where skeletons of past civilizations were taken over by the Earth, whose healing mirrored humanity's healing, too. Birdie had learned about your present in history class, where they would sit with other students on green grass under the clear blue sky. They had always been so shocked, so surprised, to learn about people who'd once wanted to hurt others. They were confused, and would raise their hand to ask their questions in class. "But *why* did the ancient humans do that? Hadn't they learned that when they hurt another, they were also hurting themselves?"

Comments:

Richard Samuels: This is a strong opening, Lark. I wonder if there's enough immediacy in the conflict, though. Maybe you need to begin with Birdie being sent back to the past.

Eli Miller: Aw, I love this! The first line especially is so great. Perfect beginning, Lark. ♥

Sable Lewis: The voice is beautiful and the writer's energy comes through their words well. I'm a little confused by the setting. How far into the future is this?

Micah Brown: This is naive as fuck and a ridiculous concept. Second person perspective is also inane and impossible to follow.

Patch Kelly: Boring.

Asha Williams: Because I prefer to give helpful critiques instead of rude criticism: I think that this is beautifully written, and I feel pulled in by the concept. I'm excited to read more!

Jamal Moore: The run-ons can be confusing.

Francis Bailey: Sorry I didn't have a chance to read.

Kasim Youngblood: I'm interested by the concept and the voice is strong. I think that *hurting others means hurting oneself* is too idealized and simplistic. What is hurt? Are we hurting ourselves if we stick up for ourselves and others feel hurt in the process? But I know you will have a chance to develop these thoughts more for the remainder of the novel.

Chapter Fourteen

IT'S ALREADY HARD ENOUGH PAYING ATTENTION IN CLASS, BUT now, I don't even *want* to pay attention with Eli beside me, holding my hands on the tabletop between us. We've been texting about that for the last couple of days—how excited we are to see each other again and hold each other's hands, along with a few more talks about how we would like to try *other things*—

"Lark," Birdie says, "if you need to use a euphemism for sex, then *you're probably not ready to try other things.*"

Eli kisses my cheek right there, in front of everyone, and I'm so happy that I barely notice when Patch gags and Micah rolls his eyes and when Kasim clenches his jaw and acts like he doesn't see me but keeps glancing up at me at the exact same time I glance up at him (okay, fine, maybe I notice Kasim, just a little). Sable doesn't even look up at us, and it's like I never even saw her at Kasim's house, that she never told me my energy is beautiful, but this doesn't hurt my feelings so much. It just feels like this is who Sable is.

What're we even talking about in class today? Right, yeah—character development. Mr. Samuels tells us this is a topic he usually lectures college students on, but we've all been in his class so much now that he thinks we're ready to dive in deeper.

"It's not just about what a character wears or what they like to eat that makes them into a living, breathing person. So, how do you develop character?" he asks. "Yes, Asha."

"Characters are supposed to have a goal," she says.

"True," Mr. Samuels says. "That helps give them agency. But the goal is a part of the external plot."

"But character *is* plot," Micah says. "Character and plot are so intertwined that you can't have one without the other."

Eli squeezes my hand and smiles at me, and I'm very tempted to lean in and kiss them. Kasim meets my eye and looks away again, glaring at his phone.

"Characters aren't just supposed to have wants," Jamal says. Their voice is hoarse, like maybe they've just started to get a cold. I hope it's not the virus. "Characters are supposed to have needs."

Mr. Samuels points at Jamal. "Okay, yes. Say more."

"The character doesn't even know what they need yet," Jamal says as they stare at the open book in front of them. "They only know what they want. They have their external goal. And their need—what they're supposed to learn, what they're supposed to change about themselves—that's what they have to figure out to actually get their goal, to get what they want. The character might not even get what they originally wanted, because they change so much by getting what they need, that they don't want their original goal anymore."

"All excellent points," Mr. Samuels says.

I frown. "But if the character doesn't get what they want, then what's the point of the story?"

Jamal just keeps an expressionless face. It's not lost on me that they don't answer, ignoring me altogether, which I've got to admit really hurts.

The awkward silence is interrupted. Kasim sits up straighter in his seat, his voice strong and steady, like he's a king announcing a new set of commandments. "The point is the character's growth," he says. "That's the point of all stories. Characters are supposed to learn and grow, like real people, and if they don't, then they face consequences. They're supposed to make mistakes and figure out what needs to change."

I hesitate. I used to look at Goodreads a lot, before I stopped because I didn't like the way a lot of people were laughing at books and authors as if it were a game, to be as mean as possible for fun. But I remember a lot of the reviews I read on there. Most readers didn't like characters *because* they made mistakes. Those were always the lowest-rated books. When I realized that, I decided I would always have characters who were absolutely perfect, so that no one would say they disliked my characters or my stories.

"But if characters make mistakes," I say, "then they're also unlikeable. No one wants to read about an unlikeable character."

Kasim rolls his eyes up at the ceiling, sending a twinge of irritation through me. "That's the point. No human in the world is likeable. We all fuck up and make mistakes. If people don't like to read about unlikeable characters, it's because they're seeing themselves reflected a little too much and they don't want to look closely at themselves."

Eli frowns. "That's a huge assumption, don't you think? Maybe people just want a break and would rather escape with a character they actually like."

Kasim lets out a loud sigh, as if, fine, he'll deign to humor Eli. "Even thinking that books are all about *escaping* defeats the true purpose of writing."

Asha shakes her head, annoyed. "You can't decide what the *true purpose* of writing is all on your own. Some people like to read and write for fun. Not everyone's trying to be the next James Baldwin or Toni Morrison, like you are, and that doesn't make you better than anyone else, either."

Kasim's eyes glint with a smirk. "I never said I was better than anyone," he says. "But since you suggested it, clearly that's what *you* think, so thank you, Asha."

"All right, all right," Mr. Samuels says, holding up his hands. "We can't say what the true purpose of writing is for everyone, okay?" he says, but Kasim just purses his lips and looks down at his phone again. "We have to decide what our purpose is individually. Figure out our own intentions."

It's not that I haven't been listening, but, well, my brain is still stuck on something Kasim said. "But not everyone gets to be likeable," I say.

Mr. S is used to me jumping around from topic to topic. "Why is that, Lark?"

"So, okay, I would read a bunch of reviews on Goodreads, right, and I would look at posts for some of my favorite books that had some of my favorite characters *ever*, and those reviews were always so much harsher than for books that had white people and cis people and straight people. Because we're not as privileged, we're not allowed to make mistakes in real life or in books and still be considered likeable, too. It's not fair, but it's true. Even if books are supposed to have characters who make mistakes and learn and grow, stories about white people and anyone else who is privileged will be considered good stories with good character development, but if we do that, our books will just be considered bad with unlikeable characters, and, well, you can't blame me or anyone else for wanting to have likeable characters, and for wanting to be likeable, too."

Mr. Samuels is nodding slowly, and I'm not sure if he gets what I mean, but he's thoughtful as he watches me. "You have a point," he eventually says. "You're going to face discrimination as writers, especially if you're writing about your marginalized identities, and especially because you're all Black. That's the society we're in, so it's the simple, unfortunate fact. But," he says, leaning away from the desk, "this just brings me back to the original question I'd asked on the first day. Do you remember it?"

"What makes a good story?" I ask. "Though, I guess technically, I answered it before you—"

"No," Mr. S says, interrupting. "I asked if you as writers should be trying to please your readers."

My answer hasn't changed from that first day. "Yes," I say. "There isn't any point to writing if our readers don't like what we write."

Kasim shakes his head. "No," he says. "Fuck what people think."

I lean forward in my seat to stare at him across the bench. "How can you say fuck what people think when you're literally writing *for* them?" I ask.

Eli takes my hand—when did I even let go of it?—but I can't stop glaring at Kasim.

He practically laughs at me, shaking his head. "Lark, you *just said* that readers are prejudiced. You can't please them even if you tried. And—no, hold on," he says, holding up a hand when I try to speak.

"Okay, fine—pretend for a second that you don't have to deal with any sort of fucked-up bigotry. Everyone treats you and your characters the same as they would treat white, cis, straight, neurotypical people. Why should you bend yourself to please other people? Why should you change your words, your story, your voice to make others happy? What about *you*, Lark?"

Maybe he didn't mean for his voice to get so loud, so intense, to the point where everyone is staring at him, even Micah and Patch. Sable glances from Kasim to me. Eli blinks at him and frowns, and I—shit, I hate that my mind jumps to the same thought that's been following me ever since Kasim posted that thread, the realization that, yeah, he's in love with me. And now I'm afraid Eli might just figure it out, too.

Kasim doesn't care that everyone's staring, because why would he? "Even if every single reader and agent and whoever else rejects you and your book," he says, voice quieter now. "Even if everyone hates you, at least you're not betraying yourself."

When Mr. S says it's time for silent writing, I kind of hate that Kasim's words are still ringing in my ears as I try to write Birdie's story. Easy enough for him to say—*fuck what everyone else thinks.* It's not that easy, Kasim.

Eli Miller @EliLovesYou17

Having summer classes with your partner basically means going on a date with them every single day and I'm not complaining @winterslark

💬 57   ⊖ 203   ♥ 1.3K

Lark Winters (they/them) @winterslark

the partner™ gave me flowers at lunch so i can 100% say this is true, makes cafeteria food taste better when youre eating with someone you love

💬 98   🔁 301   ♥ 2.1K

Eli Miller @EliLovesYou17

We're officially gross

💬 33   🔁 98   ♥ 907

Lark Winters (they/them) @winterslark

yep. yeah, I know.

💬 67   🔁 103   ♥ 989

Vree @fifthalchemist304

Lark and Eli, please be gross. Please continue to be as gross as you can. I never see two happy enby Black people together and in love, and this makes me happier than you can ever know.

💬 5   🔁 23   ♥ 58

Sylvie7 @infiniteplaylistoflove

i'm crying. i rly am. no one ever loves me like this. seeing you 2 together like this gives me hope that i can be in love someday too. thank you. 🏵️

💬 2   🔁 10   ♥ 34

🐦

Eli invites me over to their place, holding my hand on the walk over, and I'm trapped in a chaotic vortex of panic. We've been talking non-stop about how much we want to kiss each other, about what we would like to quote-unquote *try next*, and I'm pretty sure they're asking me over so that we can make out, and, yeah, I've kissed people before, but I've never gone over to their houses to make out and maybe, potentially, possibly do more.

Birdie shakes their head. "Are you *ready* to do more?"

Eli doesn't notice my panic. They tell me about the famous trans and enby celebrities who reached out to them on Insta to congratulate them and to thank them for bringing so much positive, beautiful attention to enby love. They hit 22K on Twitter and 39K on Instagram when we went public. They'd already had a pretty big following for their thirst traps and impeccable style and just for being an all-around beautiful human being, but the fact that they're no longer single seems to give them a whole new level of popularity.

"I could be like Chella Man," Eli says, our clasped hands swinging between us. "Chella got famous just for posting on Insta and even got a role on a TV show. *Titans.* How crazy would it be if we were hit up to be on TV?"

It's Friday afternoon, and they said their parents are both at work. I'm surprised to see that they live in one of those million-dollar townhouses over on Baltimore Avenue, a miniature purple Victorian mansion. We stomp up the steps, and they fiddle with the keys. It's funny—I think they might actually be a little nervous?

They turn as they open the door with a smile (that quivers a little, wow, yeah, they're just as nervous as me). "Yeah. So. This is it."

The house has pale yellow wallpaper that's stained and wooden furniture that could be from the nineties. It's a little messy inside. There are stacks of books and sheets of paper, piles of clothes in the living room—someone was in the middle of doing laundry, not that

I'm judging or anything. It all kind of reminds me of my house, too. It's just surprising, I guess, to see a huge mansion like this and see the inside is just like anywhere else.

Eli gives me a tour, showing me the kitchen with its white-and-yellow tiles and the office that's overcrowded with books. Their parents are both college professors over at UPenn. I get nervous when they take me upstairs and show me their bedroom—are we going to do that thing where we awkwardly sit on the edge of the bed and wait for someone to make the first move?—but I'm curious, too. The walls are painted a pastel yellow, shelves along the wall covered in plants, lights strung up around the window.

"I love your room," I tell them.

They sit on the edge of their bed. "Thanks."

I hesitate by their door.

Eli's smile is uncertain. "Want to sit down?"

I sit three feet away from them with two extra feet of awkwardness between us.

"Everything's been such a whirlwind," Eli says, looking at their hands, the floor—anywhere but at me. "Like a roller-coaster ride."

"Yeah, but the kind that's really slow and cute, like a small train or twirling teacups or something, because I'm afraid of heights."

Eli only laughs, shaking their head. "Has everything been okay for you?" they ask me. "I know that we're moving pretty fast."

There's a beat, and I remember Jamal telling me off in the cafeteria, Kasim saying that I need to tell Eli the truth. I bite my lip. "It's been pretty fast," I say, pushing aside the guilt, "but I kind of like that."

Eli smiles, leaning in. "I like it, too."

I mean, okay, it's not like it's a *shocker* that they kiss me, but the earlier panic turns up a few more notches, and their lips are moving against mine as we sink to our sides, onto their bed, and we kiss like that for maybe three seconds or maybe three minutes, I'm not sure which, and Eli's hands are drifting under my shirt, and my hands are awkwardly at my side, not sure where to touch them or how to touch them and—

This technically isn't the first time I've been in a bed with someone else. Kasim and I have slept in my bed before, talking and laughing, falling asleep next to each other, arms and legs bumping, skin touching, hearing each other sigh, opening my eyes to see that he'd turned over in his sleep to face me, and it was always a little surprising, too, how Kas looked when he was sleeping, like he'd let go of all the troubles in the world and finally found some peace, even if it was only for a little while—

"Hey," Eli whispers against my lips. "Where'd you go?"

Shit. I sit up. "I'm sorry. I—um—I guess I got distracted."

They sit up, too, watching me hesitantly. "Was it—did you not like . . . ?"

"No! I mean, yes! I liked it. I loved it."

They frown like they're confused.

"It's just my head, you know? I'm always getting distracted." I force a laugh.

Eli nods slowly. "Okay. Maybe we're going too fast. We can just sit and talk, too."

"Yeah. Yes. That's a good idea."

We sit in total silence. Tumbleweed blows across their floor.

Eli laughs. "Wow. This is awkward."

I groan and hide my face and rub my forehead, my temple, my cheeks, tapping them, patting them, slapping them. "It's because of me. I'm the most awkward person in the world."

"No, hey—" They take one of my hands, pulling it gently away from my face. "We're both awkward, all right?" They grin. "And that's okay. It's okay to be awkward. It doesn't mean I like you any less. You're still the Lark I'm pretty sure I'm starting to fall in love with."

Birdie twists around. "What did they saaaaay?"

Oh, my God. These are words I wouldn't have even dared to dream about hearing just a couple of weeks ago. You'd think I would feel a buzz of excitement, like I'm beginning to float. But, no—instead, I feel like I'm sinking into a pit of quicksand.

"I'm really grateful to you, Lark. I've got a lot to thank you for," they say, smiling at me so sweetly, so softly, "for posting that tweet about me in the first place."

Shame's been building more and more, this giant tower of shame threatening to fall over, and I've got Kasim's words echoing in my head—*if you really love Eli, then you need to respect them enough to tell them*—and Eli, thanking me like this, yeah, this is the last crack—

"It wasn't me."

Not that I was planning on saying it. That's so like me, isn't it? I'm always saying shit without thinking it through. When the words spill out, I'm surprised to hear them. But the second I say the truth, relief, sweet Jesus, relief swells through me, like I was standing on the bottom of the sea, trying to carry this giant rock that was weighing me down, and I finally let it go.

Eli's smile falters with confusion. "What?"

"It wasn't me, Eli."

"What wasn't you?"

"The original tweet." They're still holding my hand, and I feel like I'm trapped, so I pull away, wiping it off on my jeans. "My friend—well, not really my friend, but that's not the point—he tried to post it to his own account but posted it on mine instead, and now everyone thinks I did it. I feel like crap lying to everyone." God. I can't believe I'm actually saying this out loud. Nervousness builds in my throat and my voice cracks. "Especially you."

They squint at me in confusion, turning away for a second and then turning back to face me. "Are you serious?"

"Yeah. I'm serious."

"You're not joking?"

"No. I'm not joking."

They stare at me, and I've never seen Eli's face like this—no sun, no smile, no brightness. They look confused and hurt, like confused about *why* I would hurt them, and that makes it so much freaking worse, more terrible than I could've ever imagined. "I don't even know what to say."

My heart sinks. "I'm sorry. I shouldn't have told you that it was me."

They shake their head. "This is kind of a lot to take in," they tell me. "So—if you didn't write the thread, then who did?"

I hesitate. "It's a secret."

"Okay." They seem to consider this. "And if you didn't post that tweet, does that mean you don't actually have feelings for me?"

"No!" I say, more loudly than I mean to. "I mean—no, yes, I do have feelings for you. Everyone thought it was me, so when I was interviewed, I decided to say the name of someone who I really do love

anyway, so the thread is a lie, but my feelings for you—yes, I really do love you, Eli."

They stare at me, frowning now, jaw clenching so that their muscle jumps. It's like watching a Magic 8 Ball swirling with all the possible responses. *Outlook good. As I see it, yes. Fuck off, Lark.* This could go so wrong, so into the territory of Eli deciding they don't want to waste another second with me, them telling the whole world that I'm a liar, and wouldn't I deserve it?

"I need time, I think," they say slowly, looking away from me and frowning at their shoes. "I feel like I need to process this."

I nod, biting my lip. I probably haven't breathed in a full minute, but I take in a shaky breath now. "Okay. I understand."

"This hurts, Lark. It's—I don't know, it's like our whole relationship is a giant lie."

Fuck. "I'm really sorry."

The silence is the worst I've ever experienced, and that's not an exaggeration. I'm about to open my mouth to ask them if I should go, when they say, "Why did you even lie about the thread in the first place? I don't understand that."

"I was afraid, I think. Scared that if I said the thread wasn't me, I would get backlash, and then the longer I lied, and the more I lied about it, the more I got pulled in . . ."

They nod, watching me closely, carefully, like they're trying to figure out if they believe me, if they can trust me, and why would they? "I—yeah, I'm really upset," they say. "Time. I just need some time, okay?"

I nod. I swallow. And I try not to cry. "Yeah. Okay. I'll give you time."

Chapter Fifteen

I SIT CROSS-LEGGED ON MY BED.

People talk about meditation a lot, right?

I'm curious, and depressed and anxious and I feel like if I don't do something, I'm going to claw out of my own skin.

I take a deep breath, like I'm about to jump under the ocean, and close my eyes.

My mind is chaos, thoughts bounce around from one thing to the next—is this working? Is there any point? I wonder if Kasim has ever tried meditation. I wonder how he's doing. Does he love me? Does he hate me? But we're all made of love, right? Is hate even real, then? Or is it just something we've made up? Maybe hatred is just an illusion.

It's not working. I groan in frustration and flop back onto my bed. I curl up on my side, grab my phone, and type into the search bar: How to meditate.

A bunch of results flood my screen.

I try again: How to meditate when you're neurodivergent.

A bunch of results *still* flood my screen.

I sigh, scrolling—and then, within the first few results, something promising: *There's a misconception that your mind is supposed to be quiet during meditation . . .*

I click on the link.

There's a misconception that your mind is supposed to be quiet during meditation, and that meditation is only for people who can sit still. For many neurodivergent people, traditional ideas of meditation are difficult and feel downright impossible. But meditation can be found through dance, through walks in nature, through the act of the flow state. Meditation can be creative and is never meant to make the meditator feel confined. If you're neurodivergent like me, then let your meditation equate to exploration.

Let your mind roam. Let your thoughts explode. Eventually, a question may even come to you—a question that might just be your breakthrough.

Exploration, huh?

I decide to sit again, but let my thoughts go. Thoughts, thoughts . . . God, these thoughts, they're endless. It's hard to remember that I'm not *actually* my thoughts. That my idea of myself is created by memories and experiences that are in the past, and the past isn't real, and neither is the future, only this present moment, right here and now. So who am I, then, if I'm not this idea of myself in my head, this collection of memories?

Why do you need to be liked by everyone?

That's the question that comes to me.

I open my eyes, almost expecting to see someone sitting there, waiting for an answer.

Why? It's obvious, isn't it? I'm not safe if I'm not liked.

You weren't safe in the past. But the past is not real.

For the first time in a while, I don't have any thoughts. My mind feels emptier now, and I feel even lonelier than I did before. I pick up my phone again, open the Twitter app, and scroll.

I don't even notice it at first—not right away—but then, right there, my profile—

HOLY SHIT.

Just like that.

OH MY GOD.

It happened.

I have 53.7K followers.

I've finally, *finally* reached my goal.

Everything I'd been obsessing over for the past year. I did it. I made it past 50K.

My numbers had been growing over the past few days, but this was the final push I needed. I sit, and I grin, and I wait for it to feel like my entire life has changed.

And I wait some more.

My smile starts to fade. I realize how quiet my room is, like it's too quiet, with just the sound of my breathing and the muffled voices from the TV downstairs—sounds like my mom's watching the news. Disappointment crawls through me. I don't have an inbox full of agents instantly offering me representation. Janet Fields hasn't invited me to get lunch with her. This was everything I'd worked for, thinking that my life would change, so it's even more depressing that everything still feels the same. Even worse, I guess, is that this happened now, when I know I've hurt Eli so badly.

I shouldn't look through the comments, but I guess Twitter really does feel like an addiction, helping to soothe and numb and distract me.

Birdie makes a *yikes* expression. "That's because social media is literally addicting."

And—yeah, that's not at all surprising to see, though I wish it were. I wonder what's going on in white people's heads. Why *don't* so many white people care about race? Is it because they're ashamed? They know they benefit from white privilege, but they don't talk about the horrible things their ancestors did. Whenever I read a book with a white main character, written by a white person, they never even consider the ways that their world has been shaped by the racism they're still benefiting from. It's as if race doesn't even exist for them, and when I used to look at Goodreads, white people would complain whenever they see a book that talks about race and other issues in the character's life. *There's too much going on*, they would write. A lot of white people don't want to know that race exists for them, I guess—and that's the problem.

In a way, I think white people need to heal, too. They need to heal the shame in knowing that their ancestors were kidnappers and murderers and rapists and sadists who tortured other human beings. If Black people carry the horrors of slavery in our blood and bones, then white people must be carrying something also. But so many of them never look at it. They get angry at anyone who does. They would rather dehumanize other people than look at their own pain.

I feel a burst of inspiration.

I grab my laptop and start to type.

Lark Winters (they/them) @winterslark

why do humans dehumanize each other so much?? i think its because we need to dehumanize other people so that we can hurt them

💬 1   🔁 4   ♥ 25

our natural state is love, and we WANT to love our fellow human beings, so the only way we can trick ourselves into hating other people is by telling ourselves they are not humans worthy of the same love

💬 9   🔁 14   ♥ 37

and that's kind of sad, right?? bc we could have world peace, we rly could, if we all realized that were all worthy of love and stop dehumanizing people

💬 19   🔁 28   ♥ 52

but that goes both ways right? white ppl dehumanize black ppl, for example, and we know its wrong and want them to stop, but then we have to go by our own rules and morals too right?

💬 8   🔁 11   ♥ 31

so like for example we should not call cops pigs!!! they are humans too and we are literally dehumanizing them in the way we don't want to be dehumanized

💬 109   🔁 59   ♥ 3

i think prison should be abolished and i dont think the police system should exist, but that doesnt mean that i will engage in the same harmful behavior that i want others to stop using against me

💬 189   🔁 80   ♥ 7

alex uwu <3 @alexwawa

wow this is a really shitty take.

💬 9   🔁 16   ♥ 67

um chile anyways so @huhbigboobs

WAIT you're telling me that lark is a fucking COP
LOVER?????? THIS is the child you all choose to hype up???

💬 12   🔁 28   ♥ 106

N. Kay @nkay95

@winterslark This is an incredibly harmful comment to
post. There is a long history of police brutality against
BIPOC and especially Black communities, and to use your
growing platform to post in support of cops is thoughtless
and a slap in the face for many.

💬 91   🔁 108   ♥ 501

Lark Winters (they/them) @winterslark

sorry for not posting any updates today about my
relationship with @elilovesyou17 but thank you everyone
for the love and support!!!!

💬 109   🔁 502   ♥ 1.6K

@jellicoeflame

@winterslark @elilovesyou17 take the time you need, you
don't owe us anything <3

💬 0   🔁 0   ♥ 2

um chile anyways so @huhbigboobs

hey here's an idea, maybe you can shut up about your
relationship PERMNANTLY, I would really love that, thanks

💬 8   🔁 13   ♥ 46

comrade @patchscars

if only you all knew how annoying lark winters is irl. that "respect cops" tweet yesterday was only the beginning. they're fake and toxic as fuck and say the most problematic shit.

💬 40   ♻ 99   ♥ 209

Tithings @rosewaterborn

Hi @patchscars, can you please share how Lark is toxic and problematic? I don't want to support them if they're harmful. Please message me, my DMs are open.

💬 17   ♻ 23   ♥ 89

ancillaryx @strangerdreams

@rosewaterborn Can you let me know what @patchscars tells you please?

💬 2   ♻ 2   ♥ 6

Harrow the Outsider @harrowlin56

@patchscars oh no I hope not!! Lark has always seemed so kind

💬 27   ♻ 43   ♥ 102

alex uwu <3 @alexwawa

I believe it. Lark has only ever ignored the comments calling them out.

💬 9   ♻ 16   ♥ 37

N. Kay @nkay95

@winterslark Can you please explain why you're ignoring genuine concerns and criticisms about your recent tweet that is in support of police? Your action of ignoring comments is problematic.

💬 51   ♻ 89   ♥ 306

Chapter Sixteen

Simon Duncan <simonduncan@sdlitstudios.com>

Hi Lark,

Thanks for querying BIRDIE TAKES FLIGHT! Your writing is absolutely gorgeous, and I enjoyed the voice, but the story doesn't feel black to me, which was disappointing, seeing that your main character is described as black. We got a lot about the character's trans and queer identities, but I didn't really get a sense for the character's blackness. Maybe focus on making the book feel more culturally rich.

Besides, 50,000 words is too short for a YA novel.

Yours,

Simon

Feel Black? How does someone "feel" more Black? I *am* Black. To feel more Black would mean that someone has stereotypical ideas of what it means to be Black. To assume that I have to match a checklist in their head. I have to look a certain way, dress a certain way, speak and eat and breathe a certain way. A way that's acceptable to them.

Another reminder that I can never just exist. I can never just be. Not in this skin. This is the kind of thing that makes me wish I could grow wings like Birdie and just fly away and leave this earth and all of its bullshit behind. Wouldn't that be nice?

But still, the people who say things like this—I know that they're making mistakes. Hurtful mistakes, but mistakes that I want to forgive them for, because I don't want to keep this anger inside of me, not when I've already got so much chaos swirling around. I don't have the space for anger along with everything else.

My dream of being an author is never going to work out. I can see that clearly now. I'd wanted to be published so that I could show the world who I am and be loved by everyone—finally understood and really, truly, completely accepted. Maybe then, I would start to love myself, too.

My mom frowns at me in the kitchen as I eat dinner silently. "You all right, Lark?"

I never did have much of a poker face. "Another rejection," I tell her. I can't even begin to explain the way my social media notifications are imploding before my very eyes.

She smooths a hand over my forehead and into my hair. "I'm sorry, baby."

It's not only that. I struggle to figure out how to phrase the words in my head. "What do you think it means for a person to be toxic?"

My mom's never surprised by my random questions. "Toxic? I think it generally means a person who doesn't realize they're harming others. Or realizes they're harming others, but doesn't do anything to change their behavior."

I'm lying to so many people. I know that, and I'm not doing anything to change.

"What's going on?" she asks. "Everything okay?"

"I guess."

"If you're sure . . ." She pats my hand. "You'll let me know if you're struggling, right?" My mom is worried as she watches me. I can see it in her eyes. "Lark?"

I give her a bright smile. "Yeah—of course."

Does she believe me? "All right, baby."

Asha invites me to her house party for her seventeenth birthday, which is wild, because I've never, ever been invited to a house party before, and I'm buzzing with excitement at actually being *invited* to something, *me*, and I'm also so freaking nervous, because what do I wear and how do I act and what do I say to be likeable so that I can get invited to parties again and not be, you know, excommunicated from all semblance of a social life?

My mom's worried about me going to hang around a bunch of strangers, but I tell her that Asha said there would only be a few people, everyone wearing masks, not a big deal, and my mom makes me promise to leave if it starts to get too crowded or if people aren't wearing masks or if they start drinking. I don't think she wants me to go at all, but she knows this is kind of a big deal, being invited to my first ever party and all.

The party starts at seven, so when I show up at 6:57 P.M., I wait outside Asha's townhouse, which is a little closer to Baltimore Avenue and has a giant backyard where I can see twinkly lights are strung up. After a few minutes pass, I knock, heart pounding to match the beat. Asha opens the door, bleary-eyed and headwrap slightly askew.

"Happy birthday!" I say, arms spread wide.

She squints at me. "Lark?"

My heart drops. "Do I have the wrong day?"

"No," she says, checking her phone. "You're just kind of early."

"Oh." I pause. "I thought it started at seven."

She shakes her head. "Never mind. Come in."

I'm the only person here so far. The living room is set up for a small gathering of friends, chips open and bottles of soda out. Asha sighs and plops onto the sofa, hairpins in her mouth as she fixes her headwrap. I hand her a poem I wrote for her gift. "Sorry. I suck at poetry."

She smiles as she reads it, but I don't think she likes it very much. "This is really cute, Lark. Thank you." She glances up and folds the piece of paper. "Is Eli coming?"

I hesitate. I haven't told anyone about Eli wanting space. I texted them earlier, saying that Asha extended the invite to them, too, and they replied with an *okay*, but that was it.

I sigh. "Romance is hard."

Asha grins. "You're telling me."

Asha needs to keep getting ready, so I go outside into the back-yard and sit on a plastic chair and hold a cup of ginger ale while faint music plays from inside the house. I hear voices, more laughter, louder music. I want to go inside, but I'm also afraid to open the door and inevitably do something outrageously awkward that makes everyone stare at me, which will only make me wonder why I bother to leave the house at all.

The door opens behind me. "Lark!" Asha calls. "Why're you out here by yourself?"

When I follow Asha back inside, everything's completely different. She's hung up sheets to dim the lights, making the room glow faint reds and purples. There's a small station where Asha's set up her cards on a table so that she can do oracle readings. The music is louder, people are already dancing in the living room and in the kitchen, and all of the snacks she'd laid out are gone, though there's also stuff that other people brought—crap, I didn't even think to bring something—like chips and salsa and a plate of brownies, which, you know, are most likely *special* brownies. Asha grins and offers me one.

I take a bite and groan. "That's so good."

Asha is pulled away by a friend who squeals and hugs her. There're about ten people. I recognize a few from school, someone named Steph, a senior I think, who—oh, I see who she's talking to. Eli meets my eye. Their smile is so forced that they legit look like they're in pain. I don't know if I should go over to them, and I'm surprised when they come over to me instead.

"Hey," I say, biting my lip. "I didn't know you were going to be here."

"Steph invited me," Eli says, nodding, looking down at the cup in their hand.

The silence swells until it breaks. "I'm sorry," I say quietly. "I'm so sorry—"

"I don't want to talk about it right now," they say. Steph calls their name and waves, and Eli looks back with a sunflower smile. I miss them looking at me that way. "I know that we're both here, but we don't need to actually speak to each other."

Before I can say anything else, they've already turned away and gone back to Steph. I swallow, throat dry, when Steph smiles with a shine in her eyes and leans into Eli, hand on their arm. Do I even get to be sad right now? Maybe this is exactly what I deserve.

Kasim is here, too. He sits on the sofa across from me, looking away just as I look at him, and Sable speaks to him, hands on his cheeks, staring into his eyes super intensely. Asha might hate Kasim, but she and Sable are best friends, and, huh, I wonder if that has anything to do with why Asha doesn't like Kasim very much, now that I think about it.

I realize that I'm standing in the middle of the dance floor, spaced out and staring. Okay, it's not really a dance floor, but people are dancing all around me, twisting and grinding and laughing. An Afrobeat switches to a song with heavy drums, and someone starts doing capoeira, and everyone starts to clap as they watch the person spin around on their hands and do flips, holy shit, and before I know it, I'm clapping along, too. And the song switches to a song I *do* know and love, *if I tell you say I love you o*, and that's the thing I love about music, that it doesn't really matter how awkward or sad you're feeling, when the lights are low and everyone's dancing and singing it's so easy to get swept away in the tide of vibrations, all of us synced up to the same tune and beat, and it's easier to dance and touch and smile. Someone I don't know starts to dance with me, taking my hands and turning me around and around, laughing when I laugh, and then just like that I blink and they're gone, I don't even know where to, and it doesn't matter, because I can spin myself around and around.

Kasim and Sable are dancing, also. When did they even get up? They're only a few feet away, Kasim's back to Sable's front. He's

178

looking right at me. *I know you're feeling me—you know I'm feeling you.* Sable's head leans on his shoulder, and she's watching me, too, and I wonder what it would be like to dance with her, with him, with both of them, and maybe that's why I'm being pulled closer to them, drawn in like a magnet, and they don't seem to mind. It's not that we're dancing with each other, but more that we're dancing close, bumping into one another, Sable's leg against my leg, Kasim's hand against my hand, and I don't think they even realize it, because Kasim turns around, his back to me, and starts to kiss Sable, until we get so close that skin presses against me, I'm not even sure whose, and since we've started moving to the same beat, maybe that means we're dancing together after all. Kasim turns to face me, and it's kind of funny that we haven't even said a single word to each other, but we're dancing like this, dancing close enough to kiss each other if we wanted to—

I take a step back. That's a weird thought. Kasim stops moving, too, watching me closely. I turn on my heel. I'm not running away. I swear I'm not. But I think I just got a little confused, is all—forgot who I was and forgot who Kasim was and forgot what we were doing.

"Or," Birdie says over my shoulder, "maybe you've finally remembered."

I burst out of the door and into the backyard. There're only a few people around, standing and drinking and smoking. I take a deep breath, trying to clear my senses.

A voice is right behind me. "Lark."

I spin. I didn't even realize Kas had followed me out.

We watch each other for a long moment, but it doesn't feel awkward like it normally would, I think. It just feels intense, so many unsaid things trying to force their way to the surface, and I'm straining

to push them back down again. It's like a conversation we'd started inside continued, and Kasim refuses to look away.

"So," he says. "Where's Eli?"

I shrug. "I don't know. Inside somewhere. Why?"

"I just assumed they'd be out here with you."

Why am I so angry? Why does Kasim always piss me off so much? "Well, you were wrong. It's not any of your business, right?"

He doesn't immediately bite back. His expression is neutral, maybe even soft, which just upsets me even more. I need Kas to get angry at me, to say something sarcastic, so that I can keep being angry at him, so that we can go back to the way things were, and so that I won't have to think about the way he's looking at me right now.

"Eli's not good for you, Lark."

"What?" I say. "Why the hell would you even say that?"

"There's something off about them," Kasim tells me. "Sable agrees."

"Did she sense their energy or something?"

Kas nods. "Yeah, actually. Not that you need to be able to read energy. I get bad vibes from them, too."

"Why're you telling me this?"

"I'm just trying to help you."

"I don't think you're trying to help me. I think you're trying to sabotage my relationship." Maybe that's the real reason he said I should tell Eli the truth.

"Why would I do that, Lark?"

Because he's jealous. "I don't know. You tell me."

"I'm not trying to fight with you," he says quietly.

"Then you shouldn't have said anything."

"I've been realizing that it's important to be real," he says, "and honest about what we think, and how we feel."

No—no, I don't want to hear the next words that I'm pretty sure are about to come out of his mouth, because if Kasim tells me that he's in love with me, right here and now, then I would have to deal with the question that comes after that. The music inside switches to a slow beat, Kelsey Lu's voice. *I'm not in love, so don't forget it.*

"What do you have against Eli, anyway?" I ask him.

Kas shakes his head. "I think Eli's just in it for the follows," he says. "They're a clout chaser. They like the attention."

These words—I think these are the harshest words Kasim has ever said to me, of any fight we've ever had, any debate or disagreement. These words sting. I stand there, shocked into silence, staring at him as he stares at me, clenching his jaw with this expression, like maybe he realizes he's finally gone too far.

"So, what you're saying is that you don't think it's possible anyone would ever like me for me."

"That's not what I'm saying at all, Lark."

"Eli isn't a clout chaser. They actually like me. I know that's hard for you to believe."

"That isn't hard for me to believe."

I'm starting to cry, which just upsets me even more. Kasim takes a step forward, mouth open, like he's going to tell me something, something he's been wondering whether he should tell me for months now, maybe even for a little over a year, around the time that things got weird for us and we stopped talking and our friendship started to end—

I turn and really do run away. I rush through the backyard, slipping on the grass, and into the house, across the dance floor and past a startled Asha, who is talking to Sable on the couch.

"Lark?" Asha calls, her voice following me out the front door, onto the porch. I take a deep breath and sit on the front steps. Yeah, okay, so that was dramatic as all hell, running away crying, but what else is new?

Birdie rests their head on my shoulder. "It's okay to be dramatic, Lark."

There're footsteps behind me. I turn, expecting Asha, fully ready to apologize for making a scene at her party—and I'm surprised when I see Sable instead. She closes the door behind her, not looking at me as she sits down on the steps, too.

"Is it okay if I sit here?" she asks. She brought out her black backpack for some reason.

I nod and swallow. "Yeah."

We sit quietly, Sable opening her backpack and rummaging through it, and it's kind of crazy how with anyone else, this silence would be driving me insane—and, right, people say we should not use the words *crazy* and *insane* but I guess since I am neurodivergent and have been depressed and suicidal and I like to use these words for myself and no one else then maybe it's okay? But with Sable, it's almost comforting. Like I know she isn't judging me. She finds something—a stone. It's a pale pink, and it's smooth and cool when she puts it in my hand.

"It's a rose quartz from my crystal collection. This is what your energy feels like to me, so I decided I would like to give this to you. My love language is gift giving," she adds.

I start to cry again, for an entirely different reason, and I'm not even sure what this reason is, not really—maybe it's just the kindness, the gentleness I'm being shown when I don't even think I deserve it. I've been so awful. I've lied to so many people, and I lied to Eli and hurt their feelings, and now Sable is sitting here beside me, and even though she knows the truth, she's giving me a beautiful gift. My hand clutches around the stone and I hold it close to my chest. "I'm sorry," I say. "I don't know what's wrong with me."

Sable smiles a little as she watches me. "Nothing's wrong with you."

I manage a smile, too, and wipe my face. "Thank you for this. This is really thoughtful and kind and beautiful. I don't mean to cry."

"Crying is good for you. I'm actually kind of jealous of you, being able to cry. It's hard for me to access emotion and process and release it."

I sniff. "Really?"

She nods. "Not only because I'm autistic, I think, but because of trauma. I was taught that emotion is weak, and I'm not loveable if I express my emotions or needs."

"I'm sorry," I say. "That's so shitty. You're loveable."

"I know," she says. "I came into this world, knowing I was worthy of love, just like every human being in this world. But then I was told I'm not enough to be loved, and I began to question my worth. I started to believe that I have to do something to convince other people to love me the same way others are loved, to prove that I'm worthy, too. It took me a while to realize that I am enough exactly as I am. But maybe I'm oversharing."

"No—no, I don't mind," I tell her. "I mean, I kind of think that we might all be one and separation is an illusion and we're actually the same consciousness experiencing every single life in the universe, and

time is an illusion, so maybe I was one of your past lives and maybe I will experience your life soon and in that case, it's not actually oversharing at all."

She smiles. "I like you a lot, Lark," she says. "And I think that you're good for Kasim."

I wipe my tears with my palm. "How could I be good for him? Whenever we speak, we get into a fight." My voice gets softer, and I don't even really mean to keep speaking, not really. "It's like I don't even know how to talk to him anymore. How do you talk to him? How did you become friends with him?"

She tilts her head. "I'm honest," she says. "And not just with Kasim. With everyone. I always speak the truth of what I'm feeling and thinking, no matter whether other people will accept me or reject me."

I nod, staring at the polished stone. "I think that's what scares me the most. Being honest, just to be rejected. What's the point of that?" I ask her. "I don't want to show anyone my true self, just for other people to say I'm not good enough."

Sable considers me, her gaze soft. "But being vulnerable is the only way you can really connect to anyone. How're you supposed to connect with someone as a false version of yourself?"

There's something about Sable—her energy, maybe—that makes me feel safe, makes me feel like I can practice showing her the real Lark. "I think about Kasim sometimes," I whisper. "No—almost all the time. I hate that we're not friends anymore." I squeeze my eyes shut, waiting for Sable to laugh.

"We've spoken about you before," she says. "Kasim likes you a lot."

This makes my heart thud so loudly, I'm sure she can hear it. "But Kasim is the one who doesn't want to be my friend."

"Yes, he does. He's afraid he'll be rejected. I told him that I'm pretty sure that you like him, too."

Why does it feel like we're speaking in codes? Is she trying to suggest I'm in love with her boyfriend? I stare at the stone in my hand, because I really can't look anywhere else.

"I care about Kasim," Sable says. "If there's anything I can do to help him, I would like to do it. I think you both need to sit down and actually try to communicate. But that would require being honest with yourself, too."

I bite my lip.

Sable waits.

"I—I do like Kasim, too," I tell her. "But we get into so many fights. I feel like I can't trust him because he's so critical of everything I say and do."

This seems to confuse her. "Can't someone be critical of you and still be trustworthy?"

"I don't know. Doesn't someone hate you if they judge you?"

"So you believe that someone hates you if they're judgmental. But maybe a person can tell you what they really think because they care," she says. "Maybe that's more trustworthy—if he tells you what he really thinks, and you know that he still loves you even then, regardless of what mistakes you make."

I have to sit with that for a second. "People who've been critical of me have only ever hated me, so it doesn't feel like someone could actually care about me if I make mistakes. It feels like I have to be perfect for someone to like me."

"Maybe that's getting in the way of your relationship with Kasim. Not only Kasim," she says, "but with everybody. If you think you can only be perfect for people to care about you, then you're never really showing your true self. Because it's impossible to be perfect, isn't it?"

Birdie smiles up from the step in front of me. "I like this one."

Sable goes on. "I show Kasim my true self, whether he approves or not. I think that how we feel about others is a reflection of how we feel about ourselves. If someone doesn't love you, it's a sign of how they feel about themselves, not you. Someone who loves and accepts themselves unequivocally wouldn't spend so much energy hating others. And if you love yourself no matter what anyone thinks, then it doesn't matter if other people treat you like shit. Well," she says after a beat, "it can still hurt. But loving myself, messy and imperfect parts included, means knowing that I'm enough. Everyone is worthy of love, right?"

I can't keep my eyes off of her as she speaks, even when I feel the embarrassment rise when she doesn't look away from me, either. Is this the sort of thing Sable says to Kasim? Is this why he's in love with her? I can see that. I can understand that. I think I might be falling for her, too.

Sable stands, reaching for her backpack, ready to leave, but I don't want her to. "What are you going to tell Kasim?"

"Nothing," she says. "I think that you should talk to him yourself. I told Kasim that he should be the one to speak to you in the first place, but, well . . ." She smirks. "He likes to pretend he's braver than he actually is."

I'm nothing but a scared kid. I know that's true. Weird to think Kasim might just be a scared kid, too.

She bends over, kisses my cheek, and walks away, back into the house before I can think of anything else to say. My heart races, and, yeah, holy shit, I'm pretty sure I'm in love with Sable. Birdie face-palms.

I Love Myself

Poem by Sable Lewis

I love myself

When I see: no other Black girls on TV like me

I love myself

When I get: comments from people who hate my skin's darkness

I love myself

When I'm told: I shouldn't even exist in this world

I love myself

When they say: I can't be too angry—no, can't let this Black girl be mad or

sad or feel

I love myself

When they come, everyone of all races and sexes and creeds

They all agree that they would never be able to love someone like me

They say I'm ugly because they don't know

The power and beauty in my skin and my eyes and my nose

From the time I was a little girl, I'm shown

The only way I can have any worth in this world

Is if other people say they love me, too, yes, they agree

I am only worthy of love if you deem me worthy

I say that *I love myself* anyway, on repeat

My song drowning out the world that wants me to hate me

Comments:

Richard Samuels: This is heartbreaking, Sable. I can feel your
pain in every line. I wonder if the ending could be stronger,

somehow. This might be the sort of poem you tinker with for a while.

Kasim Youngblood: The rhymes can feel a little forced, but the writing is powerful.

Jamal Moore: The last line needs the most work. It ends too abruptly.

Patch Kelly: I'm sorry you've had to deal with so much racist and misogynistic shit.

Micah Brown: Yes, same. This is powerful, I have no other comments.

Eli Miller: Wow! Your writing is amazing. Does "I love myself" get too repetitive?

Asha Williams: I disagree, I think the repetition is the point. I think this is perfect.

Francis Bailey: Sorry I didn't have a chance to read.

Lark Winters: I don't know a lot about poetry, but this made me cry. I think it's beautiful.

alex uwu <3 @alexwawa

wait so yall really going to tell me that not only does @winterslark support cops but they said that racists are good people and they're still out here with a shit ton of likes and followers?

💬 99   🔁 104   🤍 459

Lark Winters (they/them) @winterslark

sometimes i wonder if we like it when people mess up so we feel better about ourselves as we rip them apart

💬 241   🔁 112   🤍 23

um chile anyways so @huhbigboobs

this is a bad fucking take. we're allowed to rip apart idiots, including you.

💬 56   🔁 198   🤍 677

Molls Folls @mollylanc

y'all only catching on now that they're toxic as fuck??

💬 3   🔁 4   🤍 39

FLACK DACK @lazobrw

Lark Winters has been added to my list of problematic people not to support. If anyone wants to see the list, DM me.

💬 18   🔁 40   🤍 95

N. Kay @nkay95

Can we have a serious conversation about the ways we attempt to silence others online? @winterslark's most recent post is a form of tone policing & gaslighting. It's our right to "rip apart" whoever we want, especially toxic and problematic people.

💬 94   🔁 540   🤍 3.4K

Chapter Seventeen

I NEED TO GET OUT OF MY HOUSE, BECAUSE IF I STAY IN MY room I'm pretty sure I'll throw my laptop out of my window, and then myself, because there's just no winning. It's like no matter what, I just can't say or do anything right. My followers had reached over 50K, my dream—and, just like that, I've lost more than three thousand followers overnight, and I'm not even sure *why*, or if I did or said anything wrong.

The bookstore is quiet, like usual. Just my Spotify plays. *I've been trying not to go off the deep end.* The owner, Jim, left behind a stack of flyers for me to put up on the windows—the Big Red rally is going to be at the end of the month, and different groups have organized a counterprotest against the rally, which I'm betting the entire neighborhood will come out for. There are also boxes of books that I need to cut open and unpack and organize, and I'm in the middle of doing just that, trying to figure out where the titles are supposed to go—shit, where is the memoir shelf again?

When the door opens and its bell rings, I pop up, grin on my face. "Welcome!"

Eli closes the door behind them. "Hey, Lark."

My grin freezes in place, which I'm sure makes me look terrifying, like I'm auditioning to play the zillionth version of the Joker. "Oh. Hey."

Eli stops in the middle of the floor, hands in their pockets. I have a flashback to them coming here after my interview with Patch. I'd been freaking out, so sure that I would never even be able to speak to Eli again—and even then, I would take that moment over this one any day.

"I was taking a walk," they say, "doing some thinking, and then I saw the bookstore and decided to check if you were here."

"Oh. Okay." I swallow. "I'm here. Obviously. I mean, shit, not *obviously* like you should have known that I was here, just—"

They walk in and lean against the register's counter. "Can we talk?"

I wasn't expecting this, but when is there ever a good time to have a painful conversation? I nod, pushing the box of books up against the wall, and sit at the register so the counter's in between us. "You said you were walking around, thinking," I say, unsure of where else to begin. "What were you thinking about?"

They sigh, crossing their arms. "A lot. Too much to even . . ." They sigh again. "At Asha's house," they say, "I saw the way that Kasim was looking at you."

Huh? What? Flyball out of left field knocks me in the head, leaves me for dead.

"I already knew he had feelings for you, because he's always staring at you in class," they tell me. "But at Asha's, I was surprised to see the way you were looking at him, too."

"What?" I say, panic bubbling up as laughter. "No. No—I wasn't looking at him in any kind of way, was I?"

Eli watches me closely. "If we're going to be together, we need to figure some things out. We're polyam, but we still need some ground rules."

If we're going to be together. You know that one line that's always used? *I released a breath I didn't even know I was holding.* Yeah, well, I do exactly that. There's still a chance for this to work out, then. I try not to nod too excitedly as I sit up straight, ready to force my brain to pay attention.

"We can be with other people," Eli says. "That's fine. That's not a big deal."

Most people at my school and at the Commons are polyam. I respect people who are monogamous, but I know I can't stop myself from loving multiple people at once, and I can't force my partner to love only me and to only want to be with me, either. If they love other people, it doesn't mean they love me any less. They're not hurting me by loving another person. Love is infinite, right? It's not like there's only a small amount of love that a person is given when they're born, and they can only use that amount of love for a certain number of people in their lives—and if a person is in love with multiple people and wants to be with multiple people, then why not?

It's ironic, I guess, that I'm polyamorous, but Eli is my first and only relationship, and we're already on the edge of breaking up, so maybe I'm not exactly the right expert to be talking about relationships in the first place.

Birdie shrugs. "You're allowed to have your thoughts and opinions, just the same as anyone else."

"But there's nothing going on with me and Kasim," I tell Eli, and try to ignore the jolt in my chest that tells me that this is yet another lie.

"Sure," Eli says, not meeting my eye. "Whether it's Kasim or someone else you fall for, it doesn't matter. Just as long as we talk about it and let each other know that we've got feelings for another person, or that we hooked up with another person, or whatever."

"Okay," I say, instantly agreeing, because at this point I would agree with whatever Eli wants. I hear Kasim's voice demanding the same question he'd asked in the middle of class. *What about* you, *Lark?*

"The second rule: If we do end up with someone else, we have to keep it a secret. Our relationship is public. It's a part of our brand," they say. "People online? They're not going to understand what it means for us to be polyam. They're going to say teens don't understand polyamory."

I know Eli's right about that one. Adults like to say we don't know what it means to be queer, too, or understand our own gender identities. Sigh. Why do adults make so many assumptions about what we do and don't understand, just because it doesn't fit their experience of who they were as teenagers? It's frustrating.

"They're just going to slut-shame us," Eli tells me, "or say that we're cheating on each other or something. All the bullshit things monogamous people say. We'd lose followers."

On the one hand, Eli is right. We'd be trashed online for being openly polyamorous, and so many nonbinary and queer people are excited to see our relationship. And me. My profile. I'm already dealing with so many trolls in my comments, trolls I'm afraid to even bring up to Eli. But if I figure out how to deal with them, how to work this the right way, I might just get back to 50K again, maybe even before the end of the summer.

On the other hand . . . Kasim's words come back to me. *They're a clout chaser.* Birdie whispers in my ear. "That can't be a coincidence, right? Eli talking about their followers like this?"

"I was trying to figure out if I can actually stay in this relationship or not," Eli says. "And I decided—yes. I want to be with you."

Birdie shakes their head. "What if they like the attention even more than they like you?"

But Eli's just worried about how they'll be treated online. That's fair. I am, too. That doesn't mean they don't like me. "Thank you. I know I don't deserve it, but thank you—"

"I'm still really angry with you," Eli says. "You hurt me pretty badly, Lark."

"Okay. I understand that. I do."

"We'll just take it slow," they say.

In class, Eli and I hold hands on the tabletop mechanically, like it's something we're supposed to do, and they force themselves to smile at me, but I can see their stiffness. Kasim and Sable sit together on the couch. Is it weird that I wish I was sitting with them?

"As writers," Mr. S says, then stops and says, "well, as creators—well, as *human beings*, you're going to be criticized. People are going to tear you and your work down, sometimes just for the fun of it—and sometimes, it's going to hurt. How do you handle that? How do you keep going, even knowing you'll be criticized? Patch."

Patch leans back in the bench dangerously, stretching with a grin. "I just ignore that shit. Human beings criticize. It's our nature. Might as well get used to it now."

I can't even look at them. I had trolls on my posts before, but Patch talking shit about me in my mentions was the real catalyst for

everything starting to blow up in my face. Well. Besides the catalyst of me deciding to lie about the thread in the first place, I guess.

Mr. Samuels considers what Patch said. "Okay. Asha?"

"I try to look at criticism as critiques and see if there's anything I can learn," she says. "Like, if someone says my writing is boring and why, then I'll try to see what I can do to change it."

Kasim smirks. "So, you'll change your writing and yourself just to please someone else?"

"No," Asha says slowly, annoyed, "I'll try to *get better* as a writer so that I can please other people *and* myself."

Eli raises an eyebrow at Kas. "And why're you looking down your nose at critiques, anyway? You're literally in a writing critique class."

Kasim turns slowly to meet Eli's eye, and it's like a Wild West showdown, dust blowing and a hawk crying from far overhead.

Mr. Samuels interrupts. "Well, first, there's a difference between criticizing and critiquing," he says. "What do you think that difference is? Jamal."

Jamal's arms are crossed. I can barely even look at them. There's a flare of shame whenever I do. "Criticizing someone usually has an intention to harm. Critiquing someone usually has the intention to help and to make a person better."

"Yes, exactly," Mr. S says.

I frown, thinking of Goodreads and people trashing books for fun—the same reviews I know I'll have to deal with if I'm ever published, too. "But how do you know which critiques are trying to be helpful and which ones are trying to harm?"

Mr. S leans against the table. "That's a good question."

"I think it's about boundaries."

Everyone's heads swing around, even Kasim's. Sable sits tall, looking right back at us, as if it isn't a big deal that she's speaking in class for the first time. "You don't know strangers who are critiquing you or criticizing you," she says. "I trust specific people in my life with me—my writing, and who I am as a person. If they love me and their intention is to help me, then I trust them. I don't know the strangers online who might have an intention of harming me, and since they don't know me, either, it isn't their place to decide to help me with my writing—or who I am."

There's silence for a long moment. Maybe everyone's still trying to pick their jaws up off the ground. Words start to spill out of my mouth. "But it'd be really cool, wouldn't it? If everyone learned how to love everyone, and we all knew that those critiques were always from a place of love?"

Patch rolls their eyes and Micah shakes his head, muttering something under his breath—but I see Sable give a small smile. My heart is an explosion of fireworks.

"Yes," she says, "that would be nice. But until that happens, I want to keep boundaries to protect myself. And I also agree with Kasim," she adds, looking down at him, and he looks up at her, and I wish I was the roast beef in this sandwich of love. "Not every critique needs to be taken. We don't need to change ourselves or our writing for other people's comfort."

"Beautiful, Sable," Mr. S says, nodding. "That's very good. It reminds me of another view, by—I think it's Brené Brown—yes, her: We writers, we creators, are in the ring. We're brave enough to put ourselves into that ring, to be bloodied, to show ourselves and our vulnerabilities. Everyone else watching—they're safe in their seats, many of them too afraid to come into the ring with us. We don't need to hear from the people who are in the audience. We only need to hear from those who are brave enough to come into the ring with us, to show their vulnerabilities alongside us, and—as you've all wonderfully said—we only need to listen to those who actually know us and care for us. We have the power to choose which of those critiques are helpful to our own growth, and not just for the sake of changing our writing or ourselves because we want to please others."

We're supposed to do silent writing today when the discussion ends, but Micah and Patch talk a lot more than they usually would, laughing and muttering to themselves, and there's something about the way they keep glancing at me that makes my heart thunder in my chest.

Patch leans over in their seat. "Hey, Lark—been enjoying Twitter?"

I look across the room at Kasim and Sable, but they're staring at their laptops as they type away, headphones on. Maybe I shouldn't be looking at them to rescue me from their friends anyway. Kas would probably just say that Patch and Micah have every right to call me out.

"I'm happy that people are starting to get to know the real you," Patch whispers.

I try to ignore them. I really do.

"Maybe you'll think a little more next time," they tell me, "before you say that racists are good people."

"That's not what I said," I tell them, maybe a little too loudly. A few heads look up, Jamal watching blankly. Eli looks up and glances away, pretending that they didn't hear. Asha peers across the bench with a frown.

"You okay, Lark?" she asks.

"I never said that," I tell Patch.

Micah is eager to jump in. "That's what I heard."

"That's not what I meant, okay?"

"Intention doesn't equal result," Patch says. "You're trying to gaslight us."

"What? How am I trying to gaslight you?"

"By even asking that question," Micah tells me. "By pretending you have no idea what we're talking about. By suggesting that we're spouting bullshit with that *you're crazy* tone. That's gaslighting. You always pretend to be this holier-than-thou pacifist, when really, you're just looking for attention because you want to be popular. You're egotistical and narcissistic."

"Trying to stand up for myself when I didn't say something or mean something a certain way is narcissistic?"

I look to Asha for support, but even her eyes are wide as she looks away. Maybe she isn't sure what to think, either. *Gaslighting* is one of those terms that makes everyone stop. Because negating gaslighting is gaslighting, too. And gaslighting is manipulative and abusive. And—I don't know, now I'm feeling confused. Narcissists don't even realize they're being toxic. What if I'm toxic but I just don't see it? Micah raises his chin as he stares me down, waiting for a response.

My eyes sting. "Fine. You win."

I feel strangled as I get up, picking up my laptop, and struggle to put it in my backpack, but suddenly it's too big, and my backpack won't zip back up again, and this is the most painful dramatic exit in existence, it really is. I see Sable pulling off her headphones as she watches, and I see Kasim frowning at me, and I can't tell if he heard the whole thing or not. I can feel everyone's eyes as I pick up my backpack and walk across the room in its deep silence. Micah's voice follows me in the hall. "See what I mean? Storming out instead of having a hard conversation. Toxic as fuck."

Chapter Eighteen

I GO TO ELI'S PLACE THAT AFTERNOON EVEN THOUGH WE'VE
barely talked all day, and we lie down together in their bed. We kiss for
a few minutes, and I smile and make sounds I think I'm supposed to
make, but my head is somewhere else. I think about Twitter and social
media and the people like N. Kay and Micah who say I'm toxic. I think
about Birdie and the fact that I probably won't be published. And I
think about Kasim and Sable, too. I wonder if my confused feelings for
Kas are getting tangled with my feelings for his girlfriend. I daydream
about having the kind of relationship they have with each other. It
must be amazing, right? Feeling open and honest enough to really be
myself and being loved anyway . . .

Eli pulls away.

Shit. "Sorry. I got distracted again."

They shrug and start scrolling on their phone. Why don't we ever
have anything to say to each other anymore?

"Have you ever been in a polyamorous relationship before?" I
ask them.

They nod, barely glancing up from the screen.

"What was it like?"

"It was hard," they say, and I get the feeling that I shouldn't press
for details, but to my surprise, they keep going on their own anyway.

"People assume polyamory means just having threesomes. I mean, that *did* also happen." My face burns hotter than the surface of the Earth, thanks climate change, but Eli keeps talking like it's no big deal, sure, people have threesomes all the time. I mean, maybe they do—I wouldn't know. "We tried to be a triad at one point, but my partners liked each other as friends. They weren't romantically interested in each other. And then Andre moved, and then Steph broke up with me."

"Oh." Surprise twinges through me. "I didn't realize Steph was your partner."

Eli doesn't meet my eye. "One relationship is hard enough on its own, but then make it two relationships, trying to spend time with both and communicate honestly, and then if we're all together, all of us figuring out that dynamic is like its own relationship also . . . It's a lot of work. It didn't end well."

I remember Eli mentioning that they'd related to the thread about unrequited love. "Do you still have feelings for Andre and Steph?"

Eli clenches their jaw, and I know I've officially asked one too many questions. "Yeah. I do."

"I'm sorry."

They ignore me and hold up the phone with a half-smirk. "God, I can't stand this guy."

I don't know who it is. They have their shirt off, showing their top surgery scars. I hesitate. "Why?"

"You can tell that he thinks he's amazing." Eli shakes their head, turning the phone back to keep scrolling. "Like, sir, you're not even that attractive. Calm down."

I've never heard Eli talk about another person this way before. "Well, even if you don't find him attractive, it doesn't mean that he's not."

Eli doesn't say anything, but when I look up, their mouth falls into a heavy frown as they squint at their phone. "I'm just giving my opinion."

"Sorry. I just don't like talking shit about people."

"Right, I forgot—you're so perfect and nonjudgmental." They laugh, and I automatically laugh, too, because when someone laughs, I feel like I have to join in whether I think what they're saying is funny or not.

And then I pause. And then I say, "Yeah, I don't know. I guess I just remember, when I was a kid, that my mom said if I ever talk badly about someone, it's because I'm insecure."

Eli doesn't laugh this time. They get up from the bed and walk away from me, though I don't know where they're going, and I don't think they know, either. They stand in the middle of the room. "Everyone talks shit," they say.

Is that true? "Maybe. I try not to."

"You're up on your high horse."

I frown. "I don't think I am. I just don't like to talk shit about people."

"You always think you're the only person who is ever right about everything."

I remember something Sable said. "Well, maybe what you're seeing is really a reflection of you, but you don't want to see that you're up on your high horse, so you're annoyed at me for it instead." That's what I tell them—but wow, yeah, that doesn't help at all.

Their face turns red. "You're just trying to divert the critique back to me."

Is this a critique, or is it a criticism? "I don't know. I just don't want to talk badly about anyone, okay?" God, I want this conversation to be over several minutes ago.

Eli glares. "You're talking badly about me right now, aren't you?"

"Huh?" I hesitate. Am I talking badly about them?

"You're being judgmental, right? So maybe you're actually feeling insecure, too."

The quiet is way too long. Unbearable. I have no idea if they're right and if I'm wrong, if I'm right and they're wrong, or if maybe we're both right and wrong, and that's the hardest part about it all. I just know that I don't want them to look at me this way again. "I'm sorry for judging you," I finally say.

"It's okay." They walk back over and lean against their desk, staring hard at their phone. I kind of wish they would apologize, too, because I don't think I was the only one who made a mistake—

Birdie leans against the doorframe. "Is expressing yourself in a non-harmful way ever a mistake?"

—and my feeling are hurt also, but I don't know how to ask for an apology, and I don't want them to be mad at me, not anymore, not ever again. *What about* you, *Lark?*

They sigh loudly, like they're trying to blow away all the bad vibes. Maybe they want things to go back to the way they were, too. "I have an idea," Eli says.

I try to look as excited as possible. "What's the idea?"

They shrug. "Well," they say, and there's something about their voice, or maybe the fact that they won't meet my eye, that makes me nervous. "You know, we've already kissed in photos, so—I don't know, I thought people might start to expect the next thing."

I'm confused for a solid one, two, three seconds before I realize what they're implying. "No. No, there's no way I'm doing *that* with you just for social media. I mean, I want to try it, someday, and it's been nice, um, kissing and stuff, but I'm not ready, and—"

"I'm not saying we should actually have sex," they say. More like snap, really. "We could just imply it. Couples always take pictures from bed. You could still have on a T-shirt or something, maybe one of mine so my followers might notice . . ."

I'm shaking my head, trying to clear my brain so that actual thoughts can come through. "I don't—no, I don't know."

"Why not?"

"I just don't feel comfortable with that."

"We could make it more wholesome if you want. Maybe you could be holding a flower or something."

I don't answer.

"It'd definitely boost our following. My thirst traps get the most attention."

I still don't answer.

"It's the least you could do," they say, "after you lied about the thread and everything."

Birdie grimaces. "Oof."

I shake my head. There are no good people, no bad people. I really do believe that. There are people who make mistakes. I made a mistake. And now Eli has, too. "You're trying to manipulate me into saying yes. I already said no." There's a lot I'm unsure about, but this—I know for a fact that I don't want to do this, never in a million years, not for fame and not to be published and, right now? Definitely not for Eli.

They roll their eyes. "All right. Fine." The silence has never been so loud. I'm thinking I should go when they add, "Let me ask you something. This whole *world peace* persona. It's just an act, right?"

I frown at them. "What?"

"I mean, you always come across as the type of person who talks about wanting to be positive, but you're not actually very positive at all. You like drama."

"I'm not being positive because I don't want to post after-sex photos on social media?"

"Like I said," Eli says slowly, "we wouldn't actually have sex."

And I know that they're mad—yes, they're angry, and they have every right to be. I lied to them. I hurt them. Does that mean that they get to hurt me, too?

My voice is soft. "I think I should go."

They walk me to their door, and they don't bother to hug me or kiss me goodbye when they snap it shut in my face.

I'm halfway down Baltimore Avenue when my phone buzzes with a notification. I check my screen and see that Eli uploaded an old photo of us, one we took before I told them the truth—we're leaning into each other, laughing, the sun catching our brown skin and making us glow. We looked so beautiful and happy. The likes and reposts start to explode, a bunch of comments saying that we're adorable, this is the best, etc. I scroll through the comments, the hearts, the shares. A few comments confuse me, though.

don't leave us hanging!

what's happening??

It isn't until I'm home, walking up the porch steps, that I look more closely at the original post and see the caption. *getting ready for tonight.* 😉 *so excited!!*

I pause, one foot on the step above.

I can already feel thoughts trying to defend Eli rising up.

Maybe they didn't mean it *that* way.

Birdie frowns. "But what other way could they have meant it?"

I didn't take the photos that they wanted me to, but this vague caption still got the reaction that they wanted. They didn't ask for permission. They knew I would've said no. So why did they do it anyway?

When I open the front door, I don't realize what my expression looks like until I step inside and see my mom, sitting on the couch with a mug of steaming tea, and Kasim sitting on the chair beside her, mid-laugh.

They both freeze. My mom stands up, putting the mug on the table with a clunk. "Baby, what's wrong?"

I'm always crying, so maybe that isn't what got their attention. But the tears plus what I guess must be a shocked, frozen expression?

Kasim stands up. "You okay, Lark?"

"What happened?" my mom asks. She's panicking. "Did something happen?"

"I—"

But I don't know what to say. My mom doesn't even like how much I'm on social media, and she wouldn't understand how trapped I feel in this lie. And Kasim being here definitely doesn't help.

I wipe my eyes, face hot. "I'm fine," I say, voice wavering in the most un-fine way possible.

I rush past them, up the stairs and into my bedroom. I close my door a lot harder than I mean to, and okay, I realize I'm fitting the stereotypical *crying teen slams bedroom door* trope, but hey, sometimes we just happen to fit certain roles. I pace around, pissed that the tears won't stop coming, blurring my eyes as I stare at my phone. I should

text Eli. Tell them to take it down. But they might tell me I'm being too negative or sensitive. And at this point, so many people have seen the caption. They'd notice if it suddenly disappeared, if it changed to something else. What do I do?

There's a knock on my door.

"I'm fine, Mom," I say loudly, more annoyed than I should.

The door peeks open, and Kasim sticks his head in.

I stop pacing. "Oh. Sorry. I didn't know it was you."

"Is it all right if I come in?"

I take a deep breath and drop onto the edge of my bed. "Yeah. Sure."

He slips inside, closing the door behind him with a click. "I was—uh—kind of worried that someone did something to you."

"No, I—" I stop. Technically, Eli did do something to me. I rub my face, wiping away the tears and the gathering stress. "Look at this."

I hold out my phone. He walks closer, taking it from me and inspecting the screen. He raises a brow. "Excited for tonight?"

I shake my head. "Eli—I told them I didn't want to imply that we were . . ." There's a clench of embarrassment. "They wanted to imply that we were going to—you know—and I told them not to, but they posted this caption anyway."

Kasim's gaze flicks up to mine. There's a slow, internal build that most people might not even notice, before the gradual quakes and tremors begin. I can feel the rage coming. He takes a deep, *deep*, slow breath, trying to keep the explosion inside.

"That's fucked up," he says. "That's really, *really* fucked up."

Why do I always want to defend a person when they've hurt me? "Maybe it's not that big of a deal. Not everyone saw it."

"What? Yes, it's a really big fucking deal."

"I don't know. They didn't actually say we were going to—you know."

"Eli knew what they were doing. They need to take it down."

"It's too late."

Kasim hands back my phone.

"Visiting my mom again?" I say, forcing a small smile.

He doesn't answer. He crosses his arms, leaning against the edge of my desk, watching me closely. "Why do you like Eli so much?"

I swallow. I love everyone, yes—but these days, I'm not so sure I like the way Eli's been treating me.

"Why can't you just be honest with me?" Kasim asks. "For one second. Just say what you really think. What you really feel."

I hesitate. Kasim could judge me for what I'm about to say, but he watches me with pleading eyes, and . . . "I don't know. I thought I liked them. I thought they were really confident and down-to-earth and kind."

"They're fucking horrible to you. You know that, right?"

"I guess. Yeah. I've been seeing other sides to them. But we all have other sides, right?"

Kasim watches me. "Why aren't you angry?"

"I am angry."

"Why aren't you showing it?"

"It's—well, it's not fine, but . . . I got myself into this mess, right? Maybe this is what I deserve for lying about the thread in the first place."

"What you *deserve*?" he repeats.

"I hurt Eli," I say. "It feels weird to complain to them about how they're hurting me."

"You aren't harming anyone by telling them that they've hurt you, too."

I can't even meet his eye. "I've been lying from the beginning about everything."

"Just because you made a mistake doesn't give anyone the right to harm you, Lark. You lying about this shit and still needing to come clean about it has nothing to do with the mistakes Eli has made. Yeah, you messed up—yeah, you need to change. Everyone does. Everyone needs to grow and change."

Those words hit me harder than I was expecting them to. "Even you?"

"Yeah," Kasim says like this is obvious. "Even me."

Change. God, I wish I knew how to do that. I feel so stuck, so trapped, but I want to change—I want to change so effing badly. I don't even realize I've said all of this out loud until I close my mouth and see Kasim staring at me.

For a second I don't think Kas knows what I'm talking about, but then he says, "It's not like it's easy. I'm still trying to figure out how to change, too. But I think the first step—it's probably looking at the shit we don't like, the things that we need to change, and being honest about them, right? That's the hard part, I guess."

I don't say anything to that.

"Eli doesn't get to do something like this just because you've messed up also." Kasim's reined in his earlier anger, and his voice is a lot softer now. "You don't deserve to be treated like this."

"I don't know."

"You always let people do and say whatever they want to you."

"Like you and your friends?"

I wasn't thinking it. I didn't even realize I said it, until it'd already slipped out.

Kasim shifts on his feet, uncrossing his arms and clenching the edge of the desk.

But now that it's already out, I keep going. "You and your friends have hated on me, over and over again."

"How have I hated on you?"

"You've let me know exactly how you feel about me."

He stares hard at the ground. "I haven't told you how I feel about you."

And that—yeah, I don't know what to say to that. I realize that there's no stopping it. I know what he's going to say, and I think that, right now, I'm finally ready to hear him say it.

He takes a deep breath. "I've been judgmental. I—you know, I have to admit, I was trying to protect myself."

"Protect yourself? From what?"

"From you."

"Why would you need to protect yourself from me?"

Kasim still won't look at me. "I know you've been talking to Sable a lot. I don't know what she told you, or what you think."

Why does this have to be so uncomfortable? All we want each other to know is that we care. All we have to do is be vulnerable, like Sable said. Why does it feel like this is one of the hardest things I've ever done?

"Sable told me that you like me," I tell him, "and I said that I miss you, too."

He nods. "Yeah. I miss you a lot, Lark. I feel like we go back and forth constantly, and I don't know how you actually feel about me or if you even want to be friends when you push me away so much . . ."

That's most confusing of all. "Push you away?"

He meets my gaze. "Yeah. I mean—at school, you ignore me whenever you see me."

"That's not true. *You* never say anything to *me*."

Kas frowns. "I stopped talking to you because I thought that's what you wanted. You suddenly stopped sitting with me one day, started ignoring me out of nowhere."

I could laugh, I really could. I snort in disbelief, but I don't think my reaction helps.

Kas shakes his head. "And that. You know what I mean? Laughing at me when I'm trying to be real."

"I was laughing because I can't believe that's what you think." I hear my words, realize what I'm doing. "I'm sorry. I don't mean to invalidate what you're saying. It's just that . . . this is everything I think that you do to me. You never talk to me at school. You prefer your new friends now over me."

"Huh? No, I don't."

"When you started to hang out with them more than me, you acted like you thought I was embarrassing or something. You stopped speaking to me."

"I stopped talking to you because you began to pull away. It hurt my feelings, Lark, especially since . . ." He stops for a second, taking a breath. "We were best friends. You started to pull away out of nowhere. When you got distant—I don't know, I guess I wanted to defend myself from you so you wouldn't hurt me again."

"Kasim, I only pulled away because you and your friends became a lot closer and started to get super critical of me—of everything I said, everything I did. Micah and Patch . . . they still haven't stopped

treating me like shit. You know that. I didn't feel like you even wanted to be my friend anymore."

"Yeah, of course I did. The others—they were assholes, and I talked to them about it, told them to stop messing with you. They'd started to act a lot nicer to you, but then you just . . ." He takes a breath and rubs his face.

"This is—God, I'm so confused."

He doesn't answer.

"I'm sorry," I tell him. "I didn't mean to hurt you. I thought you'd stopped caring about me. That you were relieved when I stopped hanging out with you."

"Relieved?" He shakes his head. "No. I was fucking torn up. Confused and upset and . . ." He stops talking again.

It's been over a year of this. This growing anger and resentment and hurt. And for what? Why? Because we didn't know how to communicate yet, to ask each other questions and get clear answers? Jesus. How much might've been different if we'd just figured out how to talk about our feelings?

He usually meets my eye with power and confidence, but he can't look at me now. I play with my bedsheet while Kasim pushes himself up from the edge of my desk, like he's thinking of coming to sit beside me, but decides against it. "I tried so hard to move on. To stop caring. Micah said that you were harmful and all this shit for ending our friendship without really saying anything. And yeah, you hurt me, but I think it was in the way all humans end up hurting each other. I tried so hard to stop caring about you."

Kas looks like he's on the edge of tears, which is weird because usually I'm the one who cries at everything while he laughs at me for it. Just the sight of him getting so emotional makes my eyes well up, too. And through it all, I can only think about that thread, those posts. Kasim's undeclared, unrequited love.

"What're you saying?" I ask him.

He swallows, still looking at the ground. "I think you already know."

"I need to hear you say it."

"You already know, Lark. Even before those stupid Twitter posts. Come on. It's obvious to everyone. I've been in love with you for years. You already know that." He really is crying now. "You're pretending you didn't know because . . . I mean, I don't know why. I assumed it was because you didn't feel the same way and didn't want to tell me. I thought maybe you got uncomfortable or weirded out, and that's why you started to pull away."

I feel like I've forgotten the English language. "I don't know what to say."

I see a flicker of pain on Kasim's face before he nods. "It's all right if you don't feel the same way." He takes a deep breath. "But I'd like to be friends again if that's something you want, too. I'd really like for us to work on our friendship."

I don't know. I really don't. I have so much to think about and process. I want to tell him yes, to make him happy, to help him smile again—but my throat is closing, and I feel like the world is shifting beneath my feet. How do I actually feel? What do I really want—for me? I don't think I know the answer yet.

"I just need some time, I think," I tell him, and turn away before I can see the hurt I know must be across his face.

His voice is quiet. "Yeah. All right. I'll give you time."

Fake Binary

Essay by Eli Miller

They want to shove me into a box, a fake binary of *male* and *female*. Biologically, there are as many genders as there are people in the world, an entire spectrum with ranges as diverse as the color of human skin. Socially, humans have always wanted excuses to oppress others. They want to put me into a box so that they can know whether I am oppressed or oppressor. They look at my yellow skin and want to know if I am white or Black so that they can know if I am oppressed or oppressor. They look at my house and want to know if I am rich or poor so that they can know if I am oppressed or oppressor. I offer a new conclusion: There is only one real binary in this world. Which one are you?

Comments:

Richard Samuels: These are strong parallels, Eli. I understand what you're trying to say, but I do think that this might avoid some important nuances, such as colorism within the Black community. You'll have space to develop your thoughts further.

Kasim Youngblood: The *which one are you* question turns the focus away from the writer defensively. It feels like they don't want to look at the ways they might be oppressive and harmful, too.

Asha Williams: I remember another classmate getting a comment that they could be more vulnerable in their own writing. Interesting that they've basically given the same comment here.

Sable Lewis: It started strong, I think, but saying that humans have always wanted excuses to oppress others might erase a lot of cultures where this wasn't necessarily the case before colonization.

Jamal Moore: I agree especially with the beginning on gender, but people have multiple identities that can make us all fit into categories of oppressed and oppressor.

Micah Brown: You could go into the power structures that are oppressive. Individuals benefit from power systems like capitalism and race, so to make it about the individual at the end isn't helpful in taking the system down.

Patch Kelly: I kind of feel you, but I kind of don't. So I don't know, this was okay.

Francis Bailey: Sorry I didn't have a chance to read.

Lark Winters: I really felt for you while reading and understand where you're coming from. Good job, love!

Lark Winters (they/them) @winterslark

It's in the hard times that you start to be grateful for people in your lives. Thank you @EliLovesYou17 for letting me love you, too.

💬 102   🔁 143   ♥ 562

um chile anyways so @huhbigboobs

lololol look at this kid trying to pretend they're not being called out for their problematic bullshit. This isn't a magic trick, lark. we still remember what you said

💬 21   🔁 57   ♥ 116

N. Kay @nkay95

@winterslark refuses to act truly apologetic for their harmful rhetoric. This return to inane fluff is a slap in the face.

💬 53   🔁 201   ♥ 812

Chapter Nineteen

Martin, Angie <amartin@distresslit.com>

Hi Lark,

Thanks for your query for BIRDIE TAKES FLIGHT!
I enjoyed the premise, but Birdie as a non binary
character might not resonate with the teen audience,
and I believe that Birdie's pronouns will confuse
readers. I also found it hard to believe that there
would be so many LGBTQ and non binary characters
using they and them and theirs pronouns in one story.
I've never even met one non binary person before!
Seeing several non binary people in one story is really
very hard to believe.

In any case, I appreciate you querying me, and if
you would be willing to change the pronouns and
identities of characters throughout, I would be happy
to take a second look.

Best,

Angie

🐦

The latest rejection isn't even surprising, and maybe that's what's sad-
dest of all. I'm so used to other people making their experiences, their

lives, the default—to saying that my life and my experiences are invalid, and that I should be expected to change myself for the comfort of everyone else around me. I used to do this without hesitation. I've always wanted to, if it meant I would be safe and accepted and loved.

I put Birdie's Word doc away for the night and I spend hours writing in my journal instead, bits of poetry and thoughts on this huge mess I've found myself in. Well, maybe that isn't the right phrase. I didn't really *find* myself in this mess. I put myself here, with one mistake after another. I've been trying lately—trying to look at the ways I've harmed others, like Kasim said I should. I've been trying to admit that I've made mistakes, because I'm a human being, and all humans make mistakes. Maybe realizing that each and every human being makes mistakes means we can have more compassion for others when they mess up. Maybe that means having more compassion for ourselves, too.

I know that lying was wrong. I shouldn't have taken the credit for Kasim's thread. I just don't know how to stop. The lie keeps growing, right along with the backlash I know I'll face.

I'm afraid.

It's okay to admit that to myself, isn't it? I'm afraid of the way others will treat me, and I'm even more afraid of how I'll treat myself. Because, beneath it all, I'm most afraid of the truth: I hate myself. I hate myself so much. *Why would I ever deserve love?*

People always talk about loving themselves. That's what we all say. Self-love is important. But is it enough to just say the words?

I love me. How do I actually learn to feel it? To believe it?

I guess all the thinking I'm doing is helping me start to see things from the outside, like I'm just a character in a story. Eli hurt me really badly, but I've continued our performance anyway, because I'm still so afraid to change. I've been reading about this online, too. When people are afraid of the unfamiliar and unknown, they stick with what they know, even if it isn't good for them. Kasim, in love with me? That's scary. I can safely daydream about him and Sable, but I have no idea what it would be like for Kas to treat me with that much love. Eli, treating me not-so-great? Yeah, that's something I know really well, actually. I know what it's like to be hated. I know what it's like to do anything I can to feel safe.

Eli's bright smile and golden laughter and dimples still radiate love in class, but when they meet my eye, their smile flickers a little, and I can practically read their mind. *Don't fuck this up, Lark.* We haven't talked about what went down. Not about the argument or the caption they posted. Frustration and anger that I usually try to ignore has been bottled up and building. Not even at Eli. More at myself.

Everything around me shines in a new light. I can see Kasim, sitting at the other end of the classroom's bench, not even looking at me, giving me all of the space I need. I can see myself letting Eli hold my hand and kiss my cheek in view of everyone they want to see. I can see myself staying silent about what Eli did to me. And I can see another Lark inside. Growing brighter. Getting ready. Yeah. It's time for change, isn't it?

Birdie grins, eyes shining. "Hell yes."

I catch Eli before class begins. "Can I speak with you?"

They follow me out into the hall. With other people not around, they don't try as hard to make it seem like they like me.

"Look, Eli," I say, and I can't believe the words that're about to come out of my mouth. "I'm not sure this is going to work."

They clench their jaw. "Why not? Just because things got tough? Relationships aren't always easy. We can talk it through."

I was brave enough to say that we should break up, but I'm still too afraid to tell them how upset I am about the caption. "Relationships don't always work out. It's not a big deal." That's what I say, but I can already see the messages: the disappointment of nonbinary followers who'd told me they really wanted to see this relationship work, who felt like Eli and I gave them hope. I can see the backlash, too. The people who're always excited to see me fall. Micah and Patch and others saying *looks like Eli woke up to the fact that Lark is a piece of shit. Any relationship with a narcissist is doomed to fail.*

"I want to keep trying," they tell me. "I think we're worth that."

I bite my lip, because I'm not sure what else to say or even what I feel. I follow them back into the room just as class begins.

"Trauma," Mr. Samuels says. "Every character needs to have experienced some sort of trauma in their life. And not just capital-T trauma, though that can certainly be a wound that the character needs to heal—but even traumas that are commonly experienced. Bullying," he says. "Parents who don't love us the way we need them to love us, even when they're trying their best. Losing a best friend."

I swallow and try very, very hard not to look at Kasim.

Mr. S is more fired up than usual, pacing up and down the classroom. "Every single person in the world has experienced some sort of trauma that changes the way they see life, giving them misconceptions about themselves or other people. This is a good thing to keep in mind while writing, because trauma informs so much about the character. Whether they're perfectionists because they think they need to earn love by being the best at everything they do, instead of knowing they're implicitly worthy of love. Or how about their attachment styles, and whether they're anxious or avoidant or secure? These are all things to think about when you're creating your character and their story.

"Because, really," he says, pausing at the front of the room and pointing at us, "trauma is story. It's interesting stuff, it really is—looking into neuroscience, and the way humans are programmed by their subconscious, hardwired to believe that the world is a certain way because of their experiences. Trauma can make the brain have misconceptions about the world—like thinking you're not the kind of person that can be loved, or that you can't trust other people . . . This is all created by trauma, something each and every single human being, and, so, *character*, has experienced."

Mr. Samuels slows his monologue down, and I have to admit, he really has grabbed my attention and everyone else's as he pauses, squinting thoughtfully into the sky, which is, of course, blocked by the stained ceiling.

"Good touch," Birdie whispers.

"This is my favorite topic," he says, "because it's what connects writing to real life. It's what makes writing necessary." He turns back to face us. "Characters have traumas in their own lives that they need to heal through their story, and in this way, it's almost like we living, breathing human beings are characters in stories, too. We need to learn how to heal in order to grow, to change, to expand." He smiles to himself. "Maybe that's all our lives ever are: stories."

Smaller things start to shift. I hang out with Sable at lunch instead of following Eli home after class. We sit together in the cafeteria with Asha. We don't talk about anything important. Just sitting, chilling, eating. I don't know where Kasim is, and I don't ask. Kas and I can barely be in the same room now, but for different reasons than just a month ago. Embarrassment fills the air so thick that everyone ends up looking around, searching for the source of awkwardness, like there's a bad smell.

Sable and Asha are talking about the full moon that's coming up, and I'm barely listening until Asha says, "What about you, Lark?"

"Huh?"

She gives an *oh, Lark* grin and exchanges a look with Sable, who peers at me like she might be trying to communicate telepathically, too, if only I knew how.

"What did you think of class today?" Asha asks.

"Oh. Um, it was interesting. I've never really heard about trauma talked about in that way. And, I mean, I guess it's true," I say, "the ways trauma can change how we see the world."

"I love talking about healing," Asha says. "Not physical wounds, but emotional ones. Learning about perfectionism made me realize I didn't think I was worthy of love unless I was the best. Better than everyone else. It's like I think I can only earn love by winning. God, that was a hard realization." She bites into a pear.

Sable starts doodling in her notebook. "I've liked learning about attachment styles. It makes me think more about my relationships. Not only with Kasim. Everyone in general."

"What do you think is your attachment style?"

"Avoidant," Sable says without hesitation. "I've struggled with creating social bonds because my parents rejected me a lot when I was young. Relationships scare me. I want to run away whenever someone tries to get close to me."

I frown. "Really? What about Kasim?"

"He's the only exception." She glances at Asha. "I'm working on it, though."

"I'm pretty anxious," Asha admits. "I really need people to shower me with love to feel secure. It's kind of a miracle we're friends, actually," she says to Sable, but her smile is a little tight, and I wonder if this is something she's been insecure about all along.

I've heard about attachment styles online—I even took a quiz once—and I'm definitely anxious-avoidant. I avoid relationships out of fear that I'm not enough to be loved exactly as I am. I'm afraid of loving someone and being loved back, because I've never really experienced something like that before, except from my mom, and I don't know if that counts, so I don't know what will happen, what to expect, and if I'll be abandoned in the end. Kasim has been giving me all the space I need for the last few days, which have felt like months, but I'm still scared to think about what our relationship could be if I let myself believe for even a second that I might love him, too. I'm scared of how our relationship could end.

I try to avoid thinking about him, and whenever I do, I feel a flicker of annoyance, and I realize that, underneath it all, this is why I've been so angry at him all along, why he's the only person who has ever made me mad—because I'm not actually angry at him. I'm angry at myself. I'm mad at myself for stomping down the feelings I've had for him, for

pretending that I don't love him because I've been so afraid, for—just like Kasim said—betraying *me*. Yes. Jesus Christ, yes—of course I love Kasim. And the thought absolutely terrifies me.

"I guess I'm just scared," I say, "of—I don't know, finally opening myself up and being vulnerable and real and honest, only to still be rejected as me. The real me."

Asha puts her half-eaten pear to the side. "I know what you mean. I've been realizing I don't share the real me with most people. I don't even know the real me yet, I guess. Who am I if I'm not the best at everything?"

God, I feel that one. "Yeah. I know what you mean." I have no idea who I am. Who am I when I'm not afraid? When I'm not trying to mold myself into the perfect person everyone will accept?

Asha smiles. "Something about you is different, Lark. And I'm happy I'm starting to get to know this side of you."

"Same." I really mean that. I do. I'm feeling a lot less lonely these days, showing these little bits and pieces of myself.

Birdie rests their head on their hands. "Maybe you should share the real you with a certain someone, hmm?"

When I get home, I drop my bag by the door and walk to the kitchen— then stop, surprised, when I see Taye. He and my mom look up like they're surprised, even though, hello, I live here, too—and from the way they awkwardly look at each other without saying anything, I know something is definitely up.

"Hey, Lark," Taye says. "I'm just heading out."

"Okay." I turn to watch him as he walks to the door, waving bye to us as he closes it behind him, then turn to my mom, who is slowly standing up from the table herself. "What was that?"

"What was what?"

"*That*," I say. "You're being really weird."

She doesn't answer me as she goes to the fridge, murmuring to herself about dinner. I lean against the counter, waiting, as my mom pulls out the water pitcher. She sighs after she's had a sip from a glass, still not meeting my eye.

"We have to talk, baby," she says.

This isn't good. "You're scaring me, Mom."

She turns back to me, eyes wide. "Oh, no—sorry, Lark, I didn't mean to scare you. It's just that Taye is being sent off to Baltimore for some construction work."

I frown. "Oh. Okay." I pause, then say, "How long will he be gone?"

My mom clears her throat. "It's looking like a little over a month."

Jesus, that's long. "What about Kasim?"

She meets my eye.

And it sinks in. "No," I say. "No, no, no. Kasim can't stay here!"

"He can't be in that house by himself for that long, Lark."

"He's seventeen!"

"He's going to stay with us until Taye comes back."

Oh, my God—please, let the rapture begin right here and now. I can't think of anything more awkward, more painful, than Kasim moving in right after he told me he loves me, and right as I realized—

Birdie raises their eyebrows. "Right as you've realized . . . ?"

225

He said he would give me the space I need. We can't exactly do that if we're literally stuffed into the same bedroom with each other. I shake my head. "He'll never agree to come."

"Taye already spoke to Kasim about it," she says. "It sounds like Kasim isn't happy, but he doesn't have much of a choice. He's coming tomorrow morning. He can adjust over the weekend."

I groan and let my head drop backward. I know that this isn't about me, or the drama of how he feels about me or how I feel about him—that my mom and Taye are right, and Kas needs to stay with us instead of by himself—but, yeah, I'm allowed to have my feelings, too. I'm allowed to feel uncomfortable and embarrassed and not exactly *thrilled* that he'll be moving in, because this is absolutely, without a doubt, going to be the most awkward experience known to enbykind.

"Let's do our best to make him feel welcome here. Okay?"

"Yeah. Okay."

Birdie pulls out a notepad from thin air and brandishes a pen. "Only-one-bed trope: Check!"

Kasim comes over so early that the sun hasn't had a chance to rise. I stand outside on the porch, huddled in a hoodie, watching as Taye opens his car door and slams it shut as Kasim drags himself out and grabs his duffel bag from the back seat. I feel like I shouldn't watch the next part, so I stare hard at one of the potted plants, while in the corner of my eye Taye pulls Kasim in for a hug, the kind of hug that lasts five, six, seven seconds, and probably could go on longer if Kas didn't jerk away, still not meeting Taye's eye. There's some anger in the way

he slings the duffel bag over his shoulder, the way he walks up the steps and walks past me into the house with a tight, "Hey."

Taye looks so much like Kasim that my heart automatically breaks seeing the same eyes they share as he stands at his car, looking tired and sad, needing to let Kasim live somewhere else for so long, while needing to keep it together, because he's the adult here. Why did we decide it's not okay for adults to cry?

"Good morning," he says, raising a hand.

I didn't hear my mom come outside, so I jump when she calls out from behind me. "We'll take good care of him, Taye. Call if you need anything, all right?"

We stand on the porch together, her hand rubbing my shoulder as we watch Taye get back into his car again. "Go on inside," she says. "Check on Kasim."

I try to remember that I shouldn't be so self-centered, but I can't ignore the nerves that pulse through me. Maybe there isn't any point in trying to pretend my feelings aren't there, too—no point in shaming myself and trying to hide my thoughts because I don't think they're good, or healthy, or mature. Ignoring them doesn't change the fact that they're still there, and that I'm freaking out because Kasim said that he loves me, and because I know that I'm in love with him.

I walk up the stairs, open the bedroom door, and find him standing in the middle of the room, duffel bag at his feet, like he'd been lost in thought, and me walking in snapped him out of it. He looks exactly the way Taye did outside. He's been in my room a thousand times, but now he stands rooted in one spot, like he isn't sure what to say or do. This visit is going to be different.

My voice feels small. "How're you doing?" Kasim doesn't bother to answer the question. I sit on the edge of my bed. "Do you want to get comfortable?"

He walks to the beanie bag chair, like he's thinking of falling into it, but just stares down at it instead. "Sorry that I'm all up in your space."

"Don't worry about that." My words feel so formal. "You need a safe place to stay. I'm happy that this can be that space."

"Really?"

I shrug. "Yeah. I mean—I'm not happy that it'll probably be pretty awkward, but . . . you're more important than feeling uncomfortable."

He doesn't even try to meet my eye. "Thanks, Lark."

"Do you want to talk?"

"Not really, no."

"Okay."

We're silent. Kasim still hasn't sat down. He rubs the back of his neck. "I should probably just sleep in the living room or something."

"You know my mom isn't going to let that happen."

"I don't want to make things even weirder."

"I'll probably end up on the couch."

"I'm not going to kick you out of your own room."

We stay quiet another few seconds, before Kasim finally starts pulling off his hoodie and falls into the beanie.

"It's not a big deal," I say. "I mean—well, according to you, you've had feelings for me for a while, and we shared the bed all those times, too."

"It feels different now that it's out in the open."

Even more different when there's something I still haven't told him, and I don't even know if I'm going to. Why make everything even more awkward and intense, amiright?

Birdie whispers. "No, Lark. You're wrong."

I take a deep breath and stand up, walking over to my desk and sitting in the chair and spinning around. I open my laptop to get to Spotify. Yeah, shit's weird, but the way we're acting, we're just making it worse. *I wanna believe what you say . . .*

"I'm sorry," I say. "About Taye, I mean."

He shakes his head. "What pisses me off is that I didn't have a choice. I'm really grateful—to you and your mom, I mean," he says, finally meeting my eye. "I don't want to sound ungrateful. But I wanted to stay home." Kasim starts blinking, looking up, probably not wanting to cry in front of me like this. Kas used to let me see him cry. "Fuck. I feel like I'm overreacting. He's just going to be gone for a month. But I guess, with our dad leaving—I don't know, it sounds stupid, but I'm afraid that Taye's leaving me, too."

"Taye isn't leaving you. He would never do that."

He nods, swallows. "Yeah. That's what I keep telling myself. I sound pathetic, right?"

"No. No, Jesus Christ, you don't sound pathetic." The silence is too much. I can practically feel his pain coming off in waves. "Can I give you a hug?" I ask him.

He hesitates, but only for a second. He gets out of the bag and I hug him and he hugs me, and I try to imagine transferring the same kind of comfort my mom gives me, so that he'll know he's safe and welcome—but after he relaxes into the hug, I start to feel some of his energy, too. He loves me. He really does. And it's painful for him to hug me now, like this, without knowing if I feel the same way, too—which only reminds me that, yeah, I love Kasim.

I pull back.

He laughs a little. "And just like that, it's super awkward again."

"Sorry. I guess I wasn't thinking."

"It's okay. We should be able to hug without—you know, me ruining it."

"You didn't ruin anything."

He plays with one of the locs that slipped loose. "I should go to your mom. Tell her thank you and all that."

"Yeah. Okay. I'll be here."

He leaves—maybe more like runs, not that I'm judging him for that, I'm pretty sure I'd be racing out of here, too—and I drop back into my chair and thud my head against the desk one, two, three times.

Lark Winters (they/them) @winterslark

ill be honest. im not even sure if ive actually done something wrong. but i want to be willing to learn and grow, so i apologize if i offended anyone.

💬 98   🔁 1   ❤ 12

N. Kay @nkay95

Do you call this an apology? Please Google "how to take real accountability." There is no IF you offended. You DID offend.

💬 14   🔁 36   ❤ 147

Lark Winters (they/them) @winterslark

i am sorry for offending people by saying that we should not call cops pigs and for saying that you all enjoy ripping apart others.

💬 27   🔁 1   ❤ 14

alex uwu <3 @alexwawa

lmao yall this is the weakest apology I've ever witnessed

💬 6   🔁 17   ❤ 59

um chile anyways so @huhbigboobs

the internet's forever, lark. we're not going to forget this bullshit just because you posted a fake apology. If you want to take real accountability, then QUIT.

💬 12   🔁 19   ❤ 83

Chapter Twenty

SO, HERE'S ONE THING ABOUT BEING NEURODIVERGENT: WHEN I find an obsession, I *really find an obsession*, and for some people those obsessions might be something fun and upbeat and cool, like penguins or ice cream, but no, for me, right now, it's trauma. Maybe that's not something I should say out loud. "I'm obsessed with trauma." Ha.

Ever since the last class with Mr. S, where he talked about characters and trauma, I've started to wonder if I'm a character in a story, and if I need to figure out what my trauma is to start to grow, to change, to learn how to really and truly love myself. I scroll online as I read different websites. Trauma is legit stored in our bodies. It's in our cells, which means that we have our ancestor's traumas, too, and, holy shit, that's a lot of fucking trauma—too much for me to even understand. *When you heal your own trauma, you're healing your ancestors' traumas, too.* That's beautiful. Beautiful enough to make me cry. Birdie grins and rolls their eyes.

Kasim sits in the chair beside the sofa, listening to something on his phone, *two best friends in a room, they might kiss.* He glances up and snorts. "What're you crying about now?"

I sniff. "Nothing."

Okay, I want to change myself, right? Actually learn to feel safe, learn to love myself, so that I don't care so much about what other people think. But that feels impossible when the world isn't changing with my brain. If I'm still dealing with trauma from all sides, how am I supposed to heal anything? I can't even find safe spaces in privacy, by myself, in my own head. I can't escape a world where its bones are made of hatred for people like me. And Black people. We're taught to hate ourselves, too.

I love my body. No. Really. I do. It's weird that I don't love myself, but I love my body, right? I guess it's because we're not our bodies, not really. I know that I'm cute. I had to teach myself that I am after being surrounded by my old classmates who said I was ugly, but I figured out that society brainwashes us to think only a certain type of human looks attractive, so, yeah, I just had to free my brain from those messages that white is beautiful and Black is not. It became a little easier to see the brainwashing at work, the same white man appearing over and over again on TV and movie screens and books with the same white love interests. After a while, if you're not paying close enough attention, you might start to believe it without even realizing that you do— that whiteness makes another person and their story more worthy.

I love my wide nose and big lips. I love my brown skin and the curl in my hair. I love that people who look like me have survived so much, even with our ancestors kidnapped and tortured and massacred. White people write novels of dystopian futures and fantasies where they have to escape these systems of oppression, evil monarchs and corrupt governments. They don't realize that Black people are the actual main characters. We're the humans with magic in our blood, dismantling the systems from the inside out. We're the godly beings, taught to be hated and feared. We're the rebels, fighting for our lives in the streets. Surviving, even when so many want us dead. Thriving, even with what they have done to the people who came before us. It's a miracle that I'm here.

I'm a miracle.

Black people are miraculous.

That alone should be a reason for me to love myself.

Why isn't it enough?

My phone buzzes with a notification. I put my laptop to the side, crossing my legs underneath me on the couch.

alex uwu <3 @alexwawa

can you believe @winterslark said that people are up on their high horse and like it when others are harmful?? like, we ENJOY racism??

💬 16   🔁 27   ♥ 89

The comments have been getting worse and worse, momentum building, spiraling out of my control. "I know that no one *likes* racism," I say.

Kasim looks up, eyes moving from the left to the right. "Um. What?"

"No one likes that it exists, or that it harms others. Well, except the racists, I guess."

"Lark, what're you talking about?"

"But that wasn't even really the point I was trying to make. I was just . . . I don't know, questioning the motive we've got, being on social media and talking about someone when we know that they're wrong, or when they've made a mistake."

Kasim mouths an *oh*, which means he knows what I'm talking about now, which means this mess has even reached his ears, which means that things must *really* be bad. "That's why I just try to stay away from Twitter," he says.

"And I mean, I kind of get it," I tell him. "A lot of us have to deal with so much bullshit in real life that it feels good to rip people apart

online. But sometimes the people we're jumping on aren't even racist trolls who want to go out of their way to hurt other people. Sometimes it's a person who didn't know better and made a mistake." Sometimes it's me. The number of comments, the way that people pick me apart and say that I'm not as peaceful or perfect as I pretend to be, the reposts that say I'm stupid, over and over and over again . . .

Kasim nods slowly, watching me, and I have no idea what he thinks, no idea at all, and it's kind of scary to talk about this, but . . . well, I want to work on being vulnerable, right?

My voice gets softer. "What's worse is when I don't even know if I actually made a mistake, or if I just said something a lot of people disagreed with." If my opinion isn't harmful, is it okay to think differently from everyone else?

Kasim shrugs. "People only want to think they're right. We don't really look at ourselves and the mistakes we've made, too."

"I want to respond and ask what harm I've caused. I want to type in all caps that they're literally proving my point! They *are* enjoying ripping me apart."

Instead of wanting to discuss what I said, even if they disagreed with me, they jumped at the chance to attack me in a race for as many likes and retweets as possible, like it's a competition or a game. What's scariest of all? I really could be the harmful narcissist in this, trying to convince myself that I'm not. This is such a mindfuck. I'm confused and hurt and frustrated, and I don't even know if I'm allowed to have those feelings.

"I've had too many bad experiences with Twitter to be public on there," Kas says.

"Really? Like what?"

"Like, people think only one experience is valid. There's only one way to be Black, to be trans, to be queer. Anyone who doesn't fall in line isn't valid."

"Jesus. Why do we do that to each other?"

He shrugs. "Maybe we're insecure. We're afraid that we're wrong, somehow—like, we don't accept ourselves, you know?—so we reflect that anger at anyone who is different, and don't accept them, either. Even if it's people in our own community."

"You're right. I was told once that I'm not actually queer because I didn't have a bad experience when I came out."

Kas snorts and shakes his head. "I was told I can't say I'm trans if I'm not physically transitioning. No one has the right to tell someone else what their experience is."

"It's like we feel so little power that when we see someone else living a different experience, we want to have the power to tell them no—they're not valid, because their experience isn't the same as ours."

"That's privileged shit," Kasim says. "People always expecting to be the center of the narrative. Expecting that they're the default and only their experience is right and everyone else is wrong. That's what privileged people do. We're so used to white people or cis men doing that kind of thing that it's a little harder to see when it's coming from inside our community. When we do it, too."

I think he might be right about that.

"Why're you on there, anyway?" Kasim asks me. I feel like we're back to that day when he was in my room, making fun of me for being on Twitter in the first place—except now, I can see the real concern in his eyes. "If you're stressed out from the way people are attacking you, maybe you should . . . I don't know . . ."

"Quit Twitter?" I say, already about to laugh.

He shrugs. "I was going to say take a break from it. It doesn't make you happy, right?"

I sit quietly for a second, frowning at my screen. No—I don't think Twitter has made me happy in a while. It's felt like my only real way to get published, but are the trolls, the nasty comments, being attacked—is any of it worth it?

Birdie calls from the other room. "You already know the answer to that, Lark!"

Kasim swallows and looks down at his phone. "I'm—uh—happy, I guess," he says, "that things aren't that weird between us."

I blink at him. "I mean, things are still kinda weird."

"But they're not *that* weird," he says. "At least we can still talk and have normal conversations and everything, anyway. I'm sorry," he adds, voice getting softer, "that I've made things weird."

"No—don't be sorry," I say. "I don't want you to feel sorry. I mean, when you think about it, it's actually a huge compliment, right?" I laugh nervously, just to fill in the pause that screams *tell him how you feel.*

He smiles until his phone buzzes in his hand. He tenses, staring at the screen.

"Everything okay?" I ask him.

He doesn't look at me, and I'm not even sure he actually heard me, but I'm not sure if I should repeat myself, because I learned that people don't like that, when you keep repeating yourself until they respond, and—

"It was my dad," Kas says.

My mouth falls open. Kasim's dad was barely around after he was released, but he pretty much disappeared altogether almost a year ago

now. Kas and Taye didn't know where he went or what happened, and even though Kasim never really talked about it, I know that's really messed with him.

I wish I knew what to say and how to say it. "How're you feeling?" I whisper.

He clenches his jaw, then looks away from his phone and clicks the screen off. He shrugs. "The guy's an asshole. He texted me to say he's at my aunt's place in New York—asked if I want to come see him."

"Do you? Want to go see him?"

Kasim doesn't answer me. Maybe he doesn't know the answer to that question himself. He shrugs, and I know he wants me to leave it alone, so that's the end of that conversation.

We'd both been avoiding *the* topic. I don't know about him, but I've been dreading the moment all day as time ticked by, the sky getting darker, until, finally, we have no choice but to face it.

"Come on, Lark. We've got to figure this out."

"Okay."

"Let's buy an air mattress."

"Right now? It's eleven at night. All of the stores are closed."

"I'll sleep on the floor tonight, and then buy the mattress tomorrow."

"And put it where? My room is too small."

"Fine. I'll just stay on the floor."

"I'm not letting you sleep on the floor."

We're quiet.

"Why can't I sleep on the couch again?" he asks.

"My mom's going to want to know why you're sleeping out there."

"I could try waking up and coming back upstairs really early in the morning, before she gets out of bed."

"That'd never work. What if she comes down in the middle of the night for a glass of water or something? She'd wonder why you're down there."

"Why don't we just tell your mom that we're older, and we want some more space? Yeah, we shared the bed when we were kids, and that was fine—but things are different now."

I shrug. "We could say that. But I'm pretty sure she would catch on to the fact that something else is going on."

"Would it really be that big of a deal if she found out that I'm in love with you?"

Kasim's been much more upfront about the fact that he loves me. It takes my breath away when he says it in that matter-of-face tone.

I swallow hard. "Well, maybe not. It'd just be another added layer of weird on top of everything else going on. She'd probably act like it's cute that you love me, and then she'd do that annoying smile thing whenever she sees us talking, and then she'd make a *really* big deal of making sure we don't share the same bed, and she'd probably make some kind of rule like we've got the keep the doors open, and—"

"Okay. Fine. I get it." He sighs. "I'll just sleep in the beanie bag."

"Come on, Kasim. You're not sleeping in the beanie bag."

"Why not?"

"Because that thing is uncomfortable. You'll never fall asleep."

He challenges me with a smirk.

I roll my eyes. "Fine. Good luck." I hit the lights, jump into my bed, then pull my covers up. I stare at the ceiling, listening as Kasim curls up on the bag. He turns over with a rustle, trying to get comfortable. He turns

over again. I hear him whenever he shifts and sighs, annoyed, desperate to prove me wrong. I check the time on my phone. Ten minutes. Twenty minutes. Thirty minutes go by, before I finally sit up, hitting the mattress.

"Kasim."

"What?"

"Just get in the bed. It's not that big of a deal."

"I'm fine here."

"Whenever you move around you make noise, so I can't sleep either."

He's quiet. I think he might be sulking. He hates being wrong. Then, finally, he sighs. I can see his outline moving in the dark. He hesitates before he sits on the edge of the bed. "Are you sure?"

"It's not a big deal."

"I don't want to make things awkward."

"Might be too late for that."

"More awkward, I mean. Especially when this is your own space. Bad enough that I'm intruding."

"You're not intruding. Seriously," I say when I can feel he doesn't believe me. "I want you here, okay? Yeah, things are weird, but I care about you. So get in the bed already."

He finally lies down, as close to the edge as possible. I roll my eyes and turn over, my back to him. Finally, there's enough quiet that I can get some sleep—but then I realize it's only so quiet because Kasim is barely breathing.

"Just relax," I mutter.

He lets out a deep breath. I hear him turning over behind me, so I turn back over to face him. He likes to say that he loves me so matter-of-factly because it's true. I can feel how much he loves me

now, and how much he wants me to know it. I start to think that he's imagined lying in bed with me like this, with me knowing that he loves me and welcomes and accepts him. I think he's imagined kissing me. I'm pretty sure he wants to kiss me right now. My eyes have adjusted enough to the light to see when he glances at my mouth, losing his breath again for a heartbeat.

He meets my gaze again, and he forces a smile.

"Good night, Lark."

I think I might be starting to wonder what it'd be like to kiss him, too.

"Good night, Kasim."

Lark Winters (they/them) @winterslark

thank you, @elilovesyou17 for giving me so much support, and thank you to everyone who follows me and gives so much love. ive decided to take a break from sm. see you on the other side. 🖤

💬 18   ♻ 3   ♥ 35

N. Kay @nkay95

Is anyone surprised that they would run away from a difficult conversation?

💬 12   ♻ 38   ♥ 217

um chile anyways so @huhbigboobs

LMAO!! Run, Lark, run!! If you're fast enough maybe ppl will start to forget you're annoying and harmful as fuck

💬 11   ♻ 23   ♥ 0

Chapter Twenty-One

WE BARELY SPEAK FOR MOST OF THE MORNING. WE END UP IN different places—me in my room, reading *Full Disclosure* by Camryn Garrett in bed, Kasim in the backyard, sitting by himself in the garden. I didn't expect to be so relieved to announce I was taking a break from social media. I was worried that Eli would text, demanding that I keep up our performance, but they don't bother to get in touch either, and maybe this is really more of a break from them, too. It starts to drizzle, one of those misty Sunday mornings where the sun's still shining. I hear when Kasim comes back inside and walks up the stairs. He pauses at the doorway when he sees me. His eyes are red.

I close the book. "Were you smoking?"

He falls into the beanie bag.

"Were you crying?" I ask, voice quieter.

He still doesn't answer me. He takes a deep breath. "I think I'm going to do it," he says. "I'm going to see my dad."

I sit up, legs crossed on my bed. "Really? When?"

"Today."

"That soon?" I shake my head. "How?"

"Bus ticket. It's twenty dollars both ways. Taye gave me some money before he left. This is basically all of it, but . . ."

"Does Taye know?"

"Nope. He'd just tell me not to go."

"Does my mom know?"

His gaze cuts to me. "No—and she's not going to find out."

I put my hands up defensively. "Not from me."

Kasim sighs and slouches into the bag even more. "I just want to ask him why. I know shit was hard for him. I know he was struggling. But Taye and I were, too. Why weren't we important enough for him to figure shit out, to stay with us?"

It looks like Kasim is about to start crying again, and I know that I can't hug him, but I wish there was something I could do or say to help him. "I want to come with you."

"What?"

"If you'd like me to," I tell him. "I want to come."

Kas doesn't respond for so long that I'm afraid I might've overstepped, but then he speaks, voice cracking. "I'd like that," he says, trying not to cry.

I grin. "You've been around me too much."

He grabs a pillow from my bed and chucks it at me, and I scream and try to dodge, but instead I slip off the edge and crash to the ground.

"Oh, shit," Kas says, trying (and failing) to bite back a laugh. "Shit, are you okay?"

"Lark?" my mom calls from downstairs.

I turn over, groaning, also trying not to laugh. "I'm fine!" I call back down.

Kas snorts, a laugh escaping, and his laugh is contagious so I start laughing, too, and he starts to laugh so hard that he begins to wheeze, and I fold over when I try to stand up, gasping—

"Wait, wait," I say. "My stomach hurts."

He just rolls over, laughing louder and harder, so I grab a pillow from my bed and chuck it at him, too, which he catches with a sly grin.

I point at him. "Kasim. No."

"Don't start something you're not going to finish," he says.

It shouldn't be so easy to trick my mom. We tell her that we're going to Bartram's Gardens for the day, just to get out of the house, which she gives us an odd look for, but doesn't question.

"God, I feel so guilty," I tell Kasim as we get onto the trolley, masks up. "She didn't even question us because she thinks we're so good."

Kas smirks. "It's good to be a little bad every once in a while."

The trolley is pretty empty, maybe because it's Sunday. It rides down the road, over the bridge, past the colorful townhouses and the Dog Bowl, where there's another flea market—is that Asha walking the other way? I glance at Kasim, just to catch him watching me. He looks embarrassed for a millisecond, but he doesn't look away.

"Thank you," he says. "For coming with me, I mean."

"Yeah—of course, Kas."

We make it to the bus terminal in Center City just as our 1:15 P.M. bus to Brooklyn is being called. We scramble with our money—I'd asked my mom for enough money to get me and Kasim lunch and dinner and a few extra trolley rides, in case we wanted to go somewhere else—and manage to buy tickets and get on board just before the doors close. The bus is practically empty, just a few people in the back, everyone's masks on. Still, it's really enclosed. My mom would be so pissed if she found out we lied to her and got onto a bus like this.

Kasim lets me take the window seat, and as the bus rumbles to a start, we talk for a minute, how long is the trip again, about two hours, it's kind of cold, yeah, do you want my hoodie, no, I'm good. He offers me one of his earpods, and we listen to his Spotify, *waiting for the exhale, I toss my pain with my wishes in a wishing well.* I stare out the window as we make it onto the highway and the bridge, leaving Philly behind. I haven't been back to New York in years, and I haven't been paying attention to my body—the nerves that are building, the fear I have at returning.

"You're safe," I whisper.

"What?" Kas asks, glancing at me.

I'm not going to have to deal with bullies. You're with your friend, who loves you. You're with yourself, who is learning to love you, too.

When I wake up, my head is on Kasim's shoulder. I jerk, sitting up straight, wiping my mouth. Kasim doesn't look at me, and I don't look at him. We're in a tunnel that makes me feel like we're in a sci-fi, flashing white lights, until we emerge into the anxiety-inducing, heart-pounding rush of New York City. Car horns blare, crowds of people hurry across the street, even in a pandemic, and I can see Kasim craning his head to get a look at the skyscrapers.

"Have you ever been here?" I ask him.

"Once," he mutters, "to visit my aunt. I hated it."

The bus ends up in the terminal, and we get off board, backpacks on, and look around and around for signs, getting lost when we take an escalator to the wrong floor. We finally figure out how to get to the subways, walking through the underground hallways of stained white tiles—

"Holy *fuck*," Kasim says, then grabs me, putting me in front of him, as a giant rat as big as my arm, no joke, as big as my fucking arm runs by. I yelp and grab him, trying to force him in front of me, and we grapple with each other until the rat is gone. We crack up, laughing so hard that I don't even care when people rush past us, glaring, someone muttering, "Tourists."

We take forever at the subway card machines, hitting the wrong buttons, and someone cusses us out, before another person around our age with some cool tats comes over and hits a few buttons for us with ease, shrugging when we thank them. Kas and I get onto a subway, and it's freezing, so cold that we end up huddling together, not giving a shit that one is in love with the other, as we stare at the maps on our phones.

"I'm pretty sure this is the right way," he says, shivering. I feel like we've landed in some fantasy, and we're fighting to survive as we cross the tundra. "Is this the right way?"

"I don't know," I say, squinting at my phone.

"Aren't you from here? You literally lived here, Lark."

"Yeah, but that was years ago, and I never really paid attention to where we were going. I just followed my mom."

Kasim sighs.

When the subway slows to a stop, we get out onto a platform, through turnstiles, up some moldy steps, and into the bright light. What's weird is that it feels like we stepped into a portal that took us right back to Philly. We're on a quiet, tree-lined street. There are brick townhouses, and a kid riding their bike passes by. I don't even know what part of Brooklyn this is, only that we're in Brooklyn—which looks a little more familiar, now that I think about it. We walk, Kasim telling me that the map says we're only about seven minutes away, and

I stare at the houses, the laundromat on the corner, the diner across the street, until I see it. What're the chances? The same school where I was screamed at, yelled at, pushed and spat on and punched—it's right there, down the street. It's Sunday, thank God, or I might not have been able to handle seeing other kids like us in their uniforms. I already feel like I'm struggling to breathe.

Kas frowns at me. "You okay?"

I nod, swallowing—then shake my head. "No. That's the school I went to."

I've told Kasim about how I was bullied. His eyebrows rise. "Seriously?"

"It's kind of ridiculous, right? It's just a school. It's not like I'm going to get hurt or anything. But that's how it feels."

"Do you want to stop for a second?" he asks, putting a hand on my shoulder and watching my face carefully. He guides me to the edge of the sidewalk and pauses. "Breathe. Come on, with me—one deep breath. Another. Yeah, like that."

I wipe my eyes. "Sorry, Kas. This isn't even supposed to be about me."

"You think I give a fuck? You're having a panic attack."

Am I really having a panic attack? Huh. I didn't even consider that.

His hand is still on my shoulder. It's warm, fingers gentle but firm, like he's ready to catch me if I start to fall. I look at the tattoos he has on his fingers, and I remember the way those fingers have played with Sable's—how I've wanted them to play with mine. I could just say it, couldn't I? I could just tell Kasim that I'm pretty sure I'm in love with him, too, right here and now.

"You okay?" he asks, voice low, watching me closely.

I nod. "Yeah. I'm okay."

Kasim's aunt lives in one of the brick townhouses. He hesitates next to the stoop, looking up at the door.

"Shit," he says.

"Are you all right?" I ask him.

He shakes his head. "I have no idea. I'm pissed, and the kid in me is excited to see his dad, but I'm pissed at that kid for being excited, too, and—shit, fuck it, let's just get this over with." He takes a breath and walks up the stairs of the stoop, and I stay down on the sidewalk, because I'm not sure if Kasim would really want me to be a part of his reunion with his father—but then he turns and looks at me like *what're you doing?* and we waves at me to hurry up, so I walk up the steps, too.

I take his hand. I wasn't even planning on it. It just kind of happened. I take his hand, and he looks at me, surprised, and I look at *him*, surprised, like, oops, wasn't expecting that one. But he smiles a little, then turns forward again and knocks on the door.

We stand there for a second, still holding hands.

"It's a little awkward, so I'm just going to—"

He nods, letting go. "Yeah, agreed."

The door opens. A woman, super dressed up—oh, right, it's Sunday, she's probably on her way to church or something—opens the door.

"Kasim?" she says, just like that, exaggeration on the *sim* as if she wasn't fully surprised until she was halfway through his name. She has dark brown skin and eyes that reminds me of Kas's. She walks forward automatically, arm stretched out for a hug. "What're you doing here?"

Kas adjusts his mask. "I came to see my dad," he says. "He told me he was here."

Kasim's aunt—she freezes, expression dropping, and my heart drops along with her as I glance at Kas and see him stiffening.

"Kasim," she says, slowly. "I'm sorry, but he already left."

Kas doesn't say anything to that.

She looks from Kasim to me. I awkwardly wave and instantly hate myself, but no, I take that back—I don't hate myself, because I'm trying to love myself. I really am.

"Come inside," she says. "You and your friend."

"I don't want to interrupt you if you're going—"

"Don't worry about it," she says, stepping aside and waving us in.

Kasim's aunt—she introduces herself to me as Lydia, Auntie Lydia as far as I'm concerned, which I like, because her name starts with an L, too—walks us into the living room, which has hardwood floors and sleek gray sofas and a huge flatscreen. Auntie Lydia goes into the kitchen and comes back with cups of water for us.

"Thank you," I say, and take a long sip. I didn't even realize how thirsty I was.

Kas nods his thanks when she gives him a glass but doesn't drink any of it.

She smooths out her dress and sits down opposite us.

"When was he here?" Kasim asks, his voice hoarse.

"He came a few days ago," she tells him. "Said he needed a place to stay for a little while, gave me the impression he'd be here for a few weeks. He asked for some money. Last night, he left—said he was feeling anxious. If I knew you were coming, I would've tried a little harder to get him to stay."

Kas clenches his jaw, still not drinking the water.

"He," Auntie Lydia starts, then clears her throat. "I know that it's difficult, Kasim, him not really being there for you."

Kasim shakes his head, rolling his eyes a little.

"Our dad—your grandfather," she says. "He did the same thing to us for a while, before he passed away."

Kas looks up at that, glaring—not really at her, I don't think he means to glare at her. "If my dad knows how it feels, why would he do the same fucking thing?"

I'm expecting her to reprimand him for language, but she only shakes her head. "It's because he knows how it feels that he's doing the same thing," she says.

Kasim's eyebrows pinch together for a second as he frowns, confused.

"That's what he was taught," Auntie Lydia says. "I'm not saying it's right or wrong, but that's what he was taught to do by his own father. That's how he was taught to handle his emotions and show love. And our father—that's what he was taught, too, and his father's father, back to the days when we had a father in our ancestral line that had his children taken from him, and he probably didn't think it made much sense, letting himself love a child who he wouldn't be able to love or to protect. It's all inherited, Kasim."

Kas doesn't cry a lot, so it's a shock to see him doing just that, right here and now. Seeing the tears build makes me choke up, too, and I want nothing more than to get up and hold Kasim, tell him it'll be all right, even if I don't know if it will be.

"If I have kids, I would never treat them this way," he says, voice rough.

"Good," Auntie Lydia says.

"Why wasn't I good enough for him not to do the same thing for me?" Kasim asks her. "If I know my kids would deserve better, then why couldn't he figure out that same shit for me and Taye?"

She takes a breath. "Young people—you're taught that adults have all of the answers. I don't know why that is. Maybe it's because we can't see it ourselves, how lost we are. Maybe it's because we don't want to scare you. When you're fighting to survive, it can be difficult to change."

"So you're saying it's okay that he left us? Because he doesn't know how to change?"

"I'm not saying it's okay," she says. "Not at all. I'm not saying you need to have compassion for him, or even to forgive him. And I'm sorry," she tells him. "I really am sorry that you came here, looking for answers that your father wasn't ready to give. You deserve more than that, Kasim."

His shoulders start to shake. He closes his eyes, letting out a sharp breath. I wipe my eyes with my shoulders.

"He's fighting to live," she says. "The things he's experienced in this lifetime, the traumas he's survived—he's just fighting to live by running away. I think he wants to be there for you. I really do. I just don't think he knows how."

Kasim takes a slow breath, wiping his eyes.

"The way that I see it," she tells Kas, "you have a gift. Painful, yes, but still a gift. An ability to look at the way your father has treated you, and to consciously change."

Auntie Lydia says she'd be happy to let us stay for the day, to fix us some lunch and give us money back to Philly, but Kasim—I can see

how badly he just wants to get back home. Not to my house and my bedroom, but to his home, with Taye. We mumble our thank-yous and our goodbyes and take the trip back to the terminal, onto the bus, back to Philly. It feels like an even longer trip somehow, neither of us talking much, Kasim drying his eyes every now and then.

When we see the Philly skyline on the horizon, Kasim says, "Thanks for coming with me, Lark. I think it would've been harder if I was alone right now."

I give him my hand, and this time, we're okay sitting like that, palm to palm, fingers intertwined, until the bus comes to a stop.

Chapter Twenty-Two | I

KASIM TELLS MY MOM THAT HE FEELS TOO SICK TO GO TO THE Commons on Monday. When I get back home from class, he's still in bed, his back turned to me. I'm not sure what to say. *Are you okay?* Obviously not. I'm a little scared that he hasn't been okay for a while now, and I just never saw it. I think way back, to the day before the Commons opened again—to when Kasim suggested I write about mental health and depression. Maybe that was his way of trying to tell me what was going on with him, and I was too wrapped up in my head and my feelings to ask how he was doing.

"Don't beat yourself up," Birdie tells me. "The human civilization hasn't learned how to read minds yet."

Is there a way to ask him to let me in? Is it my place to even ask something like that? It's his right, if he doesn't want to talk about how he's feeling. It's his right, if he doesn't want to open up to me and tell me that he isn't okay.

When I walk more into my room, he looks up, surprised, and tries to wipe his eyes, but he can't hide that he's crying. I sit down at my desk as he rubs a cheek with his shoulder.

"You all right?" I ask. My voice is hoarse. I'm nervous. Maybe it isn't any of my business, and he'll get mad at me for asking.

His rolls over, back to me again. "Yeah. It's just the stress of every-thing, I guess."

"Stress of your dad, you mean?"

"Yeah. That and other shit, too."

Is it okay if I hug him? I don't think it would be. We held hands yesterday, but besides that, we haven't touched—except when we're sleeping. We can't really help what we do when we're sleeping, and we wake up with one arm over one waist, legs tangled, cheek against shoulder.

"I really need to see Sable," Kas says.

That hurts my feelings. I don't know why. I'm here, right? Why can't Kasim talk to me? I don't think it's fair of me to think that, either. But I guess there's also no point in trying to hide from the truth. I can't control my feelings. I can only control the way I respond. There isn't any point in shaming myself on top of that, too. Besides, I want to see Sable also. And if I can't give Kasim what he needs, then maybe she could.

I pull my phone out. "Okay. I'll text her."

hey. this is lark. i'm worried about kas

Usually I wait a minute or two before responding to a text, so that it doesn't look like I'm always hovering over my phone like I'm desper-ate, but Sable wouldn't care about that kind of thing, especially since it's about Kasim. She replies right away. **What's wrong?**

have you spoken to him?

We've been talking on the phone but he hasn't called in a while

I hesitate, fingers pausing, then type. **can you come over?**

I'm coming.

"She's coming."

It feels good to see some of the weight rise from his shoulders.

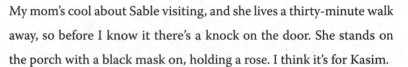

My mom's cool about Sable visiting, and she lives a thirty-minute walk away, so before I know it there's a knock on the door. She stands on the porch with a black mask on, holding a rose. I think it's for Kasim.

"Hey, Sable."

"Hi, Lark."

"Nice rose."

"It's from my grandma's garden."

Sable walks inside, and it's a little weird, having her over for the first time. She follows me up the stairs and into my bedroom. I shuffle around, tossing shoes to the side and shoving a pile of books against the wall. She barely notices. She stands in the middle of the room and stares down at Kas. And he's lying down on the bed, staring up at her. They're having another one of those telepathic conversations.

She turns to me suddenly. "Is it okay if I lie down on your bed?"

I swallow. "Yeah. Sure."

She kicks off her boots and lies down next to Kasim, and she wraps her arms around him, and that's it. That's all she does. His face is hidden in her shoulder, but from the way his body begins to shake, I know he's crying.

God, I really feel like I shouldn't be here. I head to the door to give them some privacy.

Sable speaks behind me. "Where're you going?"

I turn, and she's watching me expectantly. Kasim doesn't look up. I almost want to ask if it's really okay. But maybe this mo-

ment isn't about how awkward and embarrassed I feel. I crawl into the space between my wall and Kasim and rest my head on his shoulder and hold him. Sable and I are like a shell. Protecting him inside of us. A safe space. A real one, where no one and nothing can find him.

I have no idea how long we stay like that. Could just be five minutes, could be an hour. Kasim stops crying after a while. He kisses Sable at one point. Just a quick peck. But still. It feels weird, him kissing her while I'm hugging him. He pulls away from her and I pull away from him and he sits up with his knees up to his chest.

"Sorry," he says. He rubs an eye. They're both dry, but some salt is there. "Thanks. Sorry."

Sable sits up with him. "You don't have to be sorry for anything."

Kasim bumps his shoulder with mine and manages a small smile.

"Do you . . . I don't know. Need to talk?" I ask him.

He seems to consider the question, but then he shakes his head. "No. Not right now."

"Okay."

"I don't know. Not yet. Just being here—that's all I can take right now, I think."

"Yeah. Okay."

We're quiet for a long time, just being here, and when we eventually start a conversation, we talk in super quiet voices about nothing, about bullshit, prehistoric penguins and *Attack on Titan* and what we'd want to do if the pandemic ever ends. It's almost sundown when Sable says she should go home.

"You can sleep over," I offer, and only realize the second the words are out of my mouth how it could potentially sound. And . . . a part of me doesn't mind . . . ? Because maybe a part of me means that, too. It

might be nice. Snuggling with both of them, sleeping together, feeling safe and happy again as we all begin to kiss each other.

"I can't. My grandma." She gets up and pulls her boots back on. She kisses Kasim's cheek, and we both walk her downstairs and to the door. My mom's in the living room, TV on. She looks at me, like *excuse me, what in the world is going on?* and I have to give her a *please, it's not what you're thinking, please for the love of God don't embarrass me* look back.

I wave goodbye to Sable as she walks out, and give her and Kasim privacy while they linger on the porch. They kiss and hug. When she leaves, Kasim stands there, watching her walk up the block, and I join him.

"Thanks for inviting her over," Kas says. "When I get in my head like that—I don't know. It's like I don't even know what I need anymore."

"Yeah." I'm not even thinking when my hand searches for his and holds the tips of his fingers. "Of course."

When we decide to go to bed, I sigh and lie down. Kasim isn't asleep either. He's on his back, staring up at the ceiling. "Kasim?"

"Yeah?"

"I've been thinking."

"Okay."

"About us, I mean."

He meets my eye this time.

"I know that you love me," I tell him. My voice is barely a whisper. That's all I can manage. "And I've been thinking about it for a while

now. And I've been afraid to say it out loud. But I'm pretty sure I love you, too. I mean. I care about you a lot. I've always loved you."

Is he even breathing? I can't blame him. I'm not sure I'm breathing myself.

"But do you think that's enough?" I ask him.

"Enough for what?"

"To be in a relationship. To be together, the same way you are with Sable."

He turns onto his side to face me, and I turn onto my side to face him. "Is that what you want? To be in a relationship with me?"

"I don't know. I don't think I even know what being in a relationship with you would mean."

"It'd be a commitment, I think," he whispers. "That's what it means for me, anyway. A commitment to love each other and support each other. To work things out when it gets hard." He gives a half-grin. "And it'd just make me happy, too. To be able to say you're my partner, and I'm your boyfriend."

I bite my lip. "We've been so horrible to each other. We get into so many fights."

He breathes deeply. "Yeah. I think we've fought a lot because if I say something, you think I'm trying to attack you, and vice versa. But if we know we're not coming from a place of hate or judgment . . ."

I know he's right, but how do I know that will really last? "I'm just not sure, sometimes," I tell him, "if I'm really someone you trust—someone you feel safe with."

He doesn't answer me. I begin to wonder if he's fallen back asleep or if he didn't hear me or if he's just straight-up ignoring me.

"You trust Sable," I tell him. "Right? You trust her more than you trust me."

"Sable's been around for a lot of shit," he says. His voice is tight, clipped. It reminds me of the moments right before we'd get into a fight. See? I knew this peace wouldn't last forever. "Sable's been there for me for a while now."

I haven't been there for him. He thinks that I abandoned him, back when our friendship started to end, the same way his father did. Maybe he isn't so convinced yet that I wouldn't do the same thing again.

"I can't force you to trust me," I tell him.

He sits up, arms on his knees. "Then why does it feel like you're trying to?"

"I just want to be honest with you."

"Are you angry at me for trusting Sable more?"

"No. I'm disappointed. Not at you," I say, "but at myself, I guess— that I can't be the person I wish I was for you. To help you and be there for you."

"Don't you think that's making everything about you?" he asks, twisting to look at me.

I flinch. That reminds me of everything that I fear. That I'm just egotistical and narcissistic, and I don't even know it—that I'm toxic as hell. But I can't help the way I feel, can I? "I think I'm allowed to feel how I do. I can't help that. And me, sharing how I feel with you— that's not an attack, either, or me trying to place blame on you. I'm just opening up to you."

He clenches his jaw for a second. "Yeah. That's true."

"As long as I respond in a way that doesn't hurt anyone. That doesn't hurt you." I pause. "Is there anything I should be doing differently?"

He flops back down onto the bed with a sigh. "No, Lark. Be yourself. That's enough. Just being here with me is enough, too."

I nod. "I don't judge you or hate you or anything. I'm safe for you to be your full self with. I love you, Kasim. I really do."

His voice is low and hoarse. "I don't want you to think any less of me."

"I won't."

He tells me that he's depressed. I had no idea. God. Isn't that what people always say?

"It's getting worse," Kasim says. "It comes and goes, but it's getting worse without Taye and the way the world's just so fucked. It feels like there's no point to anything. Sometimes I don't want to be here anymore. No. Not just sometimes."

I don't know what to say. It feels like I've been punched in the chest. I don't know if there's anything I *can* say. Because just hearing these words—hearing Kasim say he doesn't want to live anymore—

"Sable," he says, "she's good to talk to about this, because she understands. She gets it. She's felt the same way before. And she doesn't try to force me to stop being depressed or suicidal because she's uncomfortable. She just listens."

I'm trying to clamp down. Trying not to cry. Because if I start crying now, I won't stop. I can't imagine a world without Kasim. It hurts so much, to know that he's hurting like this. To know I can't do anything about it.

"Are you crying, Lark?"

Fuck. I wipe my eyes.

"Don't cry. Please."

"I can't help it. Jesus, Kasim."

"This is why I didn't want to say anything. I didn't want to make you worried about me."

"I'd rather worry than not know." I want to help him. I wish I knew what to do or say.

He's quiet. Breathing. He takes my hand. Holds it on his chest. I can feel his heart beating.

"I can listen, too. If you ever need me to listen, I'm here for you," I say.

His hand tightens. "You don't think I'm crazy or fucked up?"

"No. I think we're in a fucked-up world."

Even more important then, I guess, that we have each other.

Chapter Twenty-Three I

IT'S ALMOST SCARY HOW NATURAL IT FEELS TO WAKE UP WITH Kasim, get ready with Kasim, walk down the street and into the Commons with Kasim. When we walk in through the doors, we pause, and I'm pretty sure Kas is thinking the same thing I am right now—that, with everything out in the open, he doesn't *want* to go back to acting like we did before, going off into our own separate worlds.

But Eli walks up to me with a smile, and maybe it's because I know Eli better now that I recognize the coldness in their eyes as their gaze slides from me to Kasim.

"Hey, Lark." They kiss my cheek, hold my hand, begin to walk me to the classroom. I look over my shoulder at Kas, who watches me go—but only for a second, before he turns to head over to Sable and Micah and Patch.

"Why did you walk in with Kasim?" Eli asks me.

Eli and I have been so off that we've stopped texting. I haven't even told them that Kasim has moved in with me. And the flicker of annoyance—the annoyance I think I would have wanted to ignore once upon a time, too ashamed of my own emotion because I wanted to be so liked so badly, accepted by everyone around me—yeah, it makes me not even *want* to tell them.

"Why does it matter?" I ask them.

"Because it looks bad," they say, like this is obvious. "You're my partner, walking into the Commons with someone else."

"Is anyone even looking?" I ask them, gesturing around at all the heads turned to each other, their phones. "No one's even paying attention, Eli—and if they were, it's none of their business."

Eli frowns at me. "What's going on with you?" they ask. "You're acting weird."

"I'm always weird."

They shake their head. "If someone goes online and says that you're also dating Kasim, people would trash us. You're already getting negative attention, and that's affecting me, too."

I stop and turn to face them. "And that's all that matters to you, right?"

"What?"

"You only care about social media. That's why you wanted to go out with me and be my partner in the first place."

"What're you talking about?" Eli says, but the longer I stare at them, the more their anger fades. They swallow. "I wanted to go out with you because I liked you."

"Liked?"

"I still like you," they say. "I was really angry with you. I'm still mad, to be honest," they tell me. "But we can make this work, if we want to. We just have to try." Some people pass by, laughing and chatting, and Eli pauses, stepping in closer to me, lowering their voice. "I'm sorry I snapped at you. I just didn't like seeing you and Kasim walk in together, you know?"

"Just because we walked in together, doesn't mean we're *together*," I say. I hesitate, because I can feel the edge of a lie, and lies—they've

been so easy for me to tell recently, and I want to change. Change isn't just thinking about changing, but actually doing it, right? "Kasim and I—to be honest, yeah, there's something going on between us. Even though I'm not totally sure what. But we wouldn't be public about it. That's what we agreed on."

Eli nods slowly. "But Kasim?" they ask, smile soft, which makes me wonder if their soft smiles have always been fake. "Really? He's a little—"

"A little what?"

Eli shrugs.

I frown. "Kasim's an amazing person. All people are amazing, I think, when you get to know them and all of their insecurities and pains and joys and everything that makes them human, and I've been lucky enough to get to know Kasim, and see that he's an incredible partner and friend and . . ."

I stop speaking when I see the look Eli gives me. They clench their jaw.

I take a deep breath. "It's not fair of you to speak badly about him without even really getting to know him."

The bell rings, and Eli and I walk to the classroom in silence.

"Mr. S," I say, "how do you get past writer's block?"

I've been struggling to write Birdie's story all summer, and it would've been hard enough having to write a full *novel* while getting so many rejections, but to also be dealing with the drama of the thread and Eli and now falling in love with Kasim and maybe possibly Sable and—God, it's just so hard, to the point where I've really been wondering if writing is even for me, or if I should just give up now.

We're supposed to be writing quietly. We'd already critiqued writing for the day, that was the discussion, but of course my brain didn't remember that, and now everyone looks up, surprised—Micah and Patch rolling their eyes, Eli pressing down their annoyance and shifting in their seat.

Mr. Samuels takes off his glasses and tosses them to the desk and rubs his face. "What was that, Lark?"

My voice closes in on itself, and I duck my head, ready to let the topic go—but Kasim speaks up further down the bench. "Writer's block," he says. "How do you move past it?"

There are glances around the room at Kasim, and then at me, and then back to Mr. S—and, yeah, it's frustrating that when I asked the question, it wasn't okay, but when Kas asks it, it's fine—but more than anything else, there's a swelling in my chest, the same kind of swell when I see TikToks of adorable puppies running around in circles and tiny kittens finding their furever homes. Kasim gives me a quick smile.

"Okay," Mr. S says with a sigh. "Let's talk about it, then. Anyone have any ideas for moving past writer's block? Go ahead, Asha."

"Writer's block is just a mental thing," she says. "You just need to push past it."

Eli frowns. "Really? I've heard that you shouldn't push past writer's block, because usually it's a sign that you've messed up in your book somewhere, so you need to backtrack and fix it before you can move on."

Jamal scribbles in their notebook. "I've heard the same. But I also think it might be better to just pause and think about it, before the answer comes to you."

Fran nods. "Yeah, usually in the shower."

Everyone stares at him.

"What?" he says, raising his hands. "That's *always* where I get my ideas and I figure out what to write next."

I try not to groan in frustration. These are all things I've tried, and nothing has worked—not even the shower. The few pages I've managed to write are garbage, and anything else I've written, I've just ended up deleting.

Sable traces a circle in Kasim's palm. "I think writer's block is about energy," she says.

Mr. Samuels raises an eyebrow. "Okay. Explain."

"When we sit down to write or paint or play the piano, or anything at all, we aren't alone. Energies come to us to inspire us, to help us, to get us into that flow state. It's almost meditative, and it feels like we're taken over completely, and the story practically writes itself."

I know *exactly* what she's talking about. My best writing has always been when I've closed my eyes, and it's felt like my hands are moving on their own, and I'm not even in control of myself or the writing that flows out of me. I miss that feeling. I haven't had it in a long, long time.

"Writer's block, I think, is the opposite of that flow state," Sable says. "The flow state is about freedom. It's about creativity. Writer's block is this trapped, constricted feeling, where ideas stop coming to you."

"Then," I say, sitting taller in my seat, maybe a little too excitedly, or maybe not, because fuck it, I'm really trying to be myself and do me no matter what anyone else thinks, "how do you find creativity?"

Sable smiles at me, and hopefully someone here is trained in CPR, because it really does feel like my heart stops beating.

Birdie scrunches up their face like they're in pain.

"Well," Sable says, "I think that's what creativity is: energies around us. And if we can stop and pause and breathe and let those energies find us, then the story works. But those energies can't find us if we block them by being afraid of what people will think of our writing, or thinking that it isn't good enough, or being scared that we'll never be able to finish a book. Fear is one of the worst causes of writer's block."

I'm honestly not even sure Sable is human. Like, I know she's human, because she's sitting right in front of me, but I get this overwhelming sense that she is so powerful, that she's a soul from another dimension or universe where she'd been a planet or a sun, and when she died, she decided to pop by on Earth for a short time, to see what it's like to be a human being. She's a galaxy inside of a human body. I fall more in love with her whenever she speaks.

"I try not to be afraid," she tells us. "I try to feel love for my story instead. Love, which leads to joy, which leads to excitement for the story I'm writing, which allows the story to practically write itself, instead of me writing what I think other people will want to read, or being too afraid to write what I actually want to write." Maybe my question unlocked a floodgate, and at this point, Sable can't stop speaking, even

if she wanted to. "I have a theory," she says, and everyone watches her, entranced, "that the stories we write are real—as real as you or me. Because we're all energy; that's all we are, that's what has now been proven. We are all energy, and this universe is all energy, and so is thought, and so is emotion, and so, in a way, are the characters in our stories and in the worlds we create. They're all energy, in a universe that is made of energy, and so, in a way, they are real, too."

I'm so in love with her. I'm honestly envious when Kasim smiles at Sable and wraps her hand in his. How would it feel to take both of their hands? To tell them how I feel? I look away to catch Eli watching me with a frown.

It's a quiet night, me and Kasim in my bedroom. He was on his phone until he fell asleep in my bed while I wrote at my desk. Sable energized the hell out of me, and I've spent the last couple of hours writing—just writing, nonstop, anything and everything that comes to me, letting it all flow out. It's felt so good, and it's pretty late now, going on midnight, but I almost want to text her to thank her, to tell her that I'm writing for the first time in a while—

My phone buzzes. It's a group text started by Asha with Sable, Kasim, and me.

come to the dog bowl

My mom would *kill* me if she found out that we left the house in the middle of the night to walk all the way to the park. We only run into a few people here and there, everyone walking with their heads down, not making eye contact like we would in the sunlight. The

neighborhood is a lot creepier after dark, tree branches creaking and shadows passing by.

"She didn't say anything to you?" I ask Kasim again.

He yawns, cranky that he was woken up. "*No*, Lark—I don't know what's happening."

We make it to the edge of the park, looking around for any sign of Asha and Sable, and—there, right there, at the edge of the park on the opposite end, there's a group of people laughing and talking. As we walk up to them, I can hear music is playing. Asha has a ring of flowers around her headwrap and is wearing a flowy dress as she jumps to her feet and pulls me into a hug. Sable stands up and kisses Kasim, holding his hand and pulling him over to the group, and then Kasim grabs my hand and pulls me along with them.

I recognize Steph, and Fran is there, too, and—ah.

I see.

The coven of femmes.

Kasim and I exchange glances slowly. I wouldn't consider myself femme or masc, and Kasim is *definitely* more on the masc end of the spectrum, so I'm a little nervous about why they would invite us out here.

"Welcome," Asha says, as if starting an official meeting. "It's a glorious full moon, and we wanted to come together to celebrate." She holds up the biggest blunt I've ever seen. "This is a sacred blend that will purify and cleanse and assist in our healing. So let's fucking do this."

Kasim leans into Sable, who sits in between us as the weed gets passed around the circle. "What's going on?" he whispers.

"I asked the others for permission to invite you, and Asha thought it would be a good idea to invite Lark, too."

"But what *is* this?"

"It's a healing ritual," she says.

"I didn't realize I needed healing," he says, voice tight.

And *that* sounds like a discussion I don't want to overhear. I lean away, looking for the weed, which would definitely help make all of this just a little less awkward.

"You can leave if you want to," Sable says calmly.

Kasim sighs. "No. I'll stay."

The weed makes it to him. I don't know if everyone here usually sucks on it or what, or maybe it's because of the pandemic, but instead of putting his mouth on it, Sable fans the smoke into his face. It makes its way to me, and the smoke stings my eyes and my nose and . . . it tastes weirdly like strawberries? It keeps going around and around, and I feel like I'm getting dizzy just watching it go in circles, until it's finished, and we're all laughing, I have no idea why, and maybe there doesn't need to be a reason for it, either. Asha jumps to her feet and starts to dance, and Fran is on his back, giggling as he stares up at the moon. Sable is slow dancing with Kasim to their own song, one that I can't hear, and I realize I've just been sitting here, staring off into space.

Steph is beside me. We've been talking for a while, I think. "I'm really happy," she tells me, "that you and Eli found each other. They were so upset when I broke up with them. I felt guilty, but I shouldn't, right?" she asks me. "I was doing what was right for me, and they need to do what is right for them."

"Do you believe in happily ever after?" I ask her.

"No," she says. "Happily ever after, the way we think about it now—it depends too much on another person, don't you think? We think a happily ever after means that we are loved by another person as we go off into the sunset, but—"

She starts to cough—like, really hard, like it might be the virus or something. I panic and smack her back, and she leans over and heaves. Nothing comes up. She sits back again, taking a deep breath and shaking out her face, her arms.

"—but we don't need another person to be happy."

"What was that?"

"What was what?

"Are you okay?"

She laughs and shakes her hand at me. "Yeah, I'm fine. That's just trapped energy. I was trying to get rid of that for a month. Glad it came up now." She grins and lies down next to me, eyes closed. "Happily ever after," she says, slowly, or maybe that's just my perception of time, because I can feel it, seriously, start to feel how time is an illusion. "It's like we think we need another person to be whole. To be happy. But we're already whole. We've already got all the happiness and love and joy inside of each and every one of us. We don't need another person to find our happily ever after. Everyone already has that, all on our own." Her voice gets quieter and quieter. "I think that's what Eli couldn't figure out. They wanted me to complete them. But they're complete. They're so complete."

She's still whispering when it starts to drizzle. It's just a mist at first, and then the rain—it comes down harder and harder, making the dirt slippery and muddy, and I don't even know when I started doing it, running around after Fran and laughing as we slip and fall

down the hill, into the bottom of the bowl, and when Kasim laughs as I fall on top of him, and when Asha starts screaming the words to a song and we all join in, a jumbled mess because none of us even know the words, "MARCELINE! I KNOW YOU'RE NOT REAL IN THIS DIMENSION! UNICORNS! WHAT'S UP! NIGHTOSPHERE!"

Sable laughs against my cheek. When did we lie down together? "I love unicorns."

"I know you're not really from this dimension, either," I tell her.

Her smile is soft. I'm not really thinking when I start to lean toward her, to kiss her—but I pause, because shit, I think I'm really high, and now I'm not even sure that the blunt only had weed in it, and shouldn't I ask her if she wants to kiss me? I didn't realize Kasim was lying down beside us. He watches me and Sable as we watch each other, almost kissing, and there isn't jealousy in his eyes, the way I was used to seeing jealousy in Eli's, because I'm pretty sure he's thinking that he'd like to kiss us, too.

The walk back and the rain, which is actually pretty cold for a summer night, and the water that Sable gives me and Kasim—all of that helps bring me back down to Earth. I'm covered in mud, soaking wet, and I smell like strawberry weed. My mom? She's going to freaking kill me.

Sable whispers. "I don't want to walk back home alone. Is it okay if I come over, too?"

I nod. "Yeah. We just have to sneak inside. Make sure my mom doesn't hear us."

It feels like we're suddenly in *Mission: Impossible* as I get the key from under the pot and unlock the door and wave them inside, quickly,

shush, stop laughing, Kasim, and we inch forward in the dark, up the stairs, walking as quietly as possible past my mom's door, wincing with every floorboard creak, and down the hall to my room.

I close the door and slump against it with a sigh of relief. Kasim flips on the light, and for a split second, I see how much of a disaster we all are—he snorts, and I wave my hand furiously at him, mouthing at him to be quiet and to turn the light back off.

He does what he's told. I peel my wet clothes off, and I can only see shadows and outlines, but I know Kasim and Sable are doing the same, and my throat goes dry, my heart beating so hard it's like it's trying to break out of my chest. I open up one of my drawers and pull out T-shirts and gym shorts, tossing them to where I think Kas and Sable are—

"You just hit me in the face," Kasim hisses. Sable laughs under her breath.

I have an idea. I grab my phone and flip it over so that we have dim light from the screen. I dry my hair with a towel that's hung up on my door and pass it to Sable. She wrings her hair dry and passes it to Kasim. Kasim wipes his face and shakes out his locs. And I know I'm not the only one who feels it—this quiet tension, laughter gone, as we all stand there and look at each other. I'm embarrassed. I feel like I want to jump out of my skin and hide, but Sable—she's so unapologetic, right? My phone locks itself, light fading until it's dark again, but I don't turn the screen back on. I see Sable's outline move closer to Kasim, and I hear them kiss. I feel Kasim's hand touch mine, and I let him take it, let him hang on to my fingers.

He leans closer to me. "Can I kiss you, Lark?"

I nod, because I wouldn't be able to speak anyway, and—

Kasim's lips press against mine. It feels like taking a first breath. He pulls back, just a few inches, before his hands hold my arms, pulling me closer, and he kisses me like he's been dying, and this is the one thing that will bring him back to life, and I get it, I do, because I don't think I even knew how badly I wanted to kiss Kasim until this moment, had no idea how good he would feel as we both sink onto my bed. I pull away, and Sable sits on the edge, leaning into Kasim again, kissing him, her hand taking mine, and I say something, I'm not sure what, when she asks if she can kiss me, too, and we're all on my bed, on top of my sheets, I'm not sure whose hands are on my arms, my back, under my shirt, or who is breathing hard, trying to be quiet—wait, that might be me, actually—and Kasim kisses me, my neck, and sighs against my ear, almost in relief.

"I've wanted to do that for so long," he says, quietly.

"Me, too." I didn't realize it was true until I said it, but it is—true, I mean. I've wanted to kiss Kasim and hold Kasim and lie down like this with Kasim for a while now.

Sable runs her hand up and down my arm, her chin resting on Kasim's shoulder as she watches me. That's how we all fall asleep, every now and then kissing again, but more slowly, until our breaths get slow and deep. When I wake up again, Sable is gone. There's a faint pink hue in the air, the sun starting to rise.

Chapter Twenty-Four | I

I HAVEN'T BEEN ABLE TO LOOK ANYONE IN THE EYE ALL DAY.
Kasim and I—the awkward silence is killing me, it really is, and
with Sable, it's even worse, because I can tell she doesn't feel
uncomfortable about what happened at all. In class, she just looks
between me and Kasim with a raised eyebrow, like she's wondering
why we're acting so weird, as if, sure, it's no big deal that we all
made out in my bed last night. Even weirder for me is Eli, sitting
next to me, taking my hand even though I kind of don't want them
to right now, looking at the three of us and obviously knowing
something is up.

Class has a Friday-afternoon vibe. Fran's folded over, fast asleep.
Jamal is frowning as they type away on their laptop. They haven't spoken to me in weeks now. Mr. Samuels is asking us about the responsibility we have as authors, whose words will be going out into the
world. "You'll likely make a mistake," he says. "That's only natural, isn't
it? You're human beings. So, if you get something wrong—about another race, another culture, another identity—what should you do?
What should happen?"

Patch sits up straight. "Shame," they say. "Shame. Shame. Shame."
Their voice gets louder and louder until Micah joins in, laughing, and
the two cackle together.

"But you'll probably make a mistake, too," I say, before I can think better of it—and when they both swing their heads to look at me, I feel like I'm about to get a telepathic beatdown.

"No," Patch says. "I wouldn't be such a dumbass that I would mess up with another person's identity. I would do my research, make sure I ask questions, and get it right."

Micah shakes his head. "Lark would probably mess up and then say *love and peace, we're all one, you're all bullies.*"

Kasim frowns. "Can you leave Lark alone?"

Micah and Patch—it's like they've been betrayed. They stare at Kasim with big eyes. All three stare at each other.

Sable fills in the quiet. "I don't think we should shame another person," she says. "I think we should ask for accountability."

Mr. Samuels seems intrigued. He puts one hand to his chin. "Say more about accountability."

Sable's gaze lands on me, as if she's speaking to only me. "Accountability is asking a person to look at their actions, right? To do better, without suggesting that they're a person unworthy of love. A person who has made a mistake and needs to take accountability should feel *guilt*, not shame. We all make mistakes. All of us."

"That's bullshit," Micah says, though his voice wavers a little. "We can feel however we want to feel when someone messes up. We can treat them however we want to treat them."

Sable considers him. "How you see other people is a reflection of you," she says. "So, do you hate yourself whenever you make a mistake?"

Micah's mouth opens, then snaps shut.

She continues. "I don't think anyone should hate themselves when

they make a mistake. I don't think anyone should be ashamed of themselves. Guilt is about action. Guilt lets us focus on what we need to do to make up for our mistake and how we can limit the harm we caused, while knowing with all the confidence in the world that we're still worthy of love. Each and every one of us."

Patch clenches their jaw. "You sound like all those people online who whine about cancel culture. Wah, wah, white people are being canceled for being racist!"

Sable narrows her eyes, just a little bit. "Being asked to take accountability isn't the same as being canceled. And a desire to shame a person is more about indulging the ego."

Asha's mouth falls open. Kasim bites his lip, frowning down at the table. Fran slips out his phone and starts recording. I don't blame him. I feel like I'm witnessing a war—the first fissure I've ever seen in this friend group. And it's because of me. I'm a freaking friendwrecker.

Birdie puts a hand on mine. "You didn't do anything wrong, Lark."

Micah glares. "How is it egotistical to make people face consequences?"

Sable looks at him evenly. "The goal of accountability is to end harm through learning and growth. What's the goal of shaming? Shaming is more about the person who shames, and making themselves feel like they're better than another person."

Oh, *wow*, Micah really doesn't like hearing that one. There's anger building in him as he glares at Sable, who either doesn't notice or doesn't care as she stares right back at him.

Asha speaks up quickly, taking one for the team, maybe, or to get the heat off of her friend. "I agree with Sable. Years can pass, and people on social will say, 'The internet is forever. We haven't forgotten what you did.'"

I know that Asha is right. Blacklists are created of people who should never be supported, even after they've taken accountability properly. And, when you think about it, it's like this person's mistake will follow them forever, as if it's a part of who they are and their identity now—as if they are wrong to their core. And, yeah—I can see how that's shaming, and not asking for accountability.

"I mean," Asha continues, "if a person doesn't take accountability, and others say that this person hasn't made an effort to learn and grow, then yeah, okay—it's legit to warn other people about them."

Sable says, "Maybe we would all have more compassion—not only for each other, but for ourselves."

Jamal shrugs one shoulder. They've stopped typing, are listening with a hand hovering over the keyboard. "Yes, but it should be acknowledged that there are different levels of harm. If someone is abusive, it's going to take a lot of accountability to make up for the harm."

Kasim nods. "If someone is racist, or transphobic, or anything where they feel like they're better than another group of humans—that's unforgiveable."

Jamal agrees. "Yeah, well, if someone is racist, it might be impossible for them to make up for the shit they do and say."

I'm speaking before I even realize I've opened my mouth. "But then that would mean that they're incapable of learning and growing and not being racist anymore, which would imply that they, their soul, is racist, which is impossible." Micah rolls his eyes, shakes his head, and even Kasim makes a face, like, *come on, Lark, we're trying to help you out.* But I keep going. "I think that every racist and anti-trans and anti-queer and really, super harmful person can realize that they are wrong, and that they can learn and grow and become empathetic to the fact that everyone is a

human being worthy of the same level of respect and love. If I didn't believe this, I'd have to think that cruelty is a part of the human soul, something we're born with, but I don't think that at all. Hatred is taught."

It's like I've had a second chance to explain myself, defend myself, from that first day in class at the Commons—and, for once, I feel like I've spoken, and people are looking at me like they might understand what I mean.

"And, you know, I'm not even saying that they need to be forgiven, because, yeah, that shit is so traumatizing—but I think that they can grow and change and do some good for the people they hurt, too. If we only shame and don't ask for accountability"—yes, accountability, maybe that's what I was missing all along, yes—"then that would also mean they aren't able to change and help to end the harmful cycles this society is trapped in. And they have to. We all have to change, right? And the way we all put so much energy into calling everyone else out—I think that has more to do with us not wanting to look at ourselves, and the mistakes we've made, too."

Kasim is watching me like he might be remembering why he's in love with me in the first place. Maybe it's what I'm saying or how I'm saying it, because right now, I really feel like I'm speaking with unapologetic power.

Mr. Samuels nods. "Well said. Yes, very strong points. If we make a mistake as a writer, harming another person or group of people, then it's important to take accountable, actionable steps to make up for the harm," Mr. S says. "And allowing that grace for others also allows for that grace inside of ourselves. "

But Patch still shakes their head, even if they won't make eye contact with anyone. "Nah. We don't have to accept anyone's apology when they fuck up."

"Yes," Sable says. "True. But you can decide not to accept an apology and let it end there. Boundaries set in place. No more communication or interaction."

Micah looks more thoughtful than I could've imagined, eyes downcast, too, and—yeah, as hard as it is to admit, because he and Patch messed with me so much, I know that Micah's only made mistakes, too. I know he deserves compassion also. "We're traumatized every day by racism, anti-queerness, all of these bullshit systems that're set up to kill us," he says, "and we're told by others that our pain isn't real, or doesn't deserve change or an apology. We ask for accountability for police brutality, for slurs, for systems that harm, and we're dismissed and ignored. What else are we supposed to do, then," he asks, "when the people we try to hold accountable refuse to take accountability? There's nothing else we can do *but* shame."

"I understand your frustration," Mr. S says, "and I feel your pain—believe me, I do—but maybe shaming isn't the answer that will help our world move forward. Maybe accountability is the answer we always need to return to."

We're all quiet after that. Mr. S suggests we get to silent writing, and we pull out our laptops and notebooks if they weren't already out. Eli is quiet beside me, and I wonder what they thought of the discussion, if they had any thoughts at all—or if they preferred to ignore everything that was being said. But I know I can't ignore it. I know I've made a mistake, and I know that I want to change. I want to grow.

I know what I have to do. I think I've always known, from the moment I saw Kasim's thread.

When the bell rings, only a few people get up. Jamal grabs their backpack and is out the door, not giving a crap about the drama they're leaving behind, while Eli hesitates, then slowly stands, getting their bag, too, and leaning over to kiss me on the cheek. "Talk to you later, Lark."

"Bye, Eli."

Mr. S gathers his things and slips out the door—runs, practically, as if he could feel the conversation coming. And when he's gone, the door shutting behind him, Micah and Patch glare at Sable and Kasim. Asha scoots her chair in closer to Sable, ready to defend her best friend, while I sit at the side, watching, feeling a little like the defendant in court. And Fran leans back with a grin, arms crossed, looking excitedly from one side of the table to the next, ready for the action to begin.

Kasim begins. "I want to take some accountability," he says.

Birdie nods, sounding like a sports commentator. "Nice play."

Kasim is uncomfortable. He won't meet my eye at all. "The discussion today—it made me think more, I guess, about the way we call each other out in class. I don't think we're holding each other accountable. If we were, then we would focus on the specifics, right? The things a person has done that needs to be fixed. Not whether we think they're a bad person or not."

Birdie whispers, "A solid defensive opening, but it looks like Micah is about to make a return."

Micah rolls his eyes. "Fine, all right, it's not about whether a person is bad or not—but we can still say when a person is toxic." He

gestures at me, not even bothering to say my name. "Toxic people want to get out of being shamed—or being held accountable, whatever you want to call it."

"How am I trying to get out of being held accountable?" I ask. I hate that I'm so breathless right now.

"You say the most fucked-up shit," Patch yells.

"Stop," Kasim says, loud. "Just stop."

Now that grabs everyone's attention. Micah frowns at him, like *what the hell's wrong with you?* Kas isn't looking at anyone else as he keeps talking.

"Stop fucking with Lark. I mean. Yeah. Come on. You guys are always messing with them. Everything we talked about in class—they've got a point, all right?"

Micah doesn't like this, not at all. "What point is that?"

"You're not actually trying to hold them accountable for anything." Kasim looks up, suddenly, eyes burning in the way I'm used to him looking at me whenever we get into one of our arguments and fights. "You're just fucking with them. For what? What have they actually done that deserves your bullshit, day in and day fucking out?"

There's a pause. I know this fight isn't with me—it's about me. I bite my lip and sit quietly.

"Lark's toxic as fuck," Micah eventually says. "We all know that."

"How, exactly?" Kasim asks. "Let's start there. Maybe we need to get into the specifics, the details, to really figure out if they're harmful, or if you just want someone to fuck with. How are they harmful? What have they done?"

"They said racists are good people," Patch says.

Asha shakes her head. "You know that you put words into their mouth. They didn't explain themselves really well, I'll admit," she says, looking at me, "but they never said racists are good people."

"That tweet," Micah says, arms crossed—he looks like he's sulking, like he knows he's already lost. "Saying we shouldn't call cops pigs."

Sable shrugs. "They have an opinion. They expressed it, and they said why. It isn't harming anyone to say that people shouldn't call cops pigs, and they didn't say that in defense of the police system, either."

"Their social media," Patch says. "Posting bullshit about peace and love, pulling attention away from the real issues. And then always posting about their stupid fucking relationship with Eli."

"And that's hurting who?" Asha asks. "Why don't you just ignore their Twitter account if you hate what they have to say so much? Why don't you just boost the accounts you respect?"

"So we're going to be painted out to be the villains here, right?" Micah says.

"No," Kasim tells him. "No. I mean, if we're going by the same shit we talked about, then no one's the villain. Not really. We're all toxic. We're all hiding shit from ourselves that we don't want to deal with." He clenches his jaw and meets my eye. Yeah. He's right. And him being silent, not standing up for me whenever Micah and Patch attacked me, maybe because he was hurting from the way our friendship ended, or maybe because he wasn't sure if they were right and I was wrong—I guess that was something he didn't want to look at, either. But he's looking at it now. Just like that, he's able to figure out what needs to change and take action. Is that all it takes to be a different person? Really?

I'm toxic. I'm lying to so many people, and I know that I should stop.

And change—yes, change is coming. I can feel it. It's exciting, isn't it?

Chapter Twenty-Five

I

KASIM AND I GET HOME. WE STOMP UP TO MY BEDROOM AND DROP
our bags on the bedroom floor. I feel like, if I were writing this scene in
a book, this would be the moment that the two main characters leap
at each other, desperately making out and dropping into bed and—

We stare at each other. Kas sits down on the edge of the bed. "Can
we talk?"

I nod. I sit down at my desk, knees up to my chest. "I guess we
probably should, huh?"

Kasim takes a deep breath. "It took me way too long to see that
Micah and Patch—they were just treating you like crap for no reason.
And I owe you an apology also. I really do. I should've realized that
they weren't really calling you out for anything. They were just looking
for an excuse to mess with you. It's fucked up, the way some people
twist shit around. You deserve more than that."

"Thanks, Kas."

Kas rubs the back of his neck. "And I'm sorry things have been so
awkward since—um—you know, last night."

"Not like it's your fault. It takes two . . . sets of lips . . ."

Kasim raises an eyebrow. Birdie winces.

". . . to tango . . ."

Kas nods slowly. "Yeah—okay, I'm going to ignore that."

"Please. Yes, thank you."

Kasim lets out a heavy breath. "I feel uncomfortable," he says. "I was thinking about it all day—why, I mean, because I've wanted to kiss you for so long, so I thought that once it happened, it would be like I was in heaven because I'd be so happy, right? And I am—I'm so freaking happy, Lark."

I'm blushing. I can barely look at him. "I am, too."

"It felt good and right and—fuck, I want to kiss you again."

I squeeze my face in between my knees. My voice is muffled. "Me, too."

"But I can't," Kasim says. I glance up at him, and he's frowning at his hands, palms up. "I've thought about it, and I'm uncomfortable because I still don't know what you want. We made out, sure, and it was fun—and you told me that you love me," he says, and he glances up at me, as if to check that this is still true, and when I nod, he looks back down again. "But you haven't said that you want to be in a relationship with me."

I put my head on top of my knees and spin my chair around slowly—once, twice . . . thrice? Is it thrice? Kasim is squinting at me, waiting, until I finally put my feet down on the floor. "I don't know," I tell him.

He clenches his jaw, but he holds my gaze.

"What would happen if we're in a relationship?" I ask him.

"I would be your boyfriend," he tells me.

"Yeah, but what would change?" I flap my hands back and forth, then grab onto my fingers of one hand and pull, grab onto the fingers of another hand and pull, and I really feel like I'm about to cry, goddamn it, because this is a hard conversation to have. "I feel like we've

just gotten to this good place where we can talk and laugh and not get into a fight every five minutes. We're back to being friends, and I've missed being your friend so badly, Kas—so, Jesus, this is something I've wanted for so long, and the thought of saying screw being friends, let's be in a relationship, like . . . What if it doesn't work? What if we start to fight again?"

He's shaking his head, glaring at the floor, not speaking.

"What're you thinking?" I whisper.

"I'm thinking that you're afraid, and that fear—it can make us lose out on a really good thing."

"I don't get it. Why does anything have to change? Why can't we stay friends and be happy and have the same relationship we have now?"

"Because I'm in love with you, Lark," he says, his voice rising. "Because I love you, not like a friend."

I bite my lip. Neither of us speak. I have no idea what to say to him right now.

"I—shit, I'm not going to try to force you to be in a relationship with me," Kasim says. "If that's not what you want, I'm not going to force it." He takes a deep breath. "But I'm going to need boundaries."

"Boundaries?"

"I have to think about myself, too, and—if we kiss, I'll want you to kiss me because you like me. Love me. Are willing to have that commitment with me. I don't want to kiss as friends, while I have feelings for you, and I have no idea if this is just fun for you, a whim, or—"

"This isn't just a whim."

"You want to make out with me one second, are too afraid to be in a relationship with me the next, and—the back and forth, it'll just

confuse things between us and in my head, and it'll make this hurt even more."

I let out a shaky breath. "Okay. I get it."

"It's okay if you don't want to be in a relationship with me," he says. "But I need space from you right now."

And I don't want to admit just how much that hurts to hear, too. "Okay."

"I—uh, I was thinking that maybe I should try hitting up Auntie Lydia," he says. "I think I need a break from everything. The Commons, Philly—I think I want to get out of here for the rest of the summer and just think and breathe and get back to myself."

Oh. Wow. I don't know what to say to that, and I feel like I've been punched in the gut, and my eyes are stinging, and—

It isn't about me. I know that it isn't. I swallow hard and nod. "Okay. I understand." I don't want him to go, not when I feel like I just finally got my friend back, but it isn't up to me. If this is what he needs, then I want to support him. "We should talk to my mom."

He nods, and within the hour, Kas has told my mom that he's grateful to her and everything she's done, but he wants to go to New York, and that after Kasim calls Taye and his aunt, and Auntie Lydia tells him yes, of course, he's free to come and stay however long he needs to. Kasim books a bus for the next morning—just like that, no hesitation. I sit in my room, watching as he packs up all of his stuff, not making eye contact with me.

"I'm sorry, Kas," I mumble.

He shakes his head. "You don't need to be sorry about anything, all right? This is for me. I shouldn't need you to make me happy, and getting away for a while—that'll help me get back to a place

where I can be happy on my own, whether you want to be with me or not."

I understand what he's saying, but it still massively sucks. He goes to sleep on the sofa for that one night, making my mom raise her eyebrows at me—*Did you two have another fight?* she mouths when he isn't looking, to which I only shake my head and sigh. I lie down in my bed and stare up at the ceiling all night, not able to fall asleep at all, though I must have at some point, because when I wake up and gasp and scramble out of bed and race down the stairs, Kasim is already gone.

I can't even look at Sable the next day at the Commons. I feel like I drove her boyfriend away to New York, and I feel guilty as hell . . . but she doesn't seem angry. She says hi, and even offers me a small smile. But she's definitely returned to her quieter self in class, too—maybe because she's sad that Kasim is gone, or maybe because she just doesn't have anything to say. Before I can get a chance to call her name when the bell rings, she's up, on her feet, and out the door.

I don't know if I want to be with Kasim in that way, not when I'm still so scared—but I do know what I *need* to do.

Jamal looks surprised when I sit next to them in the cafeteria. Well, maybe surprised isn't the right word. They make this face, like, *and what the flying fuck do you think you're doing?* They can be terrifyingly intimidating, but I force myself to take a deep breath.

"Can I talk to you for a second?" I ask them.

They look away, wiping their expression clean and pursing their lips as they turn the page in their book. "About what?"

"I wanted to apologize."

They pause. "Okay."

"You were right. I shouldn't have lied in the first place."

Jamal raises their chin and sits straighter in their chair, still staring down at their book.

"I'm sorry that I triggered you." I don't know the details, and I don't need to, but from the few things I've heard Jamal say about their parents, it sounds like their mom was manipulative. Maybe they've dealt with lying all of their life. "I lied because I was afraid of the backlash, and then because I saw it as an opportunity to make my profile grow, and I shouldn't have taken credit for Kasim's thread."

Jamal still doesn't speak, but I'm not sure that they're actually reading their book now. They've set it down and are staring blankly at the pages in front of them.

"It's okay if you still don't want to be around me or talk to me," I say, "but I wanted you to know that I'm planning on telling the truth. Announcing it on Medium."

They tap the bench's surface with their pen. They always take notes in books' margins. "When?"

"I don't know yet. I kind of have to talk about it with Eli first. But soon."

They're nodding. "Okay."

"I—um, I totally understand if you don't want anything to do with me from now on," I say. "That would be your right. But I'm grateful to you, because I feel like you were a catalyst, in some ways—a catalyst for my change, for putting up a boundary and getting me to start looking at myself, and . . . I'm sorry, again," I tell them, my voice quiet now.

Jamal's watching me now. "I still need to figure out how I feel about you in general," they tell me. "You know, since you'd do something like that to begin with. I don't know if I can trust you."

"Yeah. I know."

Their face softens for a second. "But I'm glad you're doing the right thing. Telling the truth." They even give the glimmer of a smile. "I hope you feel good about the decision."

Yeah. I know that I do.

Second stop: Eli's house. We haven't had a real conversation in a while now—just the quick cheek-kissing, hand-holding. Ever since I announced I was taking a break from social media, they stopped texting me and stopped wanting to spend time with me. That was just another reality I didn't want to see, I guess, and maybe it's been something Eli didn't even really want to admit to themselves, either. They haven't actually been interested in me at all—romantically, or as friends. Maybe they just wanted the fame, and even as my profile blew up, they just stayed with me out of obligation.

I don't feel safe with them. They've hurt my feelings on more than one occasion, and they've judged me constantly—and the thing is . . . I've let them. I've stuck around, stayed their partner, because I was also too afraid of the backlash, too. I should've broken up with them weeks ago. Shouldn't have even said *yes* to becoming their partner in the first place.

I'm tired. Being afraid is exhausting, and the more I tell smaller truths, take more responsibility and accountability, the more addicting it's becoming to say what I think and feel and need. I text Eli when

I'm down the block, and they swing open the door just as I'm hopping up the steps.

"Hey, Eli," I say. "We have to break up."

Their forced smile drops and they step back. "What?"

"I know it'll hurt our image, but—I'm sorry, I don't want to do this anymore. We both know it's not working."

They tilt their head to the side, confused. "Right, yeah. But we decided to keep trying."

"You decided. I kind of felt pulled along." No, that isn't right. I had enough agency. I could've made my own decisions. "Actually—I'm sorry. I'm trying to blame you when I should've just been more up-front with what I really wanted. I should've just said no from the start."

They're not bothering to smile anymore. They blink quickly with annoyance. "So, you just wasted my time, basically. That's what you're trying to say."

"I don't think I wasted your time. We both got what we'd wanted out of this."

"I could've been building a relationship with someone else. Someone who would've wanted to keep this going more than barely a month. This is a fucking joke." Eli's pissed now. "This isn't just affecting you, you know. I'm going to get so much bullshit for this online. All of these fucking trolls—trolls that *you* pissed off, by the way—and now you're just abandoning me with them."

I shake my head. "I'm sorry. It's just not what I want anymore."

"Pretty selfish of you, don't you think?"

It was harder to see before, when I was so wrapped up in this game with Eli—but I can see them clearly now. "No. I don't think it's selfish

of me to do what's best for me. I don't think it's selfish to take care of myself, my own wants and needs, and to have healthy boundaries."

They roll their eyes. "Right. Boundaries."

"I feel like you're trying to shame me into following along with you and what you want, but I have to do what's best for me. I have to break up with you," I say, then take a breath and add, "and I have to come clean."

Now that—yeah, that *really* gets their attention. "About *what*?"

"About everything. The original thread. It wasn't even mine."

"No. You can't do that, Lark."

"Yes, I can."

"That's fucking embarrassing for me, too, not just you."

"I've been lying to too many people for way too long. I have to do what's right."

"If you want to light your profile on fire, fine. But don't take me down with you."

"I'll tell the truth. You didn't know about any of this in the beginning. You were my victim at first, too." They eventually knew, sure, but I guess I also shouldn't worry about what they are and aren't doing. Eli not taking accountability for themselves, not learning or wanting to change and grow—maybe that's not my issue.

"No one's going to give a shit," they tell me. "This is going to reflect so badly on our relationship. On me and everything I've worked for."

"If you want to say that you eventually found out and kept going along with it, that's your choice. But I'm going to be honest and post an apology. I'm going to go now. Bye."

I start to walk back down the porch steps, but Eli calls out after me.

"You don't have to do any of this," they say. "Why're you doing this?"

Why do I bother to stop? "I just . . ." I hesitate. "I want to do better. I made a mistake, and I knew it was wrong, and—I don't know. I was so afraid that fucking up meant that I didn't deserve love. I want to be accountable and not just think about how I want to be a better person, but actually become that person, and still be worthy of love. You know?"

They don't say anything else, but I already feel lighter when I turn around again.

Maybe I should know by now that not everything always goes according to plan.

I get home and try not to feel sad or lonely about the fact that Kasim isn't there, and as I drop my backpack and open my laptop on my desk, I see the notifications—so many effing notifications, way too many for a profile that's on hiatus, even with the number of trolls that'd been attacking me.

And then I see it. My heart drops so hard and so fast, I feel like I'm going to be sick, or that I might start crying, or both.

Eli Miller @EliLovesYou17

I'm heartbroken. Lark Winters @winterslark lied to me about everything. They never loved me. They never even wrote the unrequited love thread that was supposedly about me.

💬 703   ♻ 3.5K   ♥ 10.3K

Eli Miller @EliLovesYou17

@winterslark is problematic and harmful. They will do anything and lie about anything for attention. Even break my heart.

💬 102   ♻ 1.1K   ♥ 6.2K

um chile anyways so @huhbigboobs

THIS SHIT IS CRAZYYYYYYY, this kid didn't even write the fucking thread?!!!

💬 39   🔁 67   ❤️ 105

alex uwu <3 @alexwawa

LMAO this is officially the wildest thing I've ever witnessed. To all of the Lark Winters simps out there, hate to say it but, we told you so

💬 65   🔁 99   ❤️ 200

Tithings @rosewaterborn

I have been looking into the problematic behavior of @winterslark for the past month. If you would like the details of their toxicity, please DM me.

💬 56   🔁 79   ❤️ 85

ancillaryx @strangerdreams

Wow, this is so disappointing, and what's worse is that it looks really bad for nonbinary Black ppl everywhere. We get so little rep already.

💬 34   🔁 76   ❤️ 119

N. Kay @nkay95

I think that we need to look at the effects of social media on children and teens, and why it is that they feel the need to go to such drastic lengths for attention in the first place.

💬 87   🔁 105   ❤️ 508

Chapter Twenty-Six

MY MOM IS REALLY WORRIED ABOUT ME. I CAN TELL. THE WAY SHE watches my every move as I get ready to go to the Commons the next morning. In an epic plot twist, she asks me if I'd like to stay home today. "You're really going through a lot right now," she says. That was a part of my accountability, too, I decided—telling her everything, from start to end, even everything with Kasim. She was disappointed with my decisions, but I can't exactly blame her for that when I've been disappointed in myself, too.

I nod. "I have to go. I don't want to hide from my mistakes anymore."

She smooths my hair down. "Okay, baby. I love you."

"I love you, too."

I knew that the Commons would be awful, but I didn't think that the Commons would be *this* awful. Everyone turns to look at me when I walk in, and it's almost like that first day—except that this time, there aren't any excited whispers. There are glares, frowns, people muttering to one another. Steph shakes her head when she sees me. Fran strides by and offers a high five, then pulls away at the last second. "High fives aren't for liars, Lark!" he calls, waving goodbye.

I see Asha, but when she meets my eye, she only frowns and gets up from her table, walking away. I start to follow.

"Bad idea," Birdie whispers.

"Asha," I say, following her up the stairs. "Asha, wait."

She turns around to face me in the hallway. "What do you want, Lark?"

I bite my lip, holding my arm close to me. "I—well, I wanted to personally apologize—"

She holds up a hand. "Why did you lie like that?"

I mean, I knew that I would get a hard time for this, and I should, shouldn't I? If I'm going to take real accountability, then yeah—this is going to be hard. "Um—a lot of different reasons I told myself, but none that really matter now."

She's nodding slowly. "I keep thinking back to all of those conversations we've had, where you pretended the thread was yours, and that you were in love with Eli, and—it feels like I'm looking at a completely different person."

I nod. "Maybe it's because that mistake was made by a person I don't really want to be anymore, and now I'm changing into the person I want to be instead."

Asha watches me carefully. "I know that everyone makes mistakes," she says, "but this was a big, *big* mistake, Lark."

"I know. You're right."

"It's not that easy to just forgive and forget," she says. "I need a break from you, all right?"

She continues on to class without me, and I'm starting to wonder if maybe I should have stayed home after all—but staying home after this mess would just make coming back a thousand times worse. When I

walk inside, everyone else is already there—including Eli. They turn and see me and there's the smallest twinge of a smirk, before they turn back around again. I take a deep breath and sit at the bench far away from them, and Fran scoots over like I smell bad or something. Jamal frowns at their book. Sable is the only person who will meet my eye, and there's some concern in her gaze, but she doesn't say anything to me—not that I should expect her to. Maybe she's upset about Kasim leaving because of me after all. Micah and Patch just snort and shake their heads.

"All of you really wanted to act like Lark was some victim," Micah says, "when they were just as toxic as we were saying all along."

I spend my afternoons in the bookstore. The anti–Big Red flyers are pasted all over the door and window, and there's a stack at the register for customers to take. The counterprotest is going to be massive. There's something calming and therapeutic about cutting open boxes, unpacking them on shelves, organizing them by title, doing it again. I wish Kasim were here, and that we were speaking. I would ask him for his opinion. What should I do next? I was going to post the apology online, coming clean about everything, but now that Eli's gotten to it first, I don't know if it will seem disingenuous to apologize or not.

I can practically hear Kasim's voice. Who cares if it seems disingenuous? Is it the right thing for you to do?

I nod at my imaginary Kasim. "Yeah, it is."

Then do it.

The door opens, and the bell rings just as I'm bending over another box. I flinch, startled, and look up. Sable waits by the entrance, hands gripping her backpack's straps.

"Hey, Lark."

My heart catches up with my head, and it starts to race around in my chest about a mile a minute. "I didn't know you were coming," I tell her.

"I stopped by your house, but your mom told me you were here." Sable tucks some hair behind her ear. "I should've texted."

"It's okay." I rub my arm, not sure what else to say.

"I wanted to tell you in person that I'm sorry about the way everyone's reacting," she says. "I've realized that I care about you, and it makes me sad to see you treated badly."

I care about you. If only there was a way to record moments like that and keep them forever. Birdie makes a face. "Isn't that literally called memory . . . ?"

I shrug and try to act nonchalant even though I'm the walking definition of chalant. "I'm the one that made the mistake. Now I should take accountability."

She nods. "Yes—speaking of accountability. I've decided to speak to Micah and Patch. I've generally stayed out of the fight," she says, "because I haven't thought that it was any of my business, but I realize that was wrong of me, and I'm sorry. I should have realized that they were bullying you and spoken up sooner than the other day in class. I'll tell them exactly what I think of the way that they treat you, and I'm sure that, the next time you see them, they'll treat you with the respect that you deserve, regardless of the mistakes you've made."

Holy shit. I blink at her, and she only looks at me, waiting for any sort of reaction. "That—thank you. That means a lot."

She nods, then looks around the store, eyeing the work I've done. I walk over to the counter, wiping my hands off on my jeans. "I've wanted to say sorry to you, too," I tell her.

"For what?"

"For Kasim. It's because of me that he—you know—left."

"It wasn't because of you," Sable says simply. "He needed space to get back to feeling like himself. You don't have anything to be sorry for." She takes a breath, then turns around. "I told you what I wanted to say. I'll see you later."

"Wait—Sable."

She turns around, mildly surprised, and I—shit, I wasn't really thinking this through, but what else is new? I've really started to like the rush I get when I tell the truth about what I'm thinking and feeling.

Sable watches me, waiting. "Is everything okay?" she asks.

Once upon a time, I would've automatically said, "Yes!" with a forced, bright smile. Now, it feels good to actually consider that question. Hmmm. "I don't know," I tell her. "I've also wanted to talk to you recently because . . . Well, I wanted to be honest about something."

"Okay."

"I thought about telling Kasim, but then I thought it would be better to talk to you about it first, because it really has to do with you more than him."

"Tell me what it is, Lark."

I take a breath and speak the words as I let it out. "I like you," I tell her. "A lot. I have a crush on you. I think I might even love you. I mean, well, I do love you, because I love all human beings, but in love

299

with you, I mean, because I think you're incredible—like, powerful and beautiful and inspiring and—"

Birdie whispers. "You're rambling."

Sable taps a boot against the floor. "I wasn't expecting that, to be honest."

My throat's dry now. "Just—I don't know, the way you interact with the world. The way you don't care about what anyone thinks. Anyone could say they don't care about what other people think, but with you, I really believe it, you know? And I admire that. And I've learned more about being honest with myself because of you."

"That's really kind."

"I feel safe with you because I think you'll tell the truth no matter what, but you don't judge me or anything. You don't look down at me. You don't hate me if I mess up. And it's the same with Kasim." I can't help it. I have to hide my hands in my face. I fold over so I won't have to look at her. "I've been daydreaming about being your partner."

Sable's quiet. I don't blame her. I just told her a lot. Maybe too much to process at once. It's possible she'll say she needs time and decide she needs to leave. That's probably what I would do. I can't always immediately know how I'm going to feel.

I risk a look at her. She's standing straight as she stares forward, thinking. "I've liked talking to you," she says. "I've liked getting to know you more, because I know you mean a lot to Kasim. But."

My heart begins to drop. I stare at my hands, hard.

"I don't know if I feel the same way."

Embarrassment. Surprise. Is it shitty of me, to be surprised? No. Maybe not. A part of me still believes we're all meant to love each

other. Maybe that's what'll happen to the human race eventually—in another thousand years, but not right now.

"No," Birdie says, "but soon."

And sad. I'm so fucking sad to hear that. My heart hasn't stopped sinking, and the tears are coming, and I don't want Sable to see me cry. "Okay."

"I mean, I know that I like you," she says, "but I don't think I want the same thing. With everything that's going on—with Kasim, and my grandma—she's sick right now, and I have to help her a lot . . . I'm at capacity. If I was your girlfriend, I would feel more responsibility toward you, and I'd like to keep things between us where they are."

I nod. I understand. I do. But it still hurts like hell. "Is it okay if I ask where things are with us?"

"I think that we're friends," she says. "Friends who love each other, and maybe kiss sometimes, and who are connected by someone we both also love." She doesn't meet my eye. "And maybe I'll want to be your girlfriend, too, when things aren't so hard. I just don't know if I want a different relationship with you right now."

I'm feeling so many things at once. I'm happy, in a weird way, because I'm glad that Sable still wants to be friends, and that she loves me, and, holy hell, that she might want to be my girlfriend someday. I remember that she's said she's afraid of relationships, and that she wants to run away, and maybe that's a part of it, too, that she really does need some time to process and figure out what she wants. I wonder if I should feel the way that Kas felt about me—if I should want to put up a boundary with her also—but I know that I don't feel the way that he did, and I don't have to. I still want Sable in my life. She

still makes me so happy, whether she's my friend or my girlfriend. I'd rather keep the relationship we have now than nothing at all.

And even though I'm happy, I still want to cry. I don't know—I guess it feels like I've worked really hard to be someone who loves myself and worked to be someone who is always honest and someone who wants to grow and change—to become someone who deserves to be loved and wanted, too.

"You deserve to be loved, Lark," Birdie tells me. "Right here, right now, exactly as you are. Everyone does. Everyone."

"But thank you," Sable says, "for telling me."

"Yeah. I'm sorry if I made things awkward."

"No. I like awkward. I like uncomfortable. That's where the hard conversations happen. That's where we're forced to be honest with ourselves and each other. That's when we start to learn and grow together."

I give her a watery smile. "Yeah. I think so, too."

"I'm going to go," Sable says. "I'll see you at class."

"Okay. Bye."

I watch her leave. I take a breath. And I let myself cry. Because, yeah—it's important to be honest. Crying is like having a hard conversation with myself. Letting myself actually feel the pain I don't want to feel. It's okay that I'm hurting, isn't it?

Birdie wraps their wings around me. "You're perfect, Lark. Absolutely perfect."

Chapter Twenty-Seven

Fields, Janet <jfields@janetfieldslit.com>

Hi Lark,

BIRDIE TAKES FLIGHT has a beautiful concept and first fifty pages. I'm truly blown away that you're only seventeen, and I would love to see the rest of your manuscript when you have a moment to send.

I'm looking forward to reading.

Best,

Janet

Oh, my God.

Oh, *my GOD*!

"What do I do?" I stand up, pulling at my hair. "Holy shit! Birdie, what do I do?!"

Birdie throws their hands up in the air. "I don't know! I'm not even real!"

I sit back down, staring at my laptop. Holy shit, oh my God, holy shit, oh my God. I bite my lip. I finally pushed through the writer's block, sure, but I'm only halfway through the manuscript. There's no way that I could ever manage to finish writing my novel in the next few days, and even if I could . . .

"I have to tell her the truth," I say. I look over my shoulder at Birdie, who sits on the edge of my bed. "Right?"

They shrug. "Yeah. Maybe you do."

I take a deep breath and begin to type.

Lark Winters <winterslark@gmail.com>

Dear Ms. Fields,

This is such a huge compliment. Thank you so much for requesting my full manuscript. I have to be honest. I have not actually finished writing the manuscript like I said that I did. I'm sorry for lying and saying that it's complete. I understand if you're not interested anymore. Either way, thank you for your time.

Sincerely,

Lark

I hesitate, but only for a second, before I decide to just get it over with and hit send. Like ripping off a Band-Aid, right? I close my eyes and try not to groan. My dream agent, my dream of getting published, is in its death throes—and I have no one else to blame but me.

I open my eyes when there's a ping on my laptop. Another email?

Lark, would you give me a call when you have a moment? My number is in my signature at the bottom of this email.

—Janet

Um.

I turn and frown at Birdie. "That's kind of weird, isn't it?" I've never heard of agents asking writers to call them unless they're offering representation, and I really don't think that Janet Fields is about to offer me rep when I've just told her that I messed up big-time. I'm terrified, but I also know I can't *not* call her, so I grab my cell and dial in the number and listen to it ring, ring, ring—

"Hello," a voice says on the other end. "Janet Fields."

I've suddenly lost my voice. I emit a low rasp. "Hi."

"Hello?" she says. "Who is this?"

"Um—this is Lark. Lark Winters?"

"Oh, good, I thought it might be you," she says. "Listen, Lark—I don't usually do this, but I wanted to have a small chat with you, because you're so much younger than any writer that usually queries, and I thought I would give you some advice. I volunteer with some teen writers in the city," she tells me, "and—well, I felt compelled to help you, if you're open to some tips."

"Yes!" I say, way too loudly now. "I mean—shit—I mean, shoot, sorry for swearing—"

She laughs. "Don't worry about it."

"Yes," I say, much softer. "I would love any advice, please."

There's some rustling on the other end. "Well, you already know the first thing I'm about to say, don't you?"

I hesitate with a lurch of embarrassment. "Don't query without finishing the manuscript yet?"

"Yes, exactly," she says, and I'm relieved that she doesn't sound too angry. "You really need to finish your manuscript before you query anyone, okay?"

I nod, even though she can't see me. "Okay."

"Secondly," she says, "my next piece of advice would be to figure out what your story is about. Not just in terms of what happens," she tells me, "but your message, or your question. Not every story has this, granted, but for me—the stories that I love—they have a message that the author so clearly wanted to convey, or had a question that the author asked of its readers. It could be anything that you think is important, that you think the world should know. There could even be multiple messages or questions in your book. This—yes, I think *this* is what acts almost like a portal for stories, allowing readers to feel the writer's passion and excitement and enthusiasm. If there's a message that you're truly excited about, then that could make your book even more electrifying. As I read the beginning of your manuscript, that's what I kept coming back to. I kept wondering if this story was about something *more* than just a teen from the future who has wings. Do you understand?"

I'm nodding, scrambling to get back to my laptop to write down everything she's saying, shit, why didn't I think to take notes before? "Yes—yes, that makes a lot of sense."

"The voice in your story—it's really beautiful," she says. "You're clearly such a talented writer, Lark, and I'm excited for you, because you have your entire life ahead of you to tell as many stories as you'd like to. It isn't easy, by any means," she adds, "but it can be so fulfilling for you to share yourself through your stories. One last piece of advice," she says.

"Okay."

"Are you ready?" she asks me. "It's not as commonly known."

"Okay," I say, laughing, because I can hear the smile in her voice. "I'm ready."

"Don't give up, Lark," she tells me. "That's the biggest advice I can offer. I can tell that writing is your dream. Every other author in the world is a human being, yes?"

"I mean. I think so."

She laughs. "Let's assume that they are—and, assuming you are, too, then that means you can do the same thing they have just as well. You'll be published one day, as long as you keep writing."

Ugh, God, it's that time again—time to cry, because I never would've thought, in a million years, that my dream agent would be so kind and generous. I try not to sniff into the phone too loudly.

"If you'd like to query me again," Janet says, "I would be more than happy to see your manuscript in the future. Just make sure it's completed, all right?"

The Big Red marchers come on July 1, just as they said they would—and, like the neighborhood promised, hundreds of people go out against them.

I don't even know what to think about Big Red coming here. Because after a while, I guess, what else is there to think? It's the same heartbreak. The same rage. And the same pain. Cracking us open over and over and over again. In a world that demands we learn how to heal ourselves—in a world that demands Black people must change ourselves so that other people feel safe because they think that our bodies are scary, our skin threatening—that same world refuses to look at how it's killing us.

I'm angry.

I don't think I've really admitted that to myself before. I always thought that there's no point in someone like me being angry in this

world. Black, queer, trans, neurodivergent. People, complete strangers, use my identities against me. They say that I don't have the same right to live, to exist. They treat me like I'm not likeable if I get mad. If I'm frustrated, and if I use my voice to fight back, and I make mistakes because I'm still a human being who needs to learn and grow, then I'll only become the unlikeable character in a book. Yeah. Maybe I don't care about what another person thinks so much anymore.

"I want to go," I tell my mom.

She hesitates. "I don't know, Lark. It might be dangerous."

"I have to go," I say.

My mom's quiet for a second, thinking, until she says, "If that's what you need to do, then you should."

It's a bright day, summer heat burning my skin. It isn't hard for me to find the crowd. Hundreds of people have already gathered at the Dog Bowl, most holding signs. I walk toward them, following the trickle of people down the street, but when we hit the park, it becomes a sea. The sun's beating down overhead and the air smells like sweat and everyone's wearing masks, everyone, but it's hard not to imagine that the virus is coating us. The sound is a mixture of chants and yells and cries and songs. Someone brought drums. The drumbeat is like a pulse, our feet stepping as one. So many bodies, so many voices, so many lives. I want to get lost in the chants. I want to add my voice to the cries. But this feeling I'm starting to get—this feeling is way too familiar. Anxiety starts to creep through me. There're so many people, so many emotions, so much movement, so much noise, so much energy. There's anger. People are shouting, and I want to join in—God, I want to join in and tell the Big Red marchers to leave, to look at me and see me and realize that I'm a human being, but I can't. I can't speak. I can barely breathe.

I'm feeling dizzy. Sparks of light are in the corners of my eyes. And I know that I have to go home.

When I've stomped up the porch steps, I pull off my mask and go to the bathroom stand in front of the sink and stare at myself in the mirror. I shouldn't have gone. I shouldn't have even left the house. I can see what Micah and Patch meant, now—that I'm all talk, always saying that I believe in peace, but I can't even do the work to actually fight for it.

My mom stands in the bathroom doorway. "Are you okay?"

"Not really," I tell her, "but I will be."

She nods. She isn't surprised. She probably knew I wasn't the kind of person who could handle something like a protest. Maybe she wanted me to see for myself instead of trying to tell me who I am.

I'm starting to cry. I don't even know why. I guess it's just everything: the anger and pain and fear mixed with the shame that I couldn't even manage to walk down a street.

"Talk to me," my mom says.

"It's embarrassing. I couldn't even march. I couldn't even be in the protest. How can I say I want to fight for change and I can't even do something as simple as that?"

My mom smooths a hand over my hair. "We all have different roles. We all have different personalities. It's okay if it was too much for you, to be fighting in the streets."

"It's like I suddenly had anxiety and it was too loud and too much was happening."

"That's okay."

"I don't want to be just talk. I want to help make actual change, you know?"

Her smile softens. "Don't you think there are multiple ways to make change?"

I shrug.

"I named you Lark for a reason."

She wanted me to use my voice to uplift the world—but is that really enough? "It just doesn't feel the same as people out in the streets, actually putting their lives at risk for what they believe in. Writing isn't the same as people who've dedicated their entire lives to fighting."

"Maybe not. But does that make your voice less important?" she asks. "Does that mean stories or speaking your truth don't have a role in activism, too? I don't know about that. Our society wouldn't be the same without the writers who came before you." She kisses my cheek. "Use your voice, Lark, in the way that you can—in the way that you know how. Use your passion help the world. It doesn't help anyone, does it? To force yourself to fit another person's idea of what it means to make change." She sighs, smiling at our reflections in the mirror. "I think just existing is enough. Just living and breathing and loving ourselves and each other. That's a way to fight back, too. Don't you think that's true?"

Yeah. In a world that wants me to hate myself, teaches me to hate myself, expects me to hate myself, learning to love myself instead can be an entire revolution.

Chapter Twenty-Eight

I

I CAN SEE THINGS MORE CLEARLY. LIKE I HAVE MORE PERSPEC-
tive. It's a little harder to remember why I've cared so much about
people's opinions. I want to write—want to get my voice out into the
world . . . But it's easier to see why now. I've always wanted other people's approval and validation. It's hard to admit, but I think that maybe
the writing has been a part of that, too. Getting someone to say yes,
my voice is worth listening to; yes, I'm worthy of being seen and loved.

My cursor blinks, and I know I'm about to write the most difficult
piece I've ever had to. It's hard to admit being wrong and owning up
to a mistake.

*As many of you know, I recently became viral for a thread about my
struggles with an unrequited love story. As many of you learned, I never actually
wrote that thread.*

*First, I want to say that I'm sorry. I'm sorry for lying. I'm sorry for
deceiving so many of you, and for accepting the praise and attention along with
the well-wishes and support. I'm sorry that I continued to lie for as long as I did.*

*I would like to give an explanation for what happened. Not as an
excuse, but because I think you all deserve to know the truth. A friend of mine
accidentally logged into my account and posted the thread about his own feelings
of unrequited love. I took the credit for the thread instead of explaining what*

*happened, and I pushed the lie further by saying I had feelings for someone I did
like at the time, my ex-partner Eli.*

*I have explained the truth to Eli, and I apologize for lying about the thread
to them, too. I wish them happiness and love on their journey. In the future, I
will always be transparent and honest with my feelings, no matter my fear of the
response I will receive.*

Sincerely,

Lark Winters

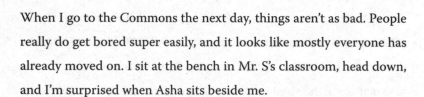

When I go to the Commons the next day, things aren't as bad. People
really do get bored super easily, and it looks like mostly everyone has
already moved on. I sit at the bench in Mr. S's classroom, head down,
and I'm surprised when Asha sits beside me.

She gives me a quick smile. "I saw your apology."

"Yeah. I should've posted it sooner. I was just scared, I think."

She sighs. "It can be scary, I guess—apologizing to so many people. Especially with the way things are online." She winces a little.
"People are being so harsh to you, you know?"

"I don't, actually," I say with a small smile. "I decided not to look
at the comments."

Asha makes a face like she's impressed. "Really? Huh. That's good
for you. The comments are a one-way ticket to hell, in my opinion."

I laugh, and then we sit quietly for a while.

"I'm really sorry, Asha," I tell her. "God. When I think back on all
of the lies I told . . . I'm just really sorry."

She nods. "I know."

I don't say anything as more people file in. Sable comes and sits on the other side of me. Jamal comes and sits across from me. Eye contact, some smiles. Eli ignores me on the other end of the bench. Micah and Patch sit down close enough to glance up at me, considering me, and look away again. It looks like things are going back to normal again, slowly but surely, except for one thing. I try not to think about how much I miss Kasim.

I notice that Sable is glaring at Micah and Patch. She nods at me and stares at them expectantly.

Patch takes a big breath and leans backward. "I'm sorry," they say.

Micah says the same thing. "Yeah. I'm sorry, too."

I stare, eyes bugging out of my head. What the hell did Sable say to scare them into an apology? I think I know what they're going to say sorry for, but I still need to hear it. "For what?"

Micah doesn't like that he has to spell it out. He half rolls his eyes.

Patch says, "For treating you like shit."

"It wasn't always treating you like shit," Micah says. "You were fucking annoying. And you deserved to be called out."

"I can admit it. I was fucking around with you." Patch shrugs. "I knew that I was. I just didn't care." *Still don't,* their tone seems to say.

"I wasn't messing around with you for no reason," Micah says. "You were fucked up."

"How was I fucked up?" I ask him.

And—yeah, suddenly, I know the truth even before Micah says it out loud. "I'm a loyal person, all right? I'm loyal to my friends. When someone treats my friends like shit, I can't just forgive them. You started ignoring Kasim one day out of nowhere. No explanation. Nothing. Stopped sitting with him, walked right by him like you weren't friends. Do you know how much that fucking killed him?"

I'm not sure what to say to that. Kas and I had a misunderstanding. One I already took accountability for with Kasim directly. I don't know if the details of that are any of Micah's business, especially here, in this classroom, in front of everybody.

"Look, we don't vibe," Patch says.

I nod. "Yeah. Agreed."

"Kas is our friend," Micah adds. "He's your friend, too. Doesn't mean we have to hang out with each other."

"Right. Yeah." I hesitate. "It also doesn't mean that we have to go out of our way to attack each other."

"If you mess up, we're going to hold you accountable," Micah says.

"Sure. Same with you," I tell him. "But I have to actually mess up. You can't say you're holding me accountable just because you don't like me, you know? Not when I haven't actually done anything wrong or made a mistake. And even if I do mess up, I don't deserve to be treated like shit. We all make mistakes, right?"

They're silent. Staring at me. My heart's hammering. They could say anything to fuck with me, but in their stares—yeah, I think they might just be more surprised than anything else. I must be like a completely different person to them, speaking up for myself.

"Respect, I guess," I say. "I respect both of you. That's all I need from you, too."

And that's how we end the conversation.

Mr. S walks in like he's unaware of the tension in the classroom. "We've only got a few more classes," he says with a big smile, "and I

want to do a check-in. Everyone, quick, answer this question: Should we be trying to write for the sake of pleasing other people?"

We groan, laugh, roll our eyes—and, at the same time, we all shout, "No!" I'm proud, just a little, that my voice might be the loudest.

When I come home, I don't even see him until I'm halfway down the block. I slow down, then walk to my porch slowly, carefully, like I'm afraid he might run away the second that he sees me. I pause by the steps, and he looks up at me.

"Hey," Kasim says.

I sit down beside him, sliding my backpack off. "I didn't know you were back."

"Taye got home earlier than he expected to a couple of days ago, so I left New York yesterday."

I swallow. I don't know what to tell him, and even if I did, I would be too afraid to say it, because I don't want to say the wrong thing that would make Kasim leave me again—but that's not right, is it?

Birdie smiles at me. "Not right at all."

Because I should be able to be myself, my full and whole self, and not hide any part of me, afraid of what other people are going to do or think. "I missed you, Kas."

He nods. "Yeah. God. I missed you a lot, too, Lark."

"Did you figure out everything you needed to in New York?"

He hesitates. "You know—yeah, I think I did. I didn't want to see it at first, because this is the kind of shit that's hard to see, but . . . I felt like I was running away from you," he tells me, "same way my dad ran away from me and Taye."

I frown. "No—no, you were just—I don't know, taking the space you needed. It's not like I'm your responsibility, the way you are to your dad."

"Maybe that's true. I don't know. Maybe two things can be true. That I left because I needed space, and that I ran away because I was too afraid of losing you."

He looks at me, watching for my reaction. I can't help the small smile, because, wow—yeah, I've missed the hell out of Kas. "Do you want to come inside?"

We both get up, and he walks in when I open the door for him. We sit in the living room, and I have no idea where my mom is, but that might be for the best, because I have a feeling this conversation is about to be uncomfortable and weird and . . . yeah, Sable was right. Those are the best kinds of conversations, aren't they?

Kasim sits down on the sofa, and I sit down beside him, legs crossed beneath me.

"Have you seen Sable yet?" I ask him.

He nods. "I saw her yesterday. We had a conversation about you."

I wince. "Really? Did she tell you about—you know . . ."

He shakes his head. "No, she didn't tell me anything. She only listened to me. I asked her for advice. I was trying to sort out my feelings for you." He turns his head to the side, smile growing, and I know I've fucked up. "What did you think she told me?"

"Ah—well, you know," I say.

"No," he says, laughing. "I don't know."

I groan and cover my face with my hands. "I kind of might have maybe probably perhaps told her that I have a crush on her, and that I think I might be in love with her."

Kasim's head swings around to look at me. I think he's genuinely surprised to hear that one. "Oh." And maybe he's wondering why I never told him that. And maybe now he's wondering how he feels about this.

"I wanted to let her know that I loved her before I told you, because—well, it's how I feel about her."

"Yeah. That makes sense." Kasim leans back on the couch. His expression is impossible to read. "What'd she say?"

I can feel my face, shoulders, dropping. "She doesn't want to be partners. She still wants to be friends, which is—you know, that's great, too. But I think I wanted to be in a relationship with her."

His expression is blank. That poker face again. "I'm sorry to hear that."

"Really?"

He makes a face, twisting his mouth to the side as he thinks. "I— yeah, I mean. I'm feeling two things at once, I guess."

"What're you feeling?"

"I'm a little mad, honestly," he says, meeting my eye. "I don't know if it's okay to be mad, but I am. You never said anything about falling for Sable."

"But those are my feelings for her. I shouldn't have to tell you that I love her."

"Yeah. But I'm still upset about it. It's not like you have to do anything or apologize for loving her. That's just how I'm honestly feeling. It's something for me to work out, I guess."

I nod. "Okay. I get that."

"There's that, and—I mean, I wanted to be in a relationship with you, and you told me no, but you wanted to be in a relationship with Sable? That's confusing as hell."

"Maybe it's because with you—we just have so much history that I'm still scared, but with Sable, it wasn't as scary."

Neither of us say anything for a while.

I tell him, "It's kind of nice to actually hear and tell you the truth without it feeling like a fight and worrying that you hate me."

He sighs. Still annoyed. "Yeah. I know."

"Can I ask about the other thing you're feeling?"

His gaze slides to mine. "Disappointed."

"Really?"

"I'd be lying if I didn't think about it—you being with me, and both of us with her. I've daydreamed of being in a triad with you."

I grin. "Really? Me, too."

"I never brought it up with Sable, because I figured I needed to work on my relationship with you first. But, yeah—I've thought it would be nice, for all of us to—you know. To be together."

"Yeah. But Sable isn't interested, so . . ."

"So there's no point in thinking about it."

"Right. Exactly."

"I'm sorry she doesn't feel the same way. I really am."

"It's okay."

"How're you feeling?" he asks me.

"It hurts."

"I'm sorry it hurts." He sounds like he means it, too.

"Like—I've been trying to work so hard on myself. On being honest and being accountable and actually learning to love myself. I think I began to believe that if I loved myself, then other people would start to love me, too. Which is a mindfuck, also, because loving myself

should be for *me* anyway—not for other people learning to love me back in the way I want them to."

"I think I get what you mean. But also," Kasim tells me, "I feel like I've got to say this: You deserve to be loved. Period. Even if you don't know how to love yourself yet. Even if you make mistakes. Even if it feels like no one else loves you. Which, anyway," Kas adds, "we both know isn't true."

We're quiet. Kasim nudges his knee with mine. "I've told you that I want to be with you, and now you're saying you daydreamed about being with me and Sable, and . . . You still haven't told me what you want, Lark."

I take a breath. What would stop Kasim from rejecting me, like I was rejected by Sable? What if I let myself be vulnerable with him, and he changes his mind? But this—I think this might be where bravery hides. This is where honesty takes courage. All of this, summed up by three words.

"I love you." He doesn't look away from me. I think he's trying to figure out if he can trust me. "I love you, Kasim."

"Really?" His voice is so quiet and legit sounds scared, so scared that I want to wrap myself around him. "Do you mean that, Lark?"

"I love you." I can say it a thousand times if it means he'll believe it. "Yeah. I do. And I want to be in a relationship with you."

That quiet lingers, and this quiet—well, I mean, come on. We know quiet. We're pretty well-acquainted with quiet. We've been though the tense, angry quiet. We've been through the sad silence where there's so much we want to say but don't know how to say it, to trust each other enough to be vulnerable and real. And then there's

this quiet. I haven't experienced it with him before. But it's exploding. It's possibilities and crossroads. It's paths untaken in the woods and quick smirks with pointy canines and playing with locs and smelling like rainstorms. It's miracles. And hope. How can ten seconds of quiet mean so much?

"Should we—" Kasim jiggles a knee up and down. "Should we?"

"I'd really like to."

He moves his hand. Hesitates. Moves it again and touches my finger. I turn my hand over and he takes it and we both get up and walk across the living room, holding hands, and walk up the stairs, holding hands (and God I really hope my mom doesn't choose this very moment to walk out of her bedroom), and we walk down the hallway, holding hands some more. My hand is damp and nervous and his is, too. I walk into my bedroom and he closes the door behind him and we stare at each other for who knows how long before he lets out a breath and takes a step toward me.

And we do the lean. We don't close our eyes. We stop, heads tilted to one another, and we really look at each other. Because, yeah—this is when everything officially changes for us. And that's scary. But it's also exciting. And it's even better, I think, deciding to trust that we're going to be there for each other. Kasim takes my hand again, and we kiss.

We kiss.

We kissed before, sure, but that kiss was nothing like this. It was almost desperate, like we'd been starving for each other for so long and we needed to feel each other so badly that we couldn't even fully enjoy the moment. But this kiss? It feels like we have all of the time in the world—not just here, in this lifetime, but in the thousands,

millions, billions, infinite number of lives we'll have after this one, always looking for each other again and again, two beings who are whole and full and complete and love each other so much that they can't wait to find each other again, to learn and grow and love together.

We pull away. We stare at each other as we sit down on the edge of my bed and lean in and kiss again, eyes closing, and we lie down on my bed, and—yeah, he feels really good, *this* feels really good. When we pull back and look at each other, I think I really understand. I get why people can look at each other for so long, unblinkingly, staring into each other's eyes. Because when I know I'm safe with Kasim—when I know he doesn't want to hurt me—I don't have to be afraid of what he thinks. I'm not so stuck in my head, and I get to see him. I get to see a whole universe inside of him. No words necessary.

We lie down on the bed together, Kasim's head on my shoulder and my arms around him and our legs tangled, and we're just breathing. I can feel that he wants me to know that I'm safe with him. I can be myself. Really, I can. I can trust him.

"I love you," Kasim says.

God, yeah. "I love you, too."

Lark Winters (they/them) @winterslark

I know that most people will be angry with what I have to say, but I've decided to stop caring.

That's a hard thing for me to do. I've always cared about what people think of me. But I realized it was because I hated myself, and I needed their love as permission to feel worthy of love, too.

I want to learn to love myself. I think I'm finally starting to. A part of loving myself has been learning to take accountability and responsibility. It's also been about creating boundaries for safety.

I made a mistake, which I took accountability for. I apologized and responded appropriately. But I can't stop existing. I can't hold on to shame for my mistakes for the rest of my life. I need to learn and grow.

I can't control other people. I can only control myself. This journey on social media has been unhealthy for me. This has been an unsafe space.

And I can't heal in a space that wants to harm me. So, with that, I will delete this account. I want to say thank you, and goodbye, to everyone who has followed me and supported me on this journey.

I love you all. I really do mean that. Sincerely, Lark

Chapter Twenty-Nine

And Birdie? When they opened their wings and flapped as hard as they could—by the gods, they lifted off the ground, and knew before anyone that they could finally fly.

I've done it. It took almost another two weeks to finish, but I finally type out those last two words.

The End.

I'm *sobbing*, because of course I am—not only because I finished writing my book, though I'm sure that's a huge part of it, too, but because I feel like I'm saying goodbye to a friend. I wipe my eyes, and Birdie smiles at me, eyes wet, too.

"Don't be sad, Lark," they say. They hug me, head resting on top of mine, feet off the ground. "I'm a piece of your imagination. I'm not going anywhere. I'll always be around."

They're gone. I'm alone, in my room, like I always was. I save the Word doc and file it away into a folder. I already know I'm not going to query it. I don't think I'm ready yet—Birdie's story needs to be revised, and I think I might need a break from the manuscript so that I can see the story more clearly, too.

My phone buzzes with a text from Kas, and—ah, shit, of course I'm late to my own birthday picnic. I scramble to jump out of my chair, grab my things, and race out of my room, down the stairs, yelling that I'll see my mom later.

When I make it to the Dog Bowl, I'm wheezing and sweating, hands on my knees, gasping, "Sorry, sorry!" Everyone cheers, a chorus of *happy birthday, Lark*. Kasim snorts and shakes his head, and I fall onto the grass beside him. I *said* that I didn't want anything, but Asha hands me a cupcake and Jamal a notebook and pen. Sable already hung out with me and Kas last night, where she gave me another crystal and we talked for hours in the backyard before we started to kiss, and she told me she's thought more about it, and she's talked it through with Kasim, and he helped her realize that she's been afraid, just like I was afraid, and well, she told me last night that she'd like to be my girlfriend, too. "I love you, Lark," she said, which was so amazing that I started to cry, of course, and we snuggled in my bed again, which is officially my new favorite thing, the three of us together. We'll have some stuff to talk about and figure out, but this is good for now. So, so, so good.

Sable lies down on her stomach on Kasim's other side, picking at the grass as she speaks to Asha, who shuffles her deck of cards, and Jamal, who looks at me for help to get away from Asha's clutches.

Everything is perfect. Absolutely everything.

Kas threads his fingers through mine and kisses my cheek. "How does it feel to be eighteen?" he asks me.

"Like everything and nothing has changed."

He smirks. "You're always so deep, Lark."

I grin at him and pretend to be offended. "Are you making fun of me?"

He kisses the corner of my mouth. "Maybe a little."

The sun's hot, the sky a bright blue. The breeze feels good. The summer grass is green, and petals and seeds float through the air. I sigh and fall backward, and Kasim lies down beside me. "What do you think is going to happen next?" I ask him.

"What do you mean?"

"There's so much change and I guess it feels like nothing's going to stop changing."

"Yeah." His finger traces the lines in my palm. "I've been thinking a lot about change. Trying to figure out if it's possible for me to change, too."

I turn my head to face him, watching him closely.

He shrugs. "It's not like I can just stop being depressed," he says. "My dad's been depressed ever since I was young. I know I can't change just like that, but—I don't know. Maybe I can figure out how to get some help."

"Like therapy?"

"I guess, yeah—like therapy."

"Maybe there're counseling sessions online. You know. FaceTime or something."

"Yeah. Maybe."

I'm staring at him too intensely, I know that I am, but I can't look away, and, hey, maybe that's just something I picked up from him, and if so, I like it. He glances at me with a smile and rolls his eyes. Once upon a time this might've been an invitation to a fight, but now . . . He rests his head on my shoulder and breathes. Just breathes.

"All these people saying the world's finally going to change because of the pandemic and protests," he says under his breath. "I don't

know. I don't think it'll happen that easily. People have to actually start to look at themselves to change first. No one wants to do that."

"Too much shame."

"Maybe."

"And some people don't want to change anyway."

"Yeah. That's true."

"But," I say, "at least there're more conversations. It feels like a lot more people are thinking about how they want to learn and grow, you know?"

I can feel his heartbeat through his chest. Calm and steady. He can probably feel mine, too. People, when they're walking together, start to step in sync. That's what our heartbeats begin to do. Line up and match each other. Maybe it's nice that we're separate instead of one being. How else would we be able to see each other? Really see and love each other, imperfections and all.

🐦

I spin around in my chair at my desk, slowly, staring out at the blue sky, thinking and thinking and thinking . . . I'm going to write a new book. I don't know what it's about yet. The cursor blinks at me, and I can't help but smile. There's something exciting about writing the first line of a novel. So many possibilities, you know?

~~Lark's~~ (Kacen's) Guide to Writing a Novel

Hey, young writers!

I've always loved writing. I started out with fanfiction by the time I was ten years old, until I began attempting my own novels around the time I was seventeen, like Lark. I'd always struggled to figure out how to actually write a novel, though, and if you're like I was, then I hope this guide can be helpful to you. Take it with a grain of salt, though—not every guide and "rule" of craft or advice has to or will work for you, but hopefully there's something in here that might resonate.

If I was talking to my teen self right now, I would tell them everything that Janet told Lark on the phone and Mr. S says in his classrooms—first, above all else, to forget what everyone will think of my writing. (Worrying about what readers want and being afraid of what they will think has always been my biggest cause of writer's block.) Second, I would show myself exactly how the theme of my book could create my character and plot, something I just did not understand how to build.

Step one: Figure out the theme!

If there was one thing you wished you could tell the entire world, that every single human being on this Earth would hear, what would it be? Beauty radiates from the inside out? Everyone is worthy of unconditional love? McDonald's is better than Burger King? The theme is a ticket right to figuring out who the character is—not just their name, age, or what their favorite color is, but who they are at their core.

For example, if I wanted to write a book with the message *beauty radiates from the inside out*, then I would need to have a character that would learn this lesson . . . so this means, in the beginning of the novel, they would believe the opposite: that beauty is only on the outside and doesn't come from within. Or, if I had a message that everyone is worthy of self-love, then I would need to have a story about a character who struggles to love themselves unconditionally, just like Lark. A theme that expresses McD's is better than BK would start with a character who eats at BK instead of McD's.

The theme is the message that the reader walks away with, but it's the very lesson that the character needs to learn, too—so, in the beginning of the novel, the character is, essentially, the opposite of the theme.

Step two completed: We've got a character.

Step two-and-a-half: But why are they the way that they are?

It's really important for me to figure out why a main character thinks and feels the way that they do, opposite of the theme I want to express. What sort of subconscious messages were they taught when they were younger that have been a detriment to them and being their authentic self? What traumas might they have encountered that pulled them away from that state of unconditional love and freedom that we're all born with? Were they told by their parents that they weren't beautiful all their life, and now they need to learn that kindness and empathy are the only forms of beauty that matter, no matter what others tell them? Were they bullied and attacked and made to feel like they were only safe if they pleased everyone around them? Did they have a horrific fear of clowns when they were younger, and were told that kings were better?

Okay, so if I have my character and I know that they're basically going to start the novel in the opposite place of the theme, then I also have the start of the plot. It's more commonly known that a plot must have a character who has an outward goal that they're fighting for—going on a magical journey to find a lost idol, going on a road trip to search for their long-lost father . . . the possibilities are endless. The infinite possibilities can be overwhelming for me at times. But if I focus on the character, and what is they need to learn for the story's message and theme, then the story starts to feel organized because there's more attention placed on what the character's conflicts need to be.

Step three: Create plot through conflict.

As the character struggles to learn their lesson/theme, outside antagonists and inner demons might get in the way of what it is they need to learn in order to get the outward goal of what it is that they want. Lark outwardly wanted validation via Twitter likes and acceptance by everyone around them, and they needed to learn that they were worthy of self-love, no matter how others treated them and no matter what mistakes they've made—so Lark's inner conflict of being a people pleaser, too afraid to truly be themselves because they were fearful they weren't worthy of unconditional love, became a major conflict. This conflict manifested itself as them lying to hide their true self and lying to please others. There were antagonists who bullied and shamed them for their mistakes, exasperating their fear and heightening their emotional stakes.

Brainstorming the number of conflicts that could become a block in the main character learning their lesson, both inner and outer, could be shown in scenes that are organized by basic plot beats that have been helpful for me to follow over the years:

- **Catalyst:** Oh no! Something new and different has happened and shakes up the main character's entire life, sometimes shattering everything they've known.
- **Promise:** The promised hook of the novel is fulfilled. Katniss goes off to the arena to fight in the *Hunger Games*, Marlin tries to find Nemo, etc. This is usually the biggest chunk of the novel, where all those brainstormed conflicts build, getting bigger and bigger until . . .
- **Pop:** It all explodes, everything comes to a head, and the main character is forced to look at their life and realize the way they've been living just hasn't been working, and it's time to really and truly change.
- **Changes:** The main character finally starts to implement those changes, maybe cutting what has been unhealthy for them out of their life altogether. (And tragedies might end with the character not learning those lessons or implementing those changes!)
- **Resolution:** Maybe the character got that outward goal they'd originally wanted from the get-go—or maybe their outward goal transformed into something else because of the way they've evolved from the inside out. Either way, we see their new state of life, enjoying the changes they've made.

This guide could go on forever! There is so much amazing advice and many, *many* books on craft out there. Two of my all-time favorites are *Save the Cat! Writes a Novel* by Jessica Brody and *Story Genius* by Lisa Cron. But, as I started this out by saying, there really aren't any rules to craft except for what works for *you*—and the only way you can figure out your own rules as a writer is by writing.

Safe journeys,
Kacen

Acknowledgments

Thank you to Beth Phelan and Gallt & Zacker Literary for being such a rock on this incredible journey.

Thank you to Maggie Lehrman for the wonderful questions and guidance, and to Emily Daluga, Margo Winton Parodi, Andrew Smith, Jody Mosley, Hana Anouk Nakamura, Melanie Chang, Elisa Gonzalez, Kim Lauber, Hallie Patterson, Jenny Choy, and the rest of the Abrams team for taking a chance on Lark and Kasim. Thank you to Sabrena Khadija for the beautiful cover and illustrations.

Thank you to my family for always cheering me on and continuing to be true believers in all my dreams.

And thank you to the readers whose support and love of stories inspires me.